PRAISE FOR IAN K. SMITH

Praise for *The Unspoken*

An Amazon Best Book of the Month: Mystery, Thriller & Suspense

"With its huge, entertaining cast and smooth sleuth, this series kickoff recalls vintage Chandler or Hammett."

—*Kirkus Reviews*

"This fine series launch from bestseller Smith (*The Ancient Nine*) introduces PI Ashe Cayne, a former Chicago PD detective . . . Ashe is just one of many well-drawn, multilayered characters. Readers will eagerly await his return."

—*Publishers Weekly*

"Ian K. Smith has created a suspense story where the pages practically turn themselves all the way to the twist at the end."

—AuthorLink

"Smith creates a fond and layered portrait of the Windy City, in all its multidimensional glory, as we traipse from fancy high-rises, to grungy boxing gyms, to tastefully decorated criminal lairs. Here's hoping for many more installments in the series!"

—CrimeReads, Most Anticipated Crime Books of 2020

"Ian K. Smith's *The Unspoken* is the start of a big, bold, original new series. Chicago PI Ashe Cayne is the perfect hero for our times. I can't wait to read his next adventure."

—Harlan Coben, #1 *New York Times* bestselling author

WOLF POINT

ALSO BY IAN K. SMITH

Novels

The Ancient Nine
The Blackbird Papers
The Unspoken

Nonfiction

Fast Burn
Mind Over Weight
Clean & Lean
The Clean 20
Blast the Sugar Out!
The Shred Power Cleanse
The Shred Diet Cookbook
Super Shred
Shred
The Truth About Men
Eat
Happy
The 4 Day Diet
Extreme Fat Smash Diet
The Fat Smash Diet
The Take-Control Diet
Dr. Ian Smith's Guide to Medical Websites

WOLF POINT

IAN K. SMITH

THOMAS & MERCER

Text copyright © 2021 by Ian K. Smith
All rights reserved.

Published by Thomas & Mercer, Seattle

www.apub.com

Amazon, the Amazon logo, and Thomas & Mercer are trademarks of Amazon.com, Inc., or its affiliates.

ISBN-13: 9781542027861 (hardcover)
ISBN-10: 1542027861 (hardcover)

ISBN-13: 9781542022712 (paperback)
ISBN-10: 1542022711 (paperback)

Cover design by Shasti O'Leary Soudant

Printed in the United States of America

First edition

To my good friend Rachael Ray. If I can produce the same artistry with the written word that you have done with food, then it will have been a journey well traveled and a life well lived. I love you!

1

"PLEASE HELP US FIND who murdered our father," Katrina Griffin said. She wore a snug yellow-and-black sundress with a matching purse that looked completely out of place in the midst of all the concrete pillars and old steel beams.

I had just finished a thirty-minute session, working the heavy bag with Arnie "the Hammer" Scazzi in the gym he owned, tucked away in the basement of Johnny's Icehouse in the West Loop. Minutes earlier, Katrina Griffin and her brother, Walter Griffin Jr., had walked up to me, introduced themselves, then asked if they could have a word with me in private. How they'd tracked me down here, I had no idea.

We now sat comfortably in Hammer's barren office. I had angled the standing fan so it blew exclusively in my direction.

"Our father was a good man," Katrina said. "He had a good life and enjoyed living it. He never would've killed himself. He wouldn't do that to our mother, and he wouldn't do it to us."

I had recognized both of them immediately when they approached me. I had seen their faces for many months in the newspapers and on television. Katrina was much shorter in person, slender, with curly shoulder-length hair and skin the color of melting chocolate. It would be difficult to believe the man sitting beside her was her brother had it not been for those eyes, a soft hazel that mesmerized, just like his father's. Walter Griffin Sr., with his heart-stopping eyes and bespoke three-piece suits, had been a legend in Chicago city politics, a bigger-than-life personality, until one easy Sunday afternoon two years ago he'd put a gun to his head and killed himself on a deserted, forgotten piece of land along the northern bank of the Chicago River.

At least that was the official account. Very few people south of Madison Street believed it. My father, who had known him for almost fifty years, was one of the doubters. I remembered him crying when he heard the news. My father rarely cried, but he had been angry. Walter Griffin had been one of the South Side's biggest supporters, never forgetting the hundreds of thousands of families who still struggled to make it to the next day. Griffin had risen to great heights downtown, but he had always found a way to give back to the distressed communities that had nurtured him.

"CPD and the ME both ruled your father's death a suicide," I said. "I'm not sure there's much more I can do that they didn't."

"That's not what we were told," Junior said. "Word around town is, you can find answers better than anybody." He leaned forward. "Word is, if anyone can get to the bottom of this, you're the one."

"Who told you that?"

"Delroy Thomas."

I nodded. I knew Thomas, but mostly just in passing. He had been the alderman of the Twenty-Seventh Ward until he was investigated by the FBI, indicted, and eventually convicted for extortion and kickbacks. After spending three years of a four-year sentence in a federal prison camp in South Dakota, he now operated a soul food restaurant in the same ward he once represented. Frequented by politicians and community activists and a smattering of local residents, Delroy's Catfish Corner held the political pulse of Black Chicago.

"Your father had a lot of powerful friends," I said. "You might be better off going to them. They're much more connected than I am and have access to certain information and records that I don't."

"That might be," Katrina said. "But you're the one who can get us the truth. Mr. Cayne, our family needs the truth."

I considered their words and the plaintiveness in their voices. They'd been young to lose their father—late twenties. I also considered how difficult this case would be and how many buried mines I would have to avoid. This case was a "heater" because of the prominence of the victim involved and his connection to other influential people. Taking it on would be dangerous. Their father had died with a lot of secrets, and there were many powerful people quietly celebrating that he had taken those secrets to his grave. It was also the middle of my golf season, and I had just gotten my handicap down to an eleven.

"I understand what you're saying and how important it is for you to have closure, but this is a bad time of year for me," I said.

"What does that mean?" Junior said.

"I have a confession to make."

Both of them tensed a little.

"I'm a golf addict. I swore an oath to the golf gods and to myself that this is the year for my handicap to finally crack into the single digits. And I only have about two more months of decent weather to get it done."

"Dad was a ten," Junior said. "He played three times a week. If someone hadn't killed him, his handicap probably would've been a nine or eight today."

"Where did he like to play?"

"Everywhere. He never had to join a course because all his friends had memberships, so he'd play on their accounts. There's no golf course in Chicago he didn't play at least once."

This time of year, Buckingham Fountain was shooting water thirty feet in the air at full throttle. Tourists stood in front of it, posing for pictures, while kids chased each other along the manicured garden paths of Grant Park. Sailboats and yachts passed each other agreeably on the calm open waters of Lake Michigan. The city braved brutal winters every year just for these hot, carefree summer months. I thought about Walter Griffin and how this had once been his city, a man who had been born and raised on the hardened streets of the West Side and had counted friends as equally in his old neighborhood as he did in the corridors of power. He would never swing a golf club again.

I turned my attention back to the Griffins. "Listen, there are plenty of other private investigators who don't play golf and who take their work very seriously," I said. "Plus, they're a lot cheaper than I am. I can give you three names. All three will work really hard for you."

"We don't want anyone else," Katrina said firmly. "We want you, and we're willing to pay whatever it takes." She reached into her purse, pulled out a sealed envelope, and placed it decisively on the desk.

I smiled. "The truth can be difficult sometimes," I said. "People think they want to hear it, but really they don't."

"We already know the truth," Junior said. "At least part of it. Our father would *never* take his own life. Not in a million years. That's not the man he was."

"And even if he wanted to kill himself, he wouldn't have done it there," Katrina said.

"What do you mean?"

"Our father was a germophobe. Everything he touched had to be clean. He even traveled with flip-flops and a Ziploc bag so he wouldn't stand barefoot in a hotel shower or touch a remote control with his bare fingers. There's no way he would go down to a dirty, nasty place like that with rats and garbage and take his own life."

"We had plans that he was excited about," Junior said. "The most excited I had ever seen him about traveling. We were two weeks away from going on safari in South Africa. My dad spent an entire year planning it. His father, my grandfather, had always wanted to go to Africa but died before he had the chance. Dad had bought all the tickets, paid for us to have our own house on a reserve for two weeks. He called us every day with the official countdown to our departure. Does that sound like a man who's also planning to kill himself?"

I had read all the stories and heard all the rumors, but I hadn't heard about the trip. I had to agree that it didn't make much sense that he would just up and put a gun to his head. Walter Griffin had every reason to love life. The consummate Chicago insider, he had been a close friend and trusted confidant of Mayor Bailey for the last thirty years. He'd sat on the most important charitable and civic boards, and his career had spanned several high-level positions in city government. Most recently the mayor had appointed him the president of the Chicago Board of Education, ultimately making him the boss of the entire Chicago public school system. Bailey had put him at CPS to help overhaul the entire corrupt and underperforming school system and lead the fight against the mayor's eternal archenemy, the Chicago Teachers Union. Griffin had won several hard-fought concessions during the last contract negotiation with CTU and was expected to win a lot more.

Then I thought about my father and how he had said Griffin's death was an immeasurable loss to the South Side, a largely depressed part of the city that had many critics but few champions. The year before he died, Griffin had spearheaded a $9 million fundraising campaign for the University of Chicago Medicine's Violence Recovery Program. It had helped thousands of families who had been victimized by violence positively reintegrate into society.

"What does your mother think?" I asked.

"She's always believed that someone killed him," Katrina said. "The second she saw it on TV, she knew they had finally gotten him."

"Who is the 'they' she was referring to?"

Junior looked at his sister, then back at me. "Someone in or near the mayor's office," he said. "She's convinced someone ordered the hit."

2

"HAVE YOU LOST YOUR goddamn mind?" Commander Rory Burke bellowed. His voice started its rumble somewhere in the hollow depths of his barrel chest, then exploded out of his mouth like a cannon.

We were sitting across from each other at Al's Italian Beef at the corner of Grand and Wells in the River North neighborhood. This was Burke's choice. I preferred Luke's Italian Beef in the Loop. Construction workers on lunch break crammed the tiny shop. Two enormous beef sandwiches big enough to feed an entire battalion sat in front of us. Burke had already chomped his way through half of his. I had gotten full just watching him.

"I didn't want to take it," I said. "I'd heard them interviewed on the news before, but there was something about seeing them in person and hearing the pain in their voices."

"Jesus Christ, you've gotten all soft on me?" Burke said. "Besides, I thought you didn't take on cases this time of year on account of your damn golf addiction."

"Usually, I don't," I said.

"But?"

"I never thought Griffin committed suicide."

"The department did their own investigation independent of the ME," Burke said. "They came to the same conclusion. He shot himself." He took a long gulp of orange soda to chase a clump of beef and bread.

I clapped softly. "The answer I expect from someone who gets a check signed by city hall every two weeks," I said. "Now tell me what you really think."

"Fuck you!" After he had inhaled almost the entire second half of the sandwich and wiped his lips with the back of his hand, Burke said, "It never added up for me either. Griffin had his hands in lots of jars, people he owed money, deals he was constantly making, old friends he was constantly helping out. Maybe too many. But a guy like that, with all he had, taking his own life and then doing it that way. Never registered for me."

"Who worked the case?"

"Gallagher and Suarez. Two of the best over in Central. They have almost fifty years between the two of them. It was before your time, but Gallagher was lead on the Girl X case back in ninety-seven." I was in middle school when the Girl X case rocked the city. A nine-year-old living in the tough Cabrini-Green housing project had been on her way to school when she was abducted from a stairwell, viciously raped, choked, and left for dead. Four years later they nailed the monster, and the judge hit him with a 120-year sentence.

"Central had jurisdiction, but did they keep the investigation local?" I asked.

"Very. None of the other areas were called in to help."

Chicago was divided into three police areas: North, Central, and South. Each area had its own division of detectives. Burke was the commander of the South area. Griffin's body and his red Cadillac convertible had been found downtown in an industrial area on the north bank of the Chicago River at a place called Wolf Point. It was mostly undeveloped land owned by the Kennedy family. That territory belonged to Central command.

"How did they run the case?" I asked.

"As best they could," Burke said. "You know heaters like this are always a pain in the ass. Everybody's looking over your damn shoulders. The paper pushers from HQ hadn't worked a case in years, but they all slid out from behind their fancy desks and got their noses in there. Albertson is the commander over there. He's smart. Rose through the ranks quickly. A little too much of a yes-man for me, but the Fifth Floor likes him."

Fifth Floor was cop speak for the mayor's office, which occupied a meandering maze of rooms on the fifth floor of city hall. The mayor and police brass always had a strained relationship. Police procedure and mandates were supposed to be independent of politics and personal agendas. They rarely were.

"I made a few calls inside," I said. "I was told they moved through it really fast. A lot of hand-waving and checking the boxes, but nothing substantive."

"I don't know all the details, but let's just say it moved much faster than I would've run it," Burke said. "Then again, I'm old school. A case like this needs time for everything to jell, to cut through the emotions and connections and let the evidence tell the story. But my goals are different. They all want their names on the supe's door. I couldn't give two shits. The brass wanted a quick resolution, so they got one."

"Even if the resolution was predetermined."

"The longer that case stayed open, the more public scrutiny it would've gotten."

"Have you seen the file?" I asked.

"Never got a chance to go anywhere near it," Burke said. "They had it flagged right away."

Heater cases were always flagged by the department. Normally, investigating officers could go to Evidence and Recovery Property Section—EARPS—and sign out the files on a case. When a case was flagged, department policy dictated that only investigators directly linked to a case or needing information from a case to help with another active case could look at the files. Their names and shield numbers were recorded. Anyone else poking around would be questioned.

"Any chance you might be able to get your hands on it?" I asked. "Getting a look at it could be a big help."

Burke took a handful of fries, dipped them first in ketchup, then made a quick pass through a heap of mayo before shoveling them into his mouth. He washed them down with another long gulp of soda.

"I'd like to help you," he said. "But there's no chance in hell I can put my signature on that file. This case was closed just over two years ago, but eyes are still on it. They want this one to stay buried. If I make the request, I won't have any cover."

"Who do you think did it?" I asked.

Burke looked around, then stared back at me with his steel-blue eyes.

"The guy had enemies," he said in a hushed voice. "You can't get as high as he was without having some."

"Where would you start?"

"That's easy," Burke said. "With the Russians. I heard he'd done some things in his real estate deals that didn't make them too happy."

Burke pushed back from the table with great effort. "I gotta take a leak," he announced.

As I watched him lumber his way between the tight tables, a photo caught my eye. A guy two tables over was reading the *Sun-Times*. There was a face on the outer page that I recognized. I was just able to make out the name. Demetrius Jackson. I kept staring at the face. I knew him, but I didn't recognize the name.

Then it clicked. He was the spitting image of Rayshawn Jackson, a young part-time college student who'd helped me with the Tinsley Gerrigan case. He worked a few days a week at nearby Saint Paul's Church, where he ran all their video equipment. Rayshawn had the most optimistic smile I'd ever seen. The picture I was now staring at had to be his older brother. From what I could read, he had been killed several years ago, and his killer had just been released from prison. I had spent many hours with Rayshawn. He knew my line of work. Yet he still had never mentioned this tragedy with his older brother.

Burke returned and sat back down. He followed my eyeline to the photograph of Demetrius Jackson.

"Awful waste of life," he said.

"You know the case?"

"Terrible. The Jackson kid is minding his own business on the train. Some gangbanger named Antoine Nelson wants to roll him for his iPhone and Louis Vuitton backpack. The Jackson kid won't give up his stuff, kicks the shit outa Nelson, gets off the train, and Nelson runs out and stabs him from behind. Jackson bleeds to death on the platform. No real witnesses, because everyone ran away, and the few who stayed long enough didn't want to snitch. DA pleads the case out, and Nelson gets only three years. Three fuckin' years for killing a decent young man who had his whole life ahead of him. Sometimes there just ain't justice."

I couldn't stop staring at Demetrius Jackson and thinking about his brother, Rayshawn, and the rest of their family. What kind of daily pain does one struggle with knowing their loved one is in the ground and the person who put them there is walking around free like nothing ever happened? Two years later, the Griffin children were still consumed by their father's death. I thought about Demetrius Jackson bleeding out on that platform, begging for his life to be saved, and Antoine Nelson callously walking away. I got that ache in my chest and that familiar tension in the back of my head.

Too often, the justice system flat out got it wrong. But sometimes justice deserved a second chance.

3

I WALKED INTO ARNIE'S Gym that night to find Mechanic working one side of the heavy bag while seventy-year-old Hammer held the other side and barked orders. Mechanic's punches were quick and forceful. One combination knocked Hammer onto the back of his heels. I stood and waited for Mechanic to take a break.

"Look who's making a cameo," Hammer said, wiping his wet forehead with the back of his hand. "You come to work or watch?"

"He needs as much practice as he can get," I said, nodding to Mechanic. "That's the only way to keep things fair."

"Too bad your golf game isn't as big as your imagination," Mechanic said, taking out his mouthpiece and spitting in a bucket.

I tapped him with a quick jab to his chest, then an uppercut to his stomach that he was too slow to block.

"Fastest damn hands I ever seen," Hammer said, shaking his head. "And you waste it all chasing that white ball on a damn golf course." He threw up his hands and walked away.

"I need to take a visit to Ukrainian Village," I said, once Mechanic and I were seated. "Thought you could make the introductions."

"What's going on?" Mechanic asked.

I explained my meeting with the Griffin kids, their father's alleged suicide, and my conversation with Burke. Dmitri Kowalski and I had been friends for almost twenty years after meeting each other while digging up roads around the city during the summer after our sophomore year in high school. He was quiet, efficient, hardworking, and strong. He'd grown up in the tough streets of the Near West Side, the son of a mason worker from Lithuania and a mother who almost drank herself into the grave until she found the church. Dmitri had gotten the nickname "Mechanic" as a fearless teenager because of his penchant for fixing problems in the neighborhood that others found too difficult to handle. He was the only guy I had ever met whom I'd think twice about going up against. Luckily for both of us we were always on the same side.

"You ever dealt with those guys before?" Mechanic said, referring to the Russians.

"Never," I said.

"They're not the friendliest. They play by different rules."

"So I've heard."

"They kill first and ask questions later."

"You think they had something to do with it?"

"Hard to say. If this happened ten, fifteen years ago, I'd say no. Back then they only moved drugs and weapons. Now they have their hands in all kinds of shit, so there's no telling."

"You have friends over there?"

"I have friends everywhere," Mechanic said. "But so do the Russians. Including cops."

"They have friends that can make murder look like suicide?"

"You need to talk to Sergei Yeltsin," Mechanic said. "He owns a bakery over in the Village. If he doesn't already know what happened, he can find out for sure."

"Is he connected?"

"To everyone and everything."

"How soon can you set it up?"

"Tomorrow afternoon. Yeltsin only takes meetings in the afternoon. He spends all morning baking."

4

I ARRIVED AT MY apartment building that night, collected my mail, and sorted through it as I rode up to the fortieth floor. I lived in a new high-rise on East Ohio Street in an expensive neighborhood called Streeterville, a couple of blocks from Navy Pier and Lake Michigan. Northwestern Memorial Hospital and its gigantic campus sat a few blocks north.

A small blue envelope slipped out of the stack of bills and junk mail. When I reached down to pick it up, I knew right away who had sent it. Her writing had always been extremely feminine and meticulous, with big loops and lots of curves. As I stared at my name and then the return address in Paris, my heart started racing so fast it was cutting off my breath. The first thing I needed to see was her surname. She still used her maiden name. She hadn't gotten married.

I made it to my apartment, struggling to slow the merry-go-round of thoughts rotating in my head. Stryker, my cockapoo, jumped on me at the door and followed me into the kitchen, where I dropped the mail on the counter and filled his bowl with food. I grabbed a Stella Artois from the refrigerator, popped the cap, and fell into the couch, staring out the window at Navy Pier's lighted Ferris wheel, which rotated into the black night. I couldn't bring myself to look at the envelope just ten feet away.

Julia Cartwright had put my heart in a metal vise and crushed it. She'd been my soul mate, my life partner, the woman with whom I was going to share kids and endless laughter and walks on the beach at sunset. Then suddenly, on my thirty-first birthday, she'd left me a simple three-sentence note explaining that she couldn't get married while she had doubts. A week later, the engagement ring I had been so proud to slip on her finger had appeared in my mailbox. She had used her parents' address in New York City for the return so I couldn't contact her. After she left, I spent a full year sitting on a couch in front of a psychiatrist who had once trained under my father.

The intercom sounded. It was Carolina. I buzzed her through the lobby and unlocked my apartment door. I hid the envelope underneath the wine cooler.

"A sight for sore eyes," I said as she walked through the door, carrying takeout from Dao, our favorite Thai restaurant, and a bottle of Chérisey Meursault Genelotte, her favorite. She looked her typical alluring self in a short floral sundress and white leather sandals with slight heels. The summer's sun had turned her naturally olive skin into a glowing bronze that made the inside of my mouth water. Her hair bounced freely on her shoulders.

"Only sore eyes?" she said, walking over to the kitchen and resting the bag on the counter where the blue envelope from Paris had once sat. "Why not a sight for all eyes?"

"Because then I would have to share you with every other human with a male organ, and I'd turn into a jealous lover."

"I've never seen you jealous," she said.

"Maybe I've been a master at disguising it," I said.

"Or maybe it's just not part of your DNA."

Carolina Espinoza and I had known each other for almost ten years. I'd met her as I was leaving the department. At the time, she'd worked in the office of the chief of detectives. When I had been summoned by the big boss and ordered to step away from the investigation of the Payton shooting, she was the one who had escorted me to his office. She was also the one who had warned me several weeks later that they were watching me. I'd known they were going to cover it up. It had been a bad shooting. The kid, Marquan Payton, had had a three-inch knife, but he'd been walking away when one of the responding officers had fired the shot that knocked him to the ground, then unloaded fifteen more shots into his bullet-riddled body. It had all been captured on the dash cam of one of the cruisers, but the written report the officers had filed hadn't matched what was in the video. I couldn't sit by and do nothing. That was not who I was. So, when the bosses had ordered me to stand down, I'd leaked the information to a reporter friend at the *Tribune*, then negotiated a settlement with my resignation.

Carolina and I had stayed in touch. She occasionally helped me with a case when I needed intel, thanks to her new position as administrative supervisor at police headquarters in the Bureau of Investigative Services. We flirted a little, threatened each other with romantic possibilities, but remained only friends. I liked her too much to bring her any closer to my sphere of damage.

"I brought over an itinerary for you to see," Carolina now said.

She plated our chicken rama with a healthy serving of white rice, peanut sauce, and steamed vegetables. She sat next to me on the couch.

"The trip you planned for me last year almost put me on the soup line," I said.

She laughed softly. "I've been very budget conscious," she said. "Instead of staying at the Mamounia, where Winston Churchill stayed, you're staying in the Palmeraie District, just outside of the old city. It's a small, charming place called Jnane Tamsna. Owned by an interior designer from Paris and her husband from Michigan."

I had decided I needed to take a vacation at the beginning of September, because it had been almost two years since my last trip. Marrakech had always interested me. Like Walter Griffin, I had never been to Africa before, and when I was a child, Morocco had always conjured images of exotic foods, bright colors, and soulful music. So, rather than making the customary first African-continent trip to South Africa, I'd chosen one of its most northern countries. Carolina had offered to make my itinerary.

"You're going to spend several days in Marrakech; then you'll camp in the Agafay Desert for a couple of nights, where you'll ride camels and watch the sunrise," she said. "After that, you go up into the Atlas Mountains for several days. I even scheduled two rounds of golf for you with one of the golf pros."

"You think of everything," I said, raising my glass in a toast. "What would I do without you?" Then I thought about the unopened letter from Julia hidden across the room, lurking like a nightmare waiting to ruin a good dream.

"I wondered the same thing." She smiled.

"I took on a new case," I said.

"In the middle of summer? You never do that."

"It's Walter Griffin," I said.

"As in the former board of ed president?"

I told her the story of how his children had come to see me and how I, too, believed he had not committed suicide. Then I told her about my conversation with Burke.

"Are you sure you want to do this?" she asked.

"I don't feel like I have a choice," I said. "They wrapped this case up into a suicide and tied it in a bow. No collateral damage. Everyone but the family has been able to go on with their lives. They deserve the truth. They deserve some kind of closure."

"Bailey and his lieutenants aren't gonna be happy if they hear you're digging around," she said.

"And I won't be happy unless I get some answers for that family."

"You think the Russians did it?"

"Burke thinks that's the first place to start," I said. "I meet with them tomorrow."

"They're very dangerous, Ashe."

"So am I with a pitching wedge in my hand, a hundred and thirty yards from the green with a soft right-to-left wind."

"This isn't a time for golf jokes."

"I know. It's a time for action."

"As in?" She inched closer to me, her thigh slightly brushing mine.

"I need you to get me a copy of the investigative file."

"I was wondering how long it would take for you to ask."

5

"THAT'S A LONG WAY with just a three iron," Penny Packer said to me as I stood behind my ball on the fourth fairway of the south course of Olympia Fields Country Club the next morning. My yardage gun had calculated a 250-yard shot to the center of the green. I grabbed a small tuft of grass and threw it up. The wind blew it forward. A helping wind would give the ball more carry than normal.

"What's the slope of the green?" I asked.

"Severe downward right to left," she said. "Anything landing left of the flag and you're dead. It's gonna roll right off the green."

Words that I wanted to hear, as this set up perfectly for my draw shot, which I had mastered last season. I went through my preshot ritual: two swings on the side of the ball, then I rested the club behind the ball and closed my eyes to visualize the ball flight. I opened my eyes, relaxed the muscles in my shoulder, and reminded myself to take a slow, smooth backswing with full rotation at the hips. A deep breath in and out, then I turned and unloaded the club. I knew by the sound of the contact between the clubface and ball that it was going to be a good shot. It started off moving slightly right as I planned; then, about a hundred yards out, it started to draw left toward the green.

We watched in silence, the most attentive three seconds in golf. The ball bounced twice, rolled a little forward and left, then stopped. Our caddie standing near the hole lifted both his hands to let me know I had hit the green and stuck.

"I see someone's been practicing and not telling," Penny said. "That shot wasn't in your bag last season."

"You're a great host," I said. "But I'm tired of walking into the clubhouse on the losing side of our scorecard."

I handed my club to the caddie walking beside us. The hot summer wind blew softly across the lush green fairway. Birds chirped above us, while a sundry of unseen critters rustled in the distant bushes. There was no place I'd rather be at that moment than right there with the smell of freshly cut grass and the sight of tightly manicured greens. A sporting nirvana.

"What do you know about Walter Griffin?" I asked.

"The school board president?" Penny asked.

"Suicide at Wolf Point."

"Walter was a good man," Penny said. "I knew him for a long time. We served together on several boards through the years. I always admired how he made the most of a tough start in life. And he had a natural way with people. Could work the room like nobody's business. You can't teach that. Why are you asking about him?"

"His children want me to find who murdered him."

Penny wrapped her arm around mine and steered me to the edge of the fairway, out of earshot of the caddie. Penny Packer was the third-richest person in Chicago. She had inherited the family's cosmetics business, then turned it into a huge conglomerate of companies ranging from women's accessories to real estate. She had been born into the seamless life of wealth and privilege, but she was funny and down to earth. She was also a fierce competitor and a phenomenal golfer.

"They ruled it a suicide," she said.

"The kids don't believe that." Peggy lifted her eyebrows. "And neither do I."

"You sure you want to get yourself mixed up in this?" she asked.

"What am I getting mixed up in?"

"Walter was born and raised on the West Side," she said. "But even with all his success and influence, he still lived on the West Side, in the same house he had lived in for thirty years, and had the same friends he knocked around with as a tough kid."

"Which means?"

"People were constantly asking him for favors," she said, "and getting him involved in things he didn't always want to get involved in. Not all those people were the most honest or reputable. But he managed to compartmentalize them like he did everything else in his life. He knew how to do business in all corners of the city."

"Would any of those corners be happy that he was no longer with us?"

"The charities definitely aren't happy. Walter was very philanthropic, and they'll miss all the fundraising he did for them. You walk into any room Walter was in, and you could be guaranteed that while he might not be the richest, he was definitely the most connected."

"Enemies?"

"Walter was a businessman," she said. "And after all, this is Chicago. It's impossible to conduct business in this city and not have enemies."

"I hear he was involved with the Russians," I said.

We reached Penny's ball resting just in the first cut of rough. She was 170 yards from the green. The caddie handed her a hybrid club. She set up next to the ball, took an easy practice swing, then addressed the ball with her clubface resting softly on the ground. In one fluid, beautiful motion, she brought the club back until it was almost parallel to the ground, then rotated her hip into the shot. The ball took off low and stayed on a perfectly straight line, landing on the front of the green and rolling about ten feet from the cup, just inside my ball. She winked at me, tossed her club to the caddie standing next to us, then walked me up the fairway.

"About a year or so before he died, Walter was betting heavy on the summer Olympic Games," she said. "All of us were. We were certain we'd get them, especially with the president being from Chicago and making a personal appeal to the committee. Walter, of course, knew all the city's plans well before most. The Summer Olympics are much bigger than the Winter Games. You need twice as many venues for the sporting events, and then there's the village where the athletes stay. It requires a lot of planning and investing, which means there's a lot of money to be made in building infrastructure. Washington Park and the West Side were right in the middle of Walter's turf, and they were certainly going to be used since they had the biggest tracts of undeveloped land. Long before it was announced that Bailey wanted to bring the Games here, Walter and his partners were allowed to buy undesirable city-owned land that had been vacant for decades. The land bank couldn't give that property away. Nobody ever wanted it, especially in those neighborhoods."

"So, he took on a lot of debt acquiring the land?" I said.

"Debt?" She laughed. "Not even close. City land is the cheapest land you can buy if you know the right people. Walter paid the princely price of one dollar per lot."

"One dollar?"

"That's it. One of the best-kept secrets. The city owns thousands of these lots, most of them in bad neighborhoods that have been abandoned or where people gave up on paying their taxes or water bills, and the city just took them over."

"What did his land have to do with the Russians?"

"They wanted the land also, but they didn't have Walter's connections, and the local aldermen weren't willing to help them. Everyone knows most of their money is laundered. So they went directly to Walter. He saw a business opportunity and flipped some of the land he had purchased for as much as half a million dollars a lot."

"Sounds like good old-fashioned capitalism to me," I said.

"It was," Penny said. "But then we never got the Olympics. Brazil did. Which they never should've, but that's a different story. Anyway, that meant all that land the Russians had paid a premium for was now worth nothing. Those kinds of people have very long memories and very little tolerance for losing, especially when it comes to that much money. They wanted Walter to buy the land back for the same price they paid for it."

"And he refused."

"Walter banked at Northern Trust. I've known the president of the bank for years. Walter didn't have much choice but to refuse the Russians. The money they had given him was long gone."

6

I HAD ARRIVED AT the corner of South Wells and West Forty-Fifth Place early enough that the rats and other night rodents were still courageous enough to walk freely in the streets. These critters didn't scurry and cower like they did in other parts of the city; in this neighborhood, they took their time and even cocked their heads back arrogantly as they returned my stare before continuing their scavenge.

Fuller Park's fifteen-block land mass squatted between two train tracks that form its east and west walls, with hardscrabble Englewood at its southern border and Bridgeport to the north—an area most famous for its racial intolerance and home to five Chicago mayors. Fuller Park consistently ranked as one of the most crime-ridden areas in the city, with more than half its residents living beneath the poverty line. The once-bustling neighborhood had been gutted when the construction of the Dan Ryan Expressway ripped through its center, destroying homes and businesses, causing residents to quickly flee the now-blighted streets.

Ever since seeing Demetrius Jackson's face, I hadn't been able to get his killer out of my mind. Antoine "Twiggy" Nelson lived here with his grandmother in a small workers' cottage–style house with dirty yellow siding and unpainted stair railings that led to a tiny porch and heavily fortified screen door. A small driveway held an old, rusted Chevy and a shiny HP4 Race BMW motorcycle that was worth substantially more than the house. I sat in my van at the opposite street corner, with a full view of the house and the nonexistent traffic that passed in front of it.

Nelson was an unrepentant murderer who'd killed a completely innocent kid. Demetrius Jackson had been minding his own business on the CTA's green line one Saturday night, heading to his aunt's house to celebrate her birthday. He was on the phone with his girlfriend, Jillian, who had just moved to New York to go to design school. She recounted to the media how she had heard Nelson confront her boyfriend and demand that he give him his cell phone and backpack. Jackson had told Nelson to get away from him. His exact words: "I'm not the one you wanna mess with." Nelson had grown even more aggressive, pointing in Jackson's face and telling him he had seconds to "give up his shit or get his ass kicked." Jackson had calmly asked to be left alone, since he was on the phone with his girl and didn't have time for petty bullshit. That had been when Nelson sucker punched him, knocking the phone to the floor. The two other passengers in the car, a sixty-year-old woman heading home from work and a teenager riding home from basketball practice, had known better than to get involved. Jackson had regained his footing, picked up the phone, and stuffed it in his pocket. He had then proceeded to pummel Nelson, who quickly retreated to the other end of the car, where he sat hunched over in pain.

Jackson had taken his phone out of his pocket and explained to Jillian what had just happened. She had begged him to leave the train as soon as possible and not continue the altercation. Jackson had agreed, as he didn't want any more trouble. He had been excited to have just gotten accepted into Columbia College, and one of his songs had been selected in a local talent competition to air on the city's hip-hop station WGCI. He had gotten off at the Garfield Boulevard station, even though it was three stops away from where he needed to go, and had decided to wait for the next train. He had taken one last look at Nelson, who was still seated at the other end of the car, then had joined the queue of passengers exiting the other cars.

Jillian and Jackson had continued to talk, discussing their plans to meet up in New York the following weekend, when suddenly she had heard him groan and yell, "Shit! He stabbed me." Other eyewitnesses at the scene had said they saw Nelson run from the train with something in his right hand. Someone had yelled, "Gun! He's got a gun!" Chaos had ensued. People had dropped bags, run out of their shoes, abandoned strollers after snatching their children, then had raced along the platform and down the stairs. But it hadn't been a gun. It had been a Buck 119 Special knife with a six-inch fixed steel blade. The knife had entered Jackson's right flank, filleting open part of his colon and right kidney, then severing the inferior vena cava—an enormous vein that transports deoxygenated blood from the lower body back to the heart.

Jillian had screamed into the phone, asking Jackson if he was okay, but all she had been able to hear was his groaning. Then she had heard a loud clap and scratchy sound as the phone hit the concrete platform. The last words he had said to her were, "Tell my family how much I love them. Let's all go see those beautiful mountains." In just the seven minutes it had taken for the police to make it to his side, Demetrius Jackson had exsanguinated alone on the Garfield Boulevard platform, lying in his own young blood, thinking about the mountaintops in the Grand Tetons he had always dreamed of visiting but now would never see.

It wasn't just the reckless loss of a promising young kid's life that incensed me, but what Nelson did afterward. Hours later he had posted a photograph of himself on Instagram, smiling with stacks of hundred-dollar bills in both hands and diamond earrings in both ears. The gold lettering on his shirt read, "Thug For Life." It should've had the word *coward* added. Two days later, he'd called up Jackson's father and told him that his son was nothing but a punk ass who got what he deserved. Antoine Nelson had never met Demetrius Jackson before that fateful night. When the judge read his sentence, Nelson had turned to Jackson's father, Cesar, smiled, and mouthed, "Fuck you!" It had taken five men to stop Cesar from jumping over the railing to get at him.

It hadn't been Nelson's only crime, just the one he'd gotten caught for. I looked at the small, battered house and the $70,000 motorcycle parked outside of it. A kid like Demetrius Jackson, who had nothing but great potential, a budding singer with a wonderful voice who would never see his parents or brother or girlfriend again, was six feet in the ground for no reason other than he wouldn't give up his cell phone and a backpack. Meanwhile, Nelson was free to run the streets, eat whatever he wanted, see his family every night, and have sex with his many girlfriends scattered throughout the city. Demetrius Jackson's body was disintegrating in a graveyard in Evergreen Park. He would never see those mountains.

At quarter past eight, Nelson opened the front door and skipped down the steps, helmet in hand. He had added a few pounds to his slight frame in prison and had grown a full beard that had been meticulously trimmed. His wide, long dreadlocks had been replaced with short twists. He wore a thick gold chain outside his powder-blue polo shirt.

He hopped on the bike, typed something into his phone, then took a right onto Forty-Fifth Place. I waited for him to turn down

Princeton before moving the van and followed him to the north-bound entrance ramp of the Dan Ryan Expressway.

Morning rush hour had almost reached its peak as eighteen-wheelers traveling through the state met up with commuters from the south suburbs heading into the city. Nelson bobbed easily among the traffic, which was making it difficult for me to follow in my transit cargo van. He stayed in the right lanes, which were moving a little faster, then a couple of miles later took the exit heading to Cermak Road in Chinatown. I continued to follow from several cars back. He headed east toward the lake, then entered the busy South Loop and headed north before pulling over at 525 South State Street, a tall residential building with a steady flow of students passing through its glass doors.

I pulled off into an alley and turned on the high-powered camera in the van, focusing it on Nelson as he parked his bike, made a phone call, then grabbed a small plastic bag from his seat storage compartment and slid it into his pants. He took his helmet off, then disappeared through the large glass doors.

I googled the address while I waited. This building belonged to Roosevelt University, a small private liberal arts school founded in the 1950s on the principle of social justice and dedicated to President Franklin Delano Roosevelt and his wife, Eleanor. Five Twenty-Five South State Street, otherwise known as University Center, was the hub of student residential life, offering all kinds of amenities, including a twenty-four-hour fitness center, meeting spaces, and computer lab. While Roosevelt didn't share the same academic prestige as Northwestern or the University of Chicago, it did share a similar sticker price, setting back undergraduates and their families more than $45,000 per year.

What was a punk like Antoine Nelson doing at Roosevelt University? I was certain he hadn't suddenly decided to become an astrophysicist. I watched the flow of students with their oversize backpacks and cherubic faces convinced they would one day save the world. It dawned on me that their parents hundreds of miles away would've gone into cardiac arrest had they known a murderer was freely mingling with their aspiring scholars.

Ten minutes later, Nelson emerged through the glass doors. He jumped on his bike and headed north on State, then made a quick right, followed by another. He wedged his bike between two parked cars in front of a modern-looking glass building on South Wabash Avenue. Google told me that this was another Roosevelt residential hall. The school had recently allowed the nearby Robert Morris University to lease several of the floors for its students.

Fifteen minutes after he went inside, Nelson sauntered through the glass doors and hopped back on his bike. This time I followed him into an exclusive, tree-lined area of the South Loop. He turned into an alley behind a row of scrubbed-brick town houses. As I drove by slowly, I saw him climb off the bike and start walking deeper into the alley.

I sped up and took a quick right on Fourteenth Street and caught Nelson as he reached the opposite end of the alley. I moved the camera and zoomed in just as a garage door opened. A tall blonde girl in black yoga pants and tight pink T-shirt, holding a small dog, greeted him. He walked in, and the garage door closed behind him.

The garage door opened about ten minutes later, but instead of Nelson, a silver Audi convertible with tinted windows emerged into the alley and headed north. I couldn't see who was in the car, so I just waited. Five minutes later, the garage door opened again, and Nelson walked out. The blonde girl said something to him as he left. She was no longer holding the dog. I tried to follow Nelson, but by the time I had made it back around the block to South Indiana, he and his bike were in the wind.

7

THE UKRAINIAN VILLAGE WAS a well-demarcated Chicago neighborhood situated in the Near West Side of the city. Bordered by Division Street to the north, Chicago Avenue to the south, and Damen to the east, the area was settled by Ukrainian immigrants at the turn of the nineteenth century. They chose this part of the city to establish a base because of their cultural and ancestral familiarity with the Poles who lived one neighborhood over.

While Russians had spread across the city, the Ukrainian Village still served as a hub that included several major churches, Ukrainian-owned banks, an elementary school, a museum, and a modern art institute as well as restaurants, stores, and other businesses. Yeltsin's was the most popular bakery in the Village, serving tiny old grandmothers and local vicars as well as gun-strapped gangsters waiting in line for chocolate tinginys. Sergei Yeltsin had immigrated as a little boy with his parents and, after a young life of running the streets, had finally settled down and taken over his father's business.

According to Mechanic, if the Russians had had anything to do with Walter Griffin's death, Yeltsin would know it.

Mechanic pulled his Viper behind a small row of storefronts, and we both got out. He tapped on the back door of the bakery, which was opened by a young girl who couldn't have been more than thirteen. She had dark, heavy eyebrows that drooped at the ends and offered her face a touch of sadness.

"We're here to see Sergei," Mechanic said.

"He's in the back," the girl said. "Follow me."

We followed her down a narrow hallway that connected to another hallway and down a flight of steps. She opened the door and nodded for us to enter. Once we had stepped in, she closed the door behind us and left.

The cavernous room was lined with rolling baking sheets along the yellow walls—an enormous baking kitchen several times the size of the retail space at the front of the building. The entire ceiling was made of glass, letting the sunshine in unimpeded. Framed movie posters hung on the walls. There was Bruce Willis in *Die Hard* next to Will Smith in *Men in Black*. Vin Diesel sat on a car in *The Fast and the Furious*, and a young Sylvester Stallone gave life to the Rocky franchise.

A short man with a large head and thick nose sat at a small table in the center of the room. He was slurping loudly from a bowl of soup. His forearms were the size of baseball bats. He nodded for us to sit in the two chairs flanking him.

"It's been a while, Dmitri," he said with a thick accent. He wiped his hands on his stained apron and gripped Mechanic's hand. I noticed a tattoo of some animal at the base of his neck.

"This is my friend Ashe," Mechanic said.

"Any friend of Dmitri is friend of mine," Sergei said with a smile. His teeth were small and bent at uncomfortable angles.

We pumped hands. His grip was strong enough to crush rocks.

"Something to eat?" he asked. "I can have more brought back for you."

"We're good," Mechanic said.

"Nice movie selection," I said, nodding to the posters.

"Ah, yes," Sergei said, grinning. "I am a fan of the Hollywood action movie. They make the best in the world."

"I figured you for something like *Silver Linings Playbook*."

Sergei scrunched up his forehead.

"Bradley Cooper and Jennifer Lawrence."

"I never heard this movie," Sergei said. "How I miss big action movie like that?"

"Cooper and Lawrence both are psychologically damaged. Cooper loses his job and wife and spends time in a mental institution. He moves in with his parents while he's on the mend. De Niro is Cooper's father, and all he wants is for him to be obsessed with the Philadelphia Eagles like he is. Lawrence has her own dark past. She and Cooper meet, and she agrees to help him reconnect with his wife if he helps her do one thing."

Sergei's eyes had glassed over. He looked at Mechanic, then back at me.

"Not my kind of movie," he said.

"Don't you want to know what she wanted him to help her with?"

"Not really, but it seem like you want to tell me. Be my guest."

"She wants him to dance with her in a competition. If he does that, she'll deliver a letter he wrote to his wife but can't get to her, because of the restraining order she took out against him."

Sergei looked at Mechanic, who shrugged and said, "He's a little different."

"How can I help you?" Sergei smiled.

"I'm looking into the death of Walter Griffin," I said. "He died along the river a couple of years ago."

"I know the name," Sergei said, nodding. "It was very bad tragedy. Lots of people upset on TV."

"A few years ago, he had some real estate dealings with a group of Russian businessmen," I said. "I was wondering if you might know anything about that."

Sergei slurped another spoonful of soup, then pushed the bowl away. "Solotov," he said. "It was very bad deal."

"How do you know this?"

"I am only a little baker in a small part of the city," he said. "But I am a friendly person. People like my vatrushkas. I hear things."

"Then you know that a lot of people believe that Griffin didn't commit suicide," I said. "Many people think he was killed by these Russian businessmen over a real estate disagreement."

"Convenient explanation." Sergei smiled again. "Always easy to blame the Russians."

"Are you saying they had nothing to do with it?"

Sergei looked at Mechanic, then back at me. "How well did you know this Mr. Griffin?" Sergei asked.

"Not well at all," I said. "I never met him before, but his family wants me to find the truth."

"Maybe you should know a little more about this man before you start asking questions and making accusations."

Sergei's tone had frosted since he'd invited us to eat with him, but he still smiled. There was a soft knock on the door. Sergei yelled for the person to enter. The girl who had escorted us earlier walked into the room. She set down a small cup of cappuccino and a plate of cookies in front of Sergei and took the bowl away, all without saying anything.

"I'm happy to learn whatever it is you have to share about Walter Griffin," I said, once the girl had left and closed the door. "I have no judgments on who he was as a person. I am only looking for the truth."

Sergei smiled, then picked up the cappuccino cup, which disappeared in his meaty hands. He took a short sip. "Let me start by saying, respectfully, your Mr. Griffin was not a saint. He portray a big man who does business and help the community, but he had a big interest for himself."

"Sounds like he was a capitalist," I said. "That might be a crime in other countries, but not here."

"He was dishonest with the land deal right from beginning," Sergei said. "He knew exactly where the city building projects if they win Olympics. So, he knew land he sold to Solotov was never going to be in the plans, and he knew Solotov only buy the land because he expected it to be one of those projects."

"We never won the bid," I said. "So everyone lost. All the land speculation was worth nothing. Griffin took a loss too."

"But he not pay millions for his land." Sergei swiped his hand across the surface of his table and held up his hand for me to see. "He pay only crumbs."

"So, they killed him because they gambled and lost."

Sergei shook his head emphatically. "They would've killed him if he lived long enough. It wasn't them. He put gun to his own head, or someone did it for him."

8

ACCORDING TO YELTSIN, THE Russians hadn't killed Walter Griffin. So, my next visit was to Delroy Thomas, the colorful former alderman of the city's Twenty-Seventh Ward on the hardscrabble West Side. He had served his constituents for five drama-filled terms before being convicted of a long list of federal crimes, including kickbacks and extortion. After serving a little more than three years of his sentence, he was released; then he returned home and promptly reentered Chicago's political boxing ring.

Thomas's loyal constituents gave him another term as a big middle finger to the government. They had always believed the Feds, in cooperation with the mayor's office, had entrapped their fearless leader as retribution for his being outspoken against what he called "the avalanche of inequities that roll down from the fifth floor of city hall." They were determined that a Black man fighting for their causes was not going to be silenced by Chicago's political elite. Thomas served the term, then passed the crown to his nephew, who now held the seat.

Delroy's Catfish Corner, a small soul food restaurant, was where Thomas now held court. The most important political and civic leaders, as well as beat reporters, gathered there daily to swap stories and trade on information.

I had heard about the place, but this was my first time venturing inside. It was just after six o'clock on a Thursday night, and the place was already jumping. Marvin Gaye crooned over the din of clanking silverware and bursts of laughter. The cramped, hot dining room had been decorated with a few banquettes along the perimeter, and weathered wood tables filled out the rest of the floor. Ceiling fans carried the smell of frying fish from the kitchen. The bar situated to the left of the room was presided over by a pleasant-looking fat man with a tall gray Afro, wearing a white shirt big enough to hang as a curtain.

A dark-skinned young woman with long braids and blue eye shadow that matched her lipstick greeted me at the door. The curves of her ample hips beneath the skinniest of waists put her jeans to the test.

"Dinner for one?" she asked. There was a trace of island in her soft voice, which made me think of warm blue water and white-sand beaches.

"I'm actually here to see Delroy," I said.

"Is he expecting you?"

"That's what I've come to ask him."

She weighed my words, then smiled. "You have jokes."

"Life is short."

"Delroy is in the back."

"Tell him Ashe Cayne is here to see him."

As she walked toward the bar and through the swinging door, I could see I wasn't the only one admiring her.

Delroy came through a couple of minutes later. He was age-less. His tight curly hair had a strand of gray here and there, and his shoulders drooped just a little, but he was still tall and thin and full of swagger. The pale-blue pinstripes of his charcoal-gray suit matched his tasseled leather loafers. He motioned me to join him at an empty table in the back.

"Glad to have you at my little joint," Delroy said as I sat down. "A long way for you to travel from downtown."

"Fifteen minutes by car," I said. "Probably double by bus."

"Metaphorically speaking." Delroy smiled, displaying a mouth full of large false teeth. He motioned, and a waitress quickly arrived at our table. "What are you drinking?" he asked me.

"Manhattan," I said. "But only if it's rye whiskey. Stirred over ice, served straight up."

"Only way to make it." Delroy looked at the waitress. "Selita, I'll take the usual."

Delroy watched her walk away, then turned back to me. "These young girls are packin' a lot more than back in my day. I don't know what the hell has happened, but I ain't complaining."

"Darwinism at its best," I said.

"Meaning?"

"Natural selection. Nature chooses which genes are most desirable and beneficial to survival, then propagates them at the expense of eliminating those that are less desirable."

"Well, thank God for Darwin, but he sure in hell got the short end of the stick."

We laughed easily. Delroy might've been as corrupt as the rest of them, but he had no shortage of charisma. I could understand why he had been reelected just months after getting sprung from prison.

"I figure you're here because of Katrina and Walter Jr.," Delroy said. "I'm the one who sent them to you."

"Why me?" I said.

"Because you don't give a damn about the politics. And you're not afraid to find the truth, no matter where it takes you or what you have to do to get it."

Selita returned with our drinks. She placed a gin and tonic in front of Delroy and the Manhattan in front of me. I could tell by the color that the big man behind the bar knew what he was doing.

"You don't think it was a suicide," I said.

Delroy sipped his drink. "I know damn well it wasn't suicide," he said. "Griff was killed just as sure as I'm sitting at this table."

"Proof?"

"I'm not the private investigator," Delroy said. "That's your job. But I know the proof is out there if somebody's serious about finding it."

"Who do you think wanted him dead?"

"C'mon, young blood. Griff was a powerful Black man in Chicago." Delroy leaned forward, and the veins in his neck popped. "He made it downtown in their world but always came back home to help his people. He won't no sellout. And he won't afraid. Who might've wanted him dead? That list could be long."

I took a sip of the Manhattan. The barman really was good. The flavors were bold, and the sweet vermouth had been mixed in a perfect ratio to the whiskey.

"How about giving me your top three on the list," I said.

"The Red Squad," Delroy said. "Walter knew too much about all the shit they was doing on the Fifth Floor. Order finally came down to eliminate him."

The Red Squad was rumored to be a small unit of rogue cops who operated solely for the mayor's interests. They gathered information on political opponents, intimidated people who threatened the city hall machine, and, if necessary, weren't afraid to help disappear people. I wasn't sure the squad really existed as an organized unit, but when I was on the force, I had heard there were certain officers who operated on both sides of the shield. They called them the Red Squad because of all the blood they had shed.

"But Griffin was Bailey's guy," I said.

"But no matter how light his skin was, he wasn't one of them. All them positions and titles and deals they gave him at the end of the day, he still shit to them."

"If Griffin was on the inside all these years, then why get rid of him now?"

"Word is Griff was about to talk," Delroy said. "The Feds had him tied to some of Bailey's boys for some shit about the Cabrini-Green land development. They did a number on those poor residents. Blacks lived in those projects for over fifty years. Forget about a second thought—city never gave them a third or fourth either. Drugs, sex, gangs, murders—the place was a real shithole. But it was all those people had, and it was prime real estate in the shadows of the Gold Coast. Those rich white developers had been trying to get that land for years. Bailey finally delivered it to them. He puts his guy in charge at the housing authority, then instead of cleaning the place up and making it livable, they condemn the buildings. Bullshit. Ran the tenants the fuck outa there before anyone could challenge them in court, tore the buildings down. Then they slowly gave leases to the private developers to start building. Completely illegal the way they did it, kickbacks and all. That land was worth a fortune, and they stole it."

"Why would Griffin talk after all these years?" I asked.

"Feds were squeezing him tight," Delroy said. "There was a lot going on. OIG was working him up on some investigation about messin' in some of the city's money. Small stuff they was trying to make into something big. At the same time, the Feds knew Griff had knowledge of the Cabrini land deal. They wanted him to spill what he knew, 'cause they wanted the big fish."

"Bailey?"

"Bailey. That muthafuckah got his hands in everything but never gets caught. So the Feds were trying to get Griff to cut a deal. I heard the offer was, he helps them out, they make the OIG shit go away."

"Did he take the deal?"

"From what I heard, he was seriously considering it. Griff won't nobody's fool. You mess with city money and get caught, they puttin' yo ass away for some time. Griff was sixty. No man at that stage in his life wants to see his grandchildren grow up in a prison visiting room."

I filed away the information about the Office of Inspector General's investigation. "Who's number two on your list?"

"Griff was betting big on the Olympics coming, like everybody else on the inside," Delroy said. "He got tied up with the Russians. Things went wrong. They killed him."

"They said they had nothing to do with it."

Delroy took a long sip of his drink, then sat back in his chair. "What the fuck they supposed to say? Stand in front of the damn Thompson Center with signs that say, 'We killed him'? The Russians are the coldest muthafuckahs on the street. Them people are made differently. Women, kids, old people—nobody's off limits with them when shit go down. They ain't human."

There was a slight commotion at the door. State Senator Billy "Hollywood" Hendricks had just walked into the restaurant. Hollywood Hendricks was the only man in Chicago who could out-slick Delroy Thomas. He was a short man with processed curly hair, reflective sunglasses, and a burgundy three-piece suit that matched his suede shoes. He was immediately swallowed in handshakes and hugs.

"Who's number three on the list?" I asked.

"Cephus Redmond."

"Cephus Redmond the car wash guy?"

"Only Cephus Redmond I know," Delroy said.

"Why would Cephus want Griffin dead?"

"Only three reasons bring a man to that darkness. Money, sex, or jealousy."

"Which one was it for Cephus?"

"What I hear, the whole damn trifecta."

9

I PULLED OFF Lake Shore Drive and slowly entered the driveway to the Sixty-Third Street Beach. It was well past midnight. The beach and surrounding parking lots had long been cleared, and the gigantic stone pavilion with all its stairwells and balconies looked like an ancient mansion that had been abandoned after a war.

I took the two envelopes sitting on the passenger seat and departed the car for the grassy ledge over the water. The waves rolled rhythmically to shore, then crashed against the rocky coastline. Julia and I would sit here for hours laughing, crying, planning our lives together, speculating on how many children we'd have and what their names might be. One night we'd decided to sneak upstairs to the second-floor promenade deck of the pavilion and in the shadows of a hot summer night made love to the sound of the water rumbling to shore and cars whizzing by.

I looked down at the envelopes sitting on the bench next to me. The small envelope from Julia still sat unopened since I had retrieved it from my mailbox. Carolina's larger envelope sat next to it. How strange life could be sometimes. Two envelopes of different sizes, carrying different messages, from two women who represented the highest and lowest points of my life.

I looked north across the black water toward downtown. A fingerlike projection of lights jutted out from the shore, leading up to the Promontory Point Field House. From this vantage, it was impossible to see Navy Pier or my building, but I could see the blinking red beacon of the lighthouse and that constant white light farther east, whose origin or purpose I had never learned despite promising Julia that one day I would satisfy our curiosity.

It had been a couple of years since she'd deserted me, and as the days went by and my life seemed to fill back up with purpose, I thought about her less. But there were moments like this—moments when I drove past a landmark she liked, a restaurant we'd frequented—that opened the wound, raw and exposed.

What did she want to say to me after all this time? Better yet, did I really want to hear it and risk another dark, downward spiral that I had barely survived after her desertion?

My hand moved past the blue envelope to pick up Carolina's. Her writing was feminine like Julia's, not as loopy but extraordinarily neat. She'd drawn a small smiley face on the back of the envelope with hearts in place of the eyes.

I opened the large envelope and pulled out a stack of papers detailing the investigation into the death of Walter Griffin. It was the entire case file that Burke wasn't able to get without raising flags. Carolina's job at headquarters gave her full clearance and access. No one would ever notice she had copied it.

Walter Griffin's Sunday morning had begun like every other Sunday. He went to the eight-o'clock church service at Mount Pleasant AME Zion Church. After service he drove to the South Shore Golf Course, a nine-hole public golf course on the southern banks of Lake Michigan. He played his regular game with Alderman Darnell Hampton from the Twentieth Ward, Cook County treasurer

Leroy Jenkins, Eddie Rankin from the University of Chicago's Office of Civic Engagement, and Moe Blight from Blight Funeral Homes. None of them reported anything unusual except that Griffin took a call as they finished the ninth hole and skipped the after-round drinks they typically shared while settling the bets. Alderman Darnell, his playing partner, said that Griffin seemed a little more distracted than normal, but he still shot three pars and a birdie that helped them win the match.

At 1:15 p.m. Griffin called his wife, Viola, and they spoke for six minutes. Her interview revealed they spoke about the match, what they planned on having for dinner that night, and a call he had gotten from one of the mayoral aides about a meeting they wanted him to attend on Monday morning with someone from the Office of Inspector General about personal charges he'd allegedly made on a credit card that had been issued to him by the Chicago Public School System. He told his wife he was going to visit his mother at the Calgary Arms Nursing Home in the West Loop; then he'd pick up some lobster from the Capital Grille on the way home.

At 1:45 p.m. he arrived at Lem's Bar-B-Q on Seventy-Fifth Street. He picked up a bucket of rib tips with extra sauce and a large order of steak fries. The interview with the cashier at Lem's said that Griffin was alone, like he always was, and looked no different than he did any other Sunday, but the cashier was surprised he ordered only one bucket of tips and one order of fries. He usually ordered two of both for the entire nursing staff. He paid cash for the food and left his customary ten-dollar tip. His behavior seemed otherwise normal.

At 2:03 p.m. Griffin walked into the Calgary Arms Nursing Home. He spent the next hour visiting his mother, as he did every Sunday. He left at 3:14 p.m.

Traffic and police cameras tracked him heading east on Madison and turning onto Upper Wacker Drive. He took a right onto Lake Street, then a short distance later turned left onto North Post Place. This effectively put him on Lower Wacker Drive, which ran exactly the same direction as Upper Wacker but felt like you were driving in a tunnel because of the road above it and the supporting concrete structures along the sides. The trail ran cold there. According to one of the notes, the cameras on Lower Wacker were out of service for technology upgrades.

At 5:37 p.m. Viola called her husband's cell phone and got his voice mail. She left him a message.

At 6:17 p.m. Viola called again, but this time his phone didn't ring. It went straight to voice mail. She left him a message and sent him a text message to call her ASAP. She was worried that she hadn't heard from him. She called several of his friends, her children, and other relatives. No one had heard from him. At 9:35 p.m. she called 911 and reported him missing. She called Alderman Hampton, who told her to sit tight, that he'd come over to the house. He arrived a little before ten and used her house as a command center, calling the superintendent of police as well as several other city-agency leaders. There was a full-out effort to locate Walter Griffin. No one had heard from or seen him since he'd left the nursing home.

Griffin's cell phone carrier was asked to ping his cell phone for a location. Illinois law clearly stipulated that actively tracking or accessing someone's cell phone records required a subpoena or judge's order, but given Griffin's status, standard protocols were ignored, and the phone company complied. The appropriate paperwork would be assembled and submitted in the morning.

At 3:35 a.m. the ping triangulated a rough location for the phone. Investigating officers were led to an area of the city called

Wolf Point in the River North neighborhood. Within fifty yards of the Kinzie Street Bridge, detectives discovered Griffin's red Cadillac convertible on the east bank of the river. The doors and trunk were locked. A handwritten note had been left on the passenger seat. Two words: *I'm sorry.*

His golf clubs and the clothes he had worn on the course earlier that morning were undisturbed in the trunk. A parking ticket had been slipped under the passenger-side wiper. It had been written by a Union Pacific Railroad police officer. Approximately seven yards away from the car, resting on a concrete embankment along the slope of the riverbank, was Griffin's CPS-issued BlackBerry. It still had battery life but had been turned off. Fresh blood had splattered along the embankment and down the side heading to the water.

At 3:55 a.m. Griffin's body was discovered at the base of the bridge abutment not too far from the red Cadillac. His waist and legs rested on the embankment, while his upper torso and face were twisted and submerged in the shallow water. A couple of feet away from his body, a single spent 9 mm cartridge was found amid a tuft of weeds and scattered trash. The officers had performed a survey of items in the vicinity of his body—a random collection of garbage items, including beer bottles, an empty soda can, cigarette butts, and a couple of potato chip bags. A Steyr 9 mm semiautomatic pistol was found in the water wedged beneath his left arm. Sixteen rounds remained in a magazine that held seventeen. The serial number had been filed off the gun.

By eight o'clock that morning, the crime scene had been cleared, Griffin's body had been carried off by police boat to the department's marine headquarters, and his car had been towed to the ME's office. His brain matter and blood had been washed and scrubbed from the asphalt, and it had been business as usual for another typical Chicago morning rush.

I looked at the crime scene photos and matched them to the written description in the report. Griffin's face had ballooned in the water, his eyes wide open and eerily lifeless. It struck me how ironic it was that a man who had been so debonair and handsome in life could look so distorted and tortured in death. I reread the ballistics report. The gun found near the body had indeed fired the bullet that killed him, but with no serial number, it was untraceable. There was no mention of any follow-up regarding the gun's ownership. Did it belong to Griffin or someone else?

Then something clicked in my head, and I scanned the pages again, making sure I hadn't missed it.

I googled the phone number to the Calgary Arms Nursing Home and made the call. A man's drowsy voice answered.

I explained that I was a private investigator working for Walter Griffin's family. "I had some questions about the last time he visited his mother."

"I can't give out that kind of information," the man said, his voice more alert. "You would need to speak to the supervisor."

"Is the supervisor available?"

"Not the one you're looking for. Mrs. Hughes works nights. You need Mrs. Evette Carson. She runs the day shift."

"What time will she be in tomorrow?"

"She won't. She's on vacation."

"For how long?"

"Sir, I can't give you that kind of information. Best I can do is take your name and number and get the message to her."

I gave him my info and asked him to let Mrs. Carson know that it was urgent. Then I looked back at the investigative report. Why hadn't anyone interviewed the staff at Calgary? And if they had, why wasn't it in the file?

10

WOLF POINT HAD A unique place in Chicago's history. This thumbnail-shaped piece of property sat at the confluence of the north, south, and main branches of the Chicago River, just west of the gigantic Merchandise Mart building and cowering in the hulking shadow of the Chicago Apparel Center. A once-bustling intersection for early explorers and traders, it got its name from a member of the Potawatomi tribe who lived there and whose name was translated as *wolf*.

Hundreds of years later, this important geographical landmark stood lifeless and deserted, accessible only by dark backstreets usually encountered only when making a wrong turn. Mechanic and I sat in my car facing the raised Kinzie Street railroad drawbridge, which was never used and remained standing at an eleven-o'clock angle over the north branch of the river. The water was to our west and behind us. It was 3:55 in the morning, the exact time the police had found Griffin's body half-submerged in the water.

Nothing moved.

"Ain't the place I'd go to kill myself," Mechanic said. "Rats and trash all over. You could set off a bomb down here, and no one would ever hear it."

"They found his car over there," I said, pointing to a flat piece of empty concrete just a few feet above the river's embankment. The blue trash bin that had been described in the report was still there. "He drove a red Cadillac."

"Which one?"

"XLR convertible."

"The man had style."

"More than guys half his age. All his suits were custom made by some tailor who flew in from Hong Kong twice a year, and his shirts were made by some guy in Brooklyn, New York."

"He had money?"

"Yes and no. He made a lot of money in his business deals, but he lost a lot of money too. I don't know how much he had when he died."

I looked around the darkness. The moon's light cut slightly through the towering buildings and rusted steel beams of the bridge. It felt so desolate and disconnected from the city. It had to be a lonely place to die. A gentle breeze blew trash across the broken asphalt.

"Something's not right," I said. "The official report says that Griffin left the note in his car, got out, and locked the doors. He made his way down the embankment. He then sat down on the ledge just above the river. He pulls out his pistol. Places the gun against his left temple, then fires with his left hand. He falls, and his body rolls over and into the shallow part of the river headfirst. The gun is found under him in the water."

"Did you see the photos?" Mechanic asked.

"I did. But I felt like something about them wasn't right. Sitting here now makes me feel the same way, but I can't say what it is."

I looked up at the Merchandise Mart. Lights still burned in several of the windows on the upper floors. Had someone up there seen what happened that night? I looked for cameras. There were none. Not one car had driven by, and we had been there for almost forty minutes. This was a perfect location to do something really bad. The killer had chosen wisely.

Mechanic read my mind. "Of all the thousands of cameras in this city, the few that would show his car driving down here just happen to be out of service," he said. "Convenient."

"Too convenient," I said.

"Forensics on his car?"

"Completely clean," I said. "Too clean. Not even his wife's prints were in the car. They found only his around the driver's window and steering wheel. Let's just say it was suicide. Why here of all places? An extremely successful and connected man and a self-described germophobe comes alone to this hellhole and puts a bullet in his head while water rats scamper at his feet? Not buying it. Someone forced him to come here. I think Griffin knew the person and knew he was going to die."

"What makes you say that?"

"A man his size with his street smarts would've put up some kind of struggle, some kind of fight to stay alive. But there were no signs of distress in the car and no bruises, scratches, or wounds on his body. The ME's report was straightforward. He was dead before his body hit the water. There was gunshot residue on his clothes and fingers. No prints could be recovered from the gun."

"So, what next?"

"I need to talk to his wife. It's time to hear what she has to say."

11

VIOLA GRIFFIN ANSWERED THE door to her immaculate home dressed in white linen pants and a silk pink-and-gold blouse that fell loosely about her petite frame. She had a short pixie cut shaped perfectly around her caramel-colored angular face. To just say that she was beautiful would be lazy. She was effortlessly stunning and all natural. Her hazel eyes sparkled as the sunlight cut through the door.

"Thanks for making the trip," she said after we were comfortably seated in the living room. The furniture was modern and stark. An array of family photos hung above the marble fireplace. "I know that getting here from downtown is a little bit of a trek."

She had a pitcher of iced lemon water and a tea service on a small table between us. She poured herself tea. I asked for the water.

"Your house is beautiful," I said.

"We put a lot of work into it," she said, gazing around. "Walter never wanted to leave, so we just made improvements. He enjoyed working downtown, then retreating here. Walter liked familiarity. Regardless of how many fancy dinners or galas or important business meetings he had to attend, he always enjoyed coming home to the neighborhood and people who loved and knew him best."

Viola Griffin was Walter's second wife. His first wife had died during childbirth, along with the baby. Viola had been raised in DC, her father a prominent lobbyist for United Airlines, her mother an art history professor at George Washington University, the same school from which Viola had graduated with a bachelor's in English. She'd taught at the University of Illinois for several years, then settled in at home to raise their children while Walter conquered the world.

"Tell me about Walter," I said.

Viola inhaled slowly, then exhaled into a smile. "Where do you want me to start?" she asked.

"Wherever you want."

"Walter was a big man," she said. "Not just in size, but in character and personality. He was so full of life. Never enough hours in the day to get done all that he wanted. He didn't know how to do anything without gusto."

"I heard he was a good golfer."

"One of his many obsessions." She smiled. "He was determined to get his handicap into the single digits. But he wanted to do it on his own. No lessons. Just by studying and tinkering and practicing."

"I suffer from a similar affliction," I said. "Going through life without golf would be like breathing without oxygen."

"Then you and Walter would've gotten along well. As frustrated as he was when his score wasn't what he wanted, he was most at peace on those quiet fairways."

I decided right away that I liked Viola Griffin. She was serene and intelligent, with a poise that came natural to her and not learned at some New England finishing school. Walter Griffin had been one lucky man to come home to her every night.

"I have to tell you that I didn't want to take this case," I said.

"But you did, because you know they killed my husband."

"I do."

"And you are the kind of man who can't let wrong stand if it's in your power to make it right."

"I am."

"Walter played golf on the last day he was alive," she said with a soft smile. "He had always said he wanted his last day on earth to include a round. It's strange what things you hold on to to give you comfort. Something like that, as small as it might seem, has helped alleviate some of the pain."

"I've heard and read bits and pieces," I said. "But would you mind taking me through what happened that day from your perspective?"

Viola Griffin drew in a deep breath and looked up briefly to gather her composure. When she was ready, she said, "It was a typical Sunday for us. Walter and I went to the early church service like we always do. We drove separate cars, because he goes right from there to play his weekly match. He called me around one o'clock and told me he and Darnell, his golf partner, had won and that he had played well. He was heading over to Lem's to pick up some food for the staff at Calgary. He went there every Sunday to see his mother unless he was out of town. He had gotten a call from Amy Donnegan about the meeting OIG wanted to have with him in the morning. I was more pissed about the call than he was. They were messing with him about nothing. But he was always so cool. He never wanted me to worry about his business. He just shrugged it off. He told me he would pick up dinner and we'd eat it in bed and catch up on TV. We were two episodes behind on *The Crown*. Walter asked me if I had spoken to the kids. I told him that Junior had called and put me on the phone with the grandkids, and I was expecting to hear from Katrina once she had gotten home from brunch with her girlfriends. And that was the last time I heard his voice."

Viola took a sip of her tea. Her eyes were wistful.

"When did you realize something wasn't right?" I asked.

"Walter is a creature of habit," she said. "He's been that way since I met him. His Sundays were very routine. I was expecting him home by five o'clock. He's out almost every night of the week with business and meetings and charity events, so Sundays were always just for us. I called him twice over the space of a couple of hours, but the second call was weird. His phone didn't ring, and it went straight to voice mail. That's when I started to panic. Not only was he really late and hadn't called to explain, but now his phone was turned off. Walter never had his phone off. Ever."

"What did you do next?"

"I called everyone I could think of. The kids, his cousins, friends, the nursing home, you name it. Calgary said he had left several hours before. No one had heard from him."

"Did you talk to his mother?"

"She'd be of no help. She has Alzheimer's. Sometimes she wouldn't even recognize Walter, yet other times she could recall every name of his elementary school teachers. It's a frustrating disease." She shook her head in resignation. "By nine thirty that night I had gone through my entire list of contacts, and I knew something really bad had happened. I could just feel it. I called 911 and reported him missing. Darnell was the first to come over. He walked in on the phone, and it never left his ear. He spent the entire time trying to coordinate things and get information from everyone. I'm so grateful he and the kids were here. I don't know what I would've done without them."

Viola took a beat and turned to the windows. Her shoulders fell in resignation. "The call came at three fifty-seven in the morning. I'll never forget the time. I looked at the clock on the TV stand.

Those numbers just burned into my heart. They had found his body downtown on the river. He left a note in the car saying, 'I'm sorry.' They told me they were looking into all the possibilities, but they felt very confident Walter had killed himself."

Viola paused, then turned toward me. "The second they said those words, I didn't believe it. And not because I was in denial or some distraught wife, Mr. Cayne. But because I know that Walter would *never* do something like that, and he definitely wouldn't do it in that way."

I nodded softly. I believed her. This woman knew her husband.

"I want you to find who did this," she said softly. "I've tried to let it go, but they're out there, and I want to know who it is. Walter deserves justice. We deserve the truth."

"I couldn't agree with you more," I said. "That's why I'm here."

Viola got up from her seat and walked over to the fireplace. She took a silver-framed portrait from the mantelpiece and brought it to me. Walter was sitting on a four-wheeler in the desert with mountains behind him. His son and daughter were sitting on their own vehicles next to him. He looked so content and in the moment.

"One of my favorite photographs of him," she said. "I took it. We were in South Africa to celebrate Katrina's nineteenth birthday. We spent a week in Cape Town, then a few days in Johannesburg. It was the most relaxed and happiest I had ever seen Walter. He was totally disconnected from his phone and work. It was just the four of us, together under the hot sun and starry nights. Walter always reminisced about the time we had there and how much he wanted to return. We were going to go back for his sixtieth birthday. We never made it."

"Was there anything troubling your husband in the days or weeks before they found him?" I asked.

"Of course," Viola said. "Walter was constantly in motion, constantly in demand, constantly working on something, always fixing problems. There were times when he felt like the weight of the world was on his shoulders. But regardless of the pressure, he never ever would've killed himself. He loved his life and his family too much."

"Can you give me some specifics about his worries?"

Viola sighed and looked out the bay window. The sun came in at the perfect angle and framed her in the soft glow.

"For one, he had invested in some taco franchises and lost a significant amount of money," she said. "One of his friends, Pernell Watson, had told him it was a sure hit. It was anything but. Walter labored so much to figure out if he should sell them or try to turn them around. I told him from the beginning it was a bad investment, but Pernell wouldn't leave him alone about it. He just had this hold on Walter. They grew up together in the Ogden Courts housing project. Pernell has always been a fast-talker, too slick for my taste. Walter knew this but couldn't tear himself away. He was just so damn loyal. To a fault."

"What interest did Pernell have in all this?" I asked.

"Walter funded most of the acquisition, but Pernell was a minor investor," Viola said. "He brought the deal to Walter. They were hemorrhaging money from day one with no end in sight, but a year later he still wanted Walter to invest more money to keep them afloat. If Walter didn't, they'd lose almost everything. I told Walter not to spend another penny and take the loss. He could make it up somewhere else. The business was nothing but a headache, and I thought Pernell was stealing him blind. They got into a big fight."

"Who won?"

"Another year and a half and a million dollars later, Walter finally closed the taco stores. It was his money. He had the final decision."

"And how did Pernell take it?"

"Not good. He and Walter stopped speaking. Pernell never forgave him."

I knew I would have to talk to Pernell Watson, and I didn't relish the thought. I had never met him before but knew his reputation. He was an infamous character around the city, dishonorable on all levels. Worst of all, he communicated mostly through intimidation. The summer was already too hot, the streets had turned violent, and I was in no mood for bullshit.

"Did your husband own any guns?" I asked.

"Two. He got them both from his father."

"Where are they?"

"Upstairs in our closet."

"Was one of them the gun used in his shooting?"

"No. I've only seen Walter hold his guns once, and that was many years ago when he took them to get cleaned. That gun they found was not his. At least not that I know of."

"I want to ask you some sensitive questions, so please don't be offended," I said.

"We hired you, Mr. Cayne," she said. "I'm not afraid of any question if it will help find my husband's killer."

I expected her to say something like that. "What about the OIG situation?" I asked. "You said it made you furious."

"Because it was nonsense," Viola said. "Politics as usual. Walter was trying his best to tame three beasts in the school system at the same time—Andrew Milton, the CEO; Shawna Simpson at the teachers union; and Jack Bailey. It was a full-on war, and he was caught right in the middle of it."

I knew his role as head of the board of education had to be stressful. CPS was the third-largest and one of the worst-performing public school systems in the country, a tangled web of corruption, political land mines, and kickbacks. Other school districts had superintendents, but Chicago called its school head the CEO after Bailey and the governor maneuvered a power consolidation to weaken unions and their bargaining rights. The board of education was reconstituted, and the CEO was given wide-ranging authority over the local school councils. The new law also gave Bailey the power to appoint all seven members of the BOE as well as the CEO, though the CEO selection tended to be made only with support from the board.

Chicago was the first city in the nation to structure its school system that way, but all the promises that had been made along with the change had yet to materialize. Six CEOs in less than ten years, and the students were still consistently at the bottom of national performance and achievement charts, and the increasing violence had made many of the schools a literal war zone. Everyone complained and threatened to bring change, hundreds of millions of dollars had been dumped into an already bloated budget, yet things had only gotten worse. Everyone quietly understood that for a system that was so broken, nothing would work short of the nuclear option. But this would never happen on Bailey's watch. Educating poor kids in a big city in the deplorable and ineffective way it had been done for decades was a big business worth too much money to too many people.

"I heard he'd stolen CPS funds—made personal charges on a credit card?"

Viola tightened her jaw and waved her hand dismissively. "Ridiculous," she said. "They found three hundred and sixty-seven dollars in charges. He used their card to fuel up his car twice because he was talking on the phone and grabbed the wrong card. He was out at dinner one night and accidentally used the CPS card instead of his own. We have our own money and plenty of it, Mr. Cayne. Walter didn't need to steal funds to buy gas or to eat. He admitted to the mistake, and he paid the money back. But they wouldn't let it go at that. After all that Walter had done for this city, they wanted to dress him down like a schoolchild who got caught cheating on a math test."

"Why did they do it to him?"

"Because he was the man in the middle, and he was taking fire from all sides. Bailey, Milton, and Simpson were in a battle to the death, and they all wanted him to fix their problems, but no one was willing to compromise. Even for someone like Walter, who thrived on making deals, their issues were too big and complicated to resolve amicably. I think OIG did this to send him a message. Regardless of how successful he was or how many important friends he had, he was still a Black man, and they still had control. The stress wore on him terribly."

I understood every word she said. My father had come home many nights from the hospital angry about what he called "the invisible plague of institutional racism." One night in particular, he had practically been frothing at the mouth. He had been the chair of the Department of Psychiatry at the time and had been invited to make a presentation to the hospital board. It had been the first time he had ever been asked to do it. He had taken his assistant with him, a white man several years younger, to run the slides for his presentation. My father had been wearing a suit and tie. His assistant had worn a button-down shirt and chinos. When they had walked into the boardroom, the chair of the board had walked over to the assistant, put out his hand, and called him Dr. Cayne and thanked him for coming. Politics, education, medicine—racism was in every corner of our society.

"What about Bailey?" I said. "They were so close for so many years. He could've stepped in and done something. Why didn't he stop the OIG investigation?"

Viola shook her head. "Only he can answer that," she said. "The official response was that the OIG is an independent watchdog. Out of the mayor's reach. No political interference."

"Even though the mayor appointed him."

"That's right. The IG serves at the mayor's pleasure but doesn't conduct his business under the mayor's favor." She took a moment, then said, "Supposedly."

Pete Dent was the city's inspector general. He had served two and a half terms and had waged a ruthless war against the mayor's political foes or anyone who decided to step outside Bailey's lines. Regardless of the effort that went into creating a facade of independence, he was nothing more than a puppet, and Bailey had exclusive control of his strings. Everyone knew that. Dent wanted to become the city's next mayor. Having Bailey and the machine coronate him as the successor would go a long way at the ballot box.

"Do you know anything about your husband talking to the Feds?" I asked.

"Feds, as in FBI?"

I nodded.

"Why would Walter be talking to the FBI?" she asked.

I didn't want to alarm her unnecessarily without confirming from an independent source what Delroy Thomas had told me about the Cabrini land deal and the Feds' attempt to flip Griffin. There was no need to introduce speculation, especially something as serious as this claim.

"Just something I heard," I said. "Doesn't mean it's true. People say things." I changed the subject. "How was your husband's relationship with Bailey?"

"Up to the last few weeks, as close as they had always been," she said. "They were together way before Jack got to the Fifth Floor. In many ways they were like brothers. They supported and protected each other, and they fought and argued just like brothers. Inseparable. Talked all the time, all hours of the day."

"Is it true they were childhood friends?"

Viola nodded softly. "Both from tough neighborhoods. Walter from North Lawndale and Jack from Bridgeport. They played football together at a time when the city couldn't be more segregated. But sports have a way of transcending differences and building bridges between even the most disparate. They've been friends their whole lives."

"Can you think of any reason they would stop being friends?"

"What exactly are you trying to ask?"

"Do you think Bailey had him killed?"

"Deep down in my soul I don't want to believe that Jack would ever do that," Viola said. "But I'm not naive either. This is Chicago. I've lived in this city for forty years, and there's one thing I learned early that's still true today. Nothing here is ever what it appears."

12

I HAD JUST COME in from my morning run around the lake. Running had always been a way I liked to clear my head. It was easy to focus on the rhythm of my steps and how it synchronized with my breathing pattern. When I finished a run, things that had been confusing me always seemed to make more sense. It was like a fog had been lifted. I sat on my balcony and looked at the empty Navy Pier. In a couple of hours it would be packed with people waiting to ride the Ferris wheel or board one of the boats that would take them out into the lake or down the Chicago River.

I picked up my phone and dialed Burke. He was an early riser also.

"What do ya need?" he answered.

"Maybe I just wanted to hear your warm voice first thing in the morning."

"Maybe the Bears might win a playoff game before I die."

"Don't bet your city pension on it."

Burke grunted.

"You hear anything about Griffin being looked at by the FBI?"

"Negative."

"Delroy Thomas told me the FBI was trying to flip him to give up information on how the Cabrini land deal went down."

"Everyone knows how that shit went down. Bailey's megadonors got development rights and minted another fortune. What did Thomas say the Feds had on Griffin?"

"It was a trade. OIG was investigating him for misusing the corporate card. They were pressing him really hard. But his wife said the charges were nothing, three hundred–plus dollars. But OIG seemed to be throwing the book at him. According to Thomas, the Feds would help get the OIG investigation dropped if he gave them names and information on Cabrini."

"An ex-con like Thomas should know," Burke grumbled. "He'd steal the suit off a dead man if he could make some money off it."

"You have anyone inside the FBI field office?"

"I did, but he retired about ten years ago and spends most his days fly-fishing down in the Florida Keys. But let me put in a couple of calls. Bad enough I got my own damn work; now I'm doing yours."

He was gone before I could tell him how much I loved him.

———

CEPHUS REDMOND OWNED Diamond Sharp Car Wash, a chain of seven brushless car washes on the South Side that had made him a rich man, something you couldn't tell by looking at him. He was dark as charcoal, fat, and ordinary looking. He didn't wear any jewelry or fancy clothes. The crown jewel of his car wash chain was a white-brick box, just beyond the intersection of State and Fifty-Eighth Street, that had proved to be a cash cow. When I'd called to learn where I could find him, I'd been told this was the location where he spent most of his time.

Cephus had been number three on Delroy Thomas's list. I pulled up to the curb and found him sitting outside on a lawn chair with a group of old-timers under the protection of a large tree. He wore a wide-collared short-sleeved shirt and linen shorts with ironed creases that looked sharp enough to cut paper. He acknowledged me with a nod and skeptical scowl as I approached.

"My name is Ashe Cayne," I said.

"I know who the fuck you are," Cephus said. "You the one wouldn't let them coppers get away with killing that boy over in Englewood."

"I am."

"Took some real balls to stand up and do that," Cephus said.

"And a good pair of feet," I said.

The other men laughed. Cephus was unimpressed.

"What can I do you for?" Cephus asked.

"I wanted to ask you a few questions about Walter Griffin."

"The father or the son?"

"The father. I heard you were good friends."

"Watcha wanna know?"

"Anything you can tell me."

"That's a lot for a short conversation."

"I have all day."

"I don't. I'm busy."

The men laughed again.

"Okay. How about we start with your thoughts on his suicide."

He leaned back in his chair and smiled. "You think I got some kinda crystal ball? How the hell I know why Griff put a gun to his head?"

"So, you think he killed himself?"

"That's what the examiner come back with. Somebody important as Griff, you figure they gonna do whatever it takes to get to the truth."

"Lots of people don't think he did it."

"Lots of people don't always know what's going through another man's mind."

"Did you?"

"Did I what?"

"Did you know what was going through his mind?"

"I ain't no damn mind reader. Head doctor neither. All of us got some problems. Sometimes them problems get too heavy. Griff obviously had some shit he couldn't handle."

"What shit might that be?" I asked.

Cephus nodded at the two other men. They gathered their beer bottles and walked inside the car wash.

"Why all these questions?" Cephus said. "Walt dead and gone. Can't nothing bring him back now."

"Gone but not forgotten," I said. "His kids want answers."

"But they might not like the answers you find."

"They're adults."

Cephus wiped his forehead with the towel slung around his shoulder. He took a long pull of beer. As he swallowed the cold brew, his wide throat inched like a pregnant caterpillar crawling on hot pavement. "Walt was a complicated man," Cephus said. "Caught between two worlds. He grew up a street kid from the West Side and always had that in him till the day he died. But even when we was young, he started to get in good on the North Side. He was the only one of us had the ambition like that. The white boys liked him. Light skinned, good looking, them pretty damn eyes. He was an *acceptable* Negro. Black-skinned kid like me ain't stand a chance. Didn't bother me none, though. I knew the rules and accepted 'em. They made Walt feel important downtown. They also put a lot of opportunity in front of him. They cut him in on different kindsa deals, contract here and there, investments. They invited him on all kinds of boards and shit like that where he could network and rub shoulders with the rich and powerful. So he had to balance both worlds, remain true to the rest of us and where he come from, yet climb the ranks and be part of their shit. He won't always in an easy position. A lot of times them worlds collided. Sometimes they wanted him to do their biddin', which meant he had to come back and get our people to get behind some city proposal we didn't really want or go along with some deal that gave us the short end of the stick. Ain't easy being pulled in two different directions. Get pulled hard enough, something gotta give."

"You think it's possible somebody killed him?"

Cephus shook his head slowly as he gazed up toward the sky. The hot sun made his skin shine. An ambulance, siren blaring, raced down State Street and hung a right on Garfield. It was probably heading to the new trauma center at the University of Chicago. This was the kind of day when the body count exploded. People were hot and miserable and impatient. Just the wrong look at a traffic light could trigger violence.

"Anything's possible, I guess," Cephus said. "But it takes a lot of hate or anger to kill a man. Walt had his conflicts like anybody else. But bad enough that someone would put a bullet in him? That's a tough one to swallow."

"How close were you?"

"Close enough. Known each other since grade school. My grandmother looked after him time to time."

"He have any specific problems you know about?"

"We all got problems, man." Cephus wiped his forehead again and swung the towel back across his shoulder. "Griff's money was runnin' tight. Not many people knew that."

"How tight?"

"He came to me secretly about a year before he died. He needed money. Half a million dollars. Said he couldn't go anywhere else 'cause he needed to keep it quiet. He didn't want Viola to know. I knew it was bad because he and Viola was real close. He told her everything."

"What did he need it for?"

"I didn't get into the details. He said he was in some kind of deal that was taking longer than expected. All his own money was tied up, and he owed some guys. They was putting pressure on him. He needed to take care of 'em right away."

"And you just wrote him a check for half a million dollars?"

"Check?" Cephus smiled. "Hell nah. I gave it to him in cash."

"That's a lotta cash."

"Washing cars ain't the prettiest business, but it makes some money."

"Did Walter pay whoever it was he owed?"

"I assumed so. He never came back for more."

"Did he pay you back?"

"Not a dime."

"How did that make you feel?"

"I ain't feel nothin'. I've lost more money in a weekend playing craps over at the Horseshoe."

I thought about what Delroy Thomas had said about why Cephus might've wanted Griffin dead. The money part of the motivation trifecta didn't fit. Cephus seemed to have plenty of it. But that didn't mean he was clear.

There was still sex and jealousy, and either one had sent many men to an early grave.

13

IT TOOK A LITTLE more work than I had expected, but I finally had some clarity on the ownership of the town house at 1322 South Indiana that Nelson had visited a couple of days ago. Golden Crest LLC, a company based in Beverly Hills, had purchased the property a little more than a year ago in an all-cash transaction for a little over a million dollars. Golden Crest was owned by the Farrington Family Trust, chaired by Garrett L. Farrington III. Garrett had three daughters by three different women. The youngest daughter was twenty-two-year-old Brittany Farrington, a sophomore at Roosevelt University. She was the girl with the small dog who had let Nelson into the garage.

I wasn't sure exactly what my plan was, but sometimes when you just knocked around, something fell. I walked up the steep steps and rang the buzzer. A shapely short girl with long chestnut-colored hair and tight yellow shorts answered.

"I'm looking for Brittany," I said.

"Who are you?" she asked. I could hear a hint of Boston in her voice. She had a friendly disposition.

"I'm here to help her out," I said.

"Help her how? Is she in trouble?"

"Not yet," I said. "That's why I want to talk to her."

"She's not here right now," the girl said. "But I can give her a message."

"Who are you?" I asked.

"Tammy O'Brien, her roommate."

"Do you know when she'll be back?"

"She has two classes today. She won't be back till after three, probably closer to four."

"Maybe I'll just come back then."

"I can give her a message if you want," Tammy repeated.

"Just tell her that Avis Roeper stopped by," I said.

"Okay, Avis. I'll tell her."

I turned down the steps and walked south down Indiana. I had parked my car around the block, away from the cameras on the corner of the building. I would come back later to see if Brittany Farrington and I could reach a mutual understanding.

———

I SPENT MOST OF the day in my office sifting through the three potential reasons for Griffin's death and who might have been involved. Now I had returned to the alley and sat outside Brittany Farrington's town house. Fifteen minutes later, the garage door opened. The silver Audi emerged with its convertible top down. Tammy sat in the driver's seat behind a large pair of dark sunglasses, her hair tucked into a baseball cap. She was alone. She drove in my direction and exited the alley on Fourteenth Street before turning right and heading west.

I spent the better part of the next hour watching the quiet alley. Some guy a few doors down showed up in a loud Mustang with a baby strapped in the back seat. An HVAC contractor parked his car behind a town house closer to the center of the alley; a young woman opened her garage door, and he followed her in. A few minutes before four o'clock, a shiny midnight-blue Porsche Cayenne SUV entered the alley. Brittany Farrington sat behind the wheel with her tiny dog on her lap. She was already in the garage by the time I jumped out of the car. I walked around the corner to the front of the town house, climbed the steps, and rang the bell. Seconds later the door opened.

"You must be Avis Roeper," she said. "Tammy told me you came earlier."

"I did," I said.

"She said you left some cryptic message about wanting to help me."

"I did."

We stared at each other for a moment.

"Oookayy," she said, shrugging. "Help me do what?"

"Help you not go to jail."

"What are you talking about?" she asked. "Why would I go to jail?"

"Because your boyfriend is gonna get you in trouble."

Brittany scrunched her face. "How is Vince gonna get me in trouble?"

"Your other boyfriend," I said. "Antoine Nelson."

"I don't know anyone by that name. I think you're confusing me with someone else." She started closing the door, but I blocked it with my foot.

I opened my wallet and flashed my old shield. She looked down at it, and her thin lips pursed. "Maybe you know him as Twiggy."

Recognition settled on her face.

"Maybe I can come in, and we can talk about this," I said.

"Are you arresting me?"

"Nope. Like I said before, I'm here to help you."

She opened the door for me to enter.

"Nice house," I said, taking a seat in a wide living room that had obviously been decorated by someone who knew how to spend a lot of money. The furniture was modern and minimalist. Original abstract paintings hung on the walls in ornate frames with elegant brass picture lights.

Brittany sat across from me while her tiny dog with a pink bow tie sat at her feet.

"What do you want from me?" she asked.

"I want to know what you and Twiggy are up to."

"He's a friend; that's all," Brittany said.

"A friend?"

"Yes. Another friend of mine introduced us last summer."

"Why would a pretty girl like you from Beverly Hills want to hang out with an ex-con like Twiggy?"

"Twiggy is an ex-con?"

"He didn't tell you?"

"He's a basketball player," she said.

"And I'm a principal dancer in the Joffrey Ballet."

"You're very handsome and in shape, but you don't look like a ballet dancer. You look too tough."

"The cop-and-badge thing, that's my alter ego," I said.

She looked at me, confused.

"Your father paid a lot of money for this house and for your school," I said. "I'm sure he didn't send you all the way out here to make friends with the likes of Twiggy."

"Well, we're not *friends* friends," she said. "It's more like we just know each other."

"Know each other enough for him to come to your house."

"How do you know that?"

"The cop-and-badge thing," I said.

Brittany shifted nervously in her seat, her hands clenched tightly on her lap. "You're going to arrest me," she said. "I want a lawyer before I say anything else. I want to call my father."

"Why would I arrest you?"

"You're trying to trap me."

"Trap you how?"

"You know what's going on."

"I do, but I want you to explain it to me. If you do that, then this visit and conversation never happened."

"What do you want me to explain?"

"Why don't you start from the beginning."

Brittany picked up the tiny dog and cradled her. The dog looked at me with a slight degree of superiority.

"One of my friends at school said a guy she was sleeping with could get some good stuff. She met him one night at Tao. They weren't serious or anything, but he was cute, and they hooked up sometimes. One night he gave her some Pink Lady. She said it was the best shit she'd ever had, so she kept hooking up with him, and he kept giving it to her."

"Sex for synthetic opioids?"

"Not at all. Emma can afford to pay for anything she wants. Her father owns half of Milwaukee. She said the sex was good and the drugs were good, so they had a good arrangement."

"Does Emma know that her lover is an ex-con?"

"Really? I don't think so. He said he was a basketball player at Chicago State. What did he do?"

"Killed a guy because he wouldn't let him steal his phone and backpack."

Brittany's eyes widened. "He killed someone?"

"Stabbed him to death. So, your friend is cavorting with a murderer. Just a little detail she might want to know the next time she's looking for someone to help her get high."

Brittany sat there with her mouth open, a look of terror frozen across her face.

"So, Emma is the one who introduced you to Twiggy?" I said.

"Yes. He asked her if any of her friends wanted to try some. Emma brought me some one night, and I liked it."

"Tammy too?"

"What does Tammy have to do with this?"

"I just figured, you being roommates and all."

"Tammy is too afraid to do anything. It's not her thing."

"So, how many friends in your network is Twiggy supplying?"

"I don't know. That's not any of my business. He gives me a bag a week, and that's it. I don't have social conversations with him."

"Does he come the same day every week?"

"Always on Thursday morning," she said.

"You need help, Brittany," I said. "You're young, rich, and pretty, and you're gonna throw it all away messing around with a piece of shit like Twiggy."

"I'm completely fine," she said. "I know what I'm doing. I grew up in Beverly Hills. I've handled much worse."

I nodded. Sometimes you have to let people learn it their way for them to really appreciate the lesson.

"So, now what?" she asked.

"This conversation never happened," I said, standing to leave and walking to the door.

"You're not gonna do anything? I don't have to go to the station and be interviewed?"

"Not as long as you help me."

"Do what?"

"I want to have a private conversation with Twiggy."

"I can give you his number."

She told me his number, and I typed it into my phone. "I might want you to help me get the conversation started," I said.

"Can't you just call him?"

"I could, but it might be better to arrange a meeting. Would you be willing to help me with that?"

She nodded nervously.

"One more thing," I said. "Don't mention a word of our conversation to Emma or Twiggy. Remember, no matter how innocent he might look, this guy is a murderer. Everyone is under surveillance. If you say something, I'll know you did, and my next visit will be with a lot of cars and bright flashing lights."

She didn't need to verbalize a response. Her eyes said it all.

14

"SHAWNA SIMPSON IS MEANER than a junkyard dog with an abscess in his ass," my father said. "She runs that teachers union like a five-star general."

We were seated in the formal dining room of his town house with an elegant spread of roasted duck à l'orange, steamed white asparagus, and burnt aubergine raita. My father, Dr. Wendell Oliver Cayne, sat at the head of the long polished walnut table like he always had. This was our weekly dinner, something we had initiated after my mother lost her battle with cancer five years ago. Sometimes these dinners were extremely pleasant; other times I'd rather be plucking my eyeballs out with hot tweezers. Tonight was somewhere in between. Almost an hour into the evening and he still hadn't brought up his regrets about the professional career I might've had if I hadn't given up on tennis right before high school. Small victories.

"How do you know Simpson?" I asked. I'd been filling him in on Walter Griffin's CPS woes.

"I knew her older sister better," my father said. "Jenny Simpson was smart as a whip. Could've been anything she wanted. Threw it all away for love. Had three kids before she was twenty-five, and her husband left her when she was pregnant with her fourth. Last I heard she was running a shelter somewhere in the south burbs. Her kids are supposed to be damn near geniuses. We lost touch."

"I need to talk to Shawna Simpson."

"Don't go to her without your facts straight. She'll put her foot up your ass so far, the size of her shoe will be imprinted on the back of your tongue."

"You paint such beautiful pictures."

"I'm telling you not what I think but what I know. Shawna is a tough woman. She and Bailey hate each other. She lives and breathes for that union. Bailey lives and breathes to destroy the union. The city isn't big enough to withstand both of them. Someone's gonna get hurt. Bad."

"Hard to bet against Bailey. He has the jackhammer of the entire city government at his disposal."

"Yes, but Shawna has the battering ram of the people and a sole focus on what's best for the city's teachers. This has been going on for years. Someone will eventually win, but there will be a lot of carnage by the time this is over."

We sat silently for a moment. I attempted some of the red wine he had pulled out of the cellar before he'd spent the better part of five minutes earlier explaining its provenance and why it went perfectly with the meal. I would've fallen asleep had the chairs not been so uncomfortable. All I wanted was an iced root beer. He purposely didn't stock any in the house, so he knew I wouldn't ask.

"You need to find out who killed Walter?" he asked. "He wasn't a perfect man, but he was a good man. He's done a lot for our people. Never forgot where he came from. That nine million he raised for the violence recovery program over at the University of Chicago was monumental."

"You know a guy named Cephus Redmond?"

"Never heard of him."

"He owns a bunch of car washes on the South Side. Makes a lot of money. Knew Griffin most of his life. He says Griffin had some money problems that a lot of people didn't know about. He thinks Griffin killed himself."

"Still don't believe it," my father said, shaking his head. "Walter Griffin meant too much to so many people. Whenever we caught up with each other at a dinner or event, he always had a smile on his face. Couldn't stop talking about how proud he was that Junior had gotten married and given him two grandboys. He gushed about them. One was gonna play for the Bears and the other for the White Sox. I've dealt with many suicidal patients in my career. He might've had some money problems, but Walter was not suicidal."

I shared with him Delroy Thomas's theory of the FBI trying to flip Griffin for information on the Cabrini land deal as a trade to get him off the hook with the OIG investigation. I told him about my conversation with Viola. When I was done, he said, "Are you sure you want to continue with this case?"

"It's too late to back out now," I said. "I gave the family my commitment."

"It's never too late," he said. "Return the retainer and move on."

"I can't do that."

"Why?"

"Because I have that feeling inside of me that something bad happened, and I want to find out who was mixed up in it. I won't be able to rest until I have some answers."

"You can't save the world, Ashe. Admirable goal but a fool's errand."

"Agreed. But I can try to bring some peace to the family. They have a right to know what happened."

Pearline, my father's housekeeper and cook, entered the dining room with another basket of warm bread. She had started working with my father about a year ago. One of the deacons in my father's church had recommended her. She had moved to Chicago from Cape Verde and hadn't been able to get a full-time job. She was a couple of years older than me, extremely courteous, a great cook, and easy to look at. Sometimes I thought his glances at her lingered a little long.

When Pearline had left the room, my father said, "Walter Griffin was a very busy man." We were halfway through the meal, and he was now leaning back in his chair, steadying his wineglass. He liked to take a break during dinner. He felt it was the best way to enjoy a good meal. "Walter mixed with some very powerful but equally duplicitous people. You should be careful about the feathers you ruffle. I liked and respected Walter a lot, but he wasn't a saint. None of them are."

"Especially Bailey. He sits above it all, the master puppeteer."

My father unleashed one of his all-knowing smiles. "Everyone knows that Jack Bailey is a tyrannical megalomaniac who shags his female aides on the Fifth Floor, then takes photo ops with his wife when he needs to present this great family-man image to the public. He learned at the knees of his miserable father, who ran this city for twenty years like a dictator of a third world country. Bailey has bodies buried all over this town, and many of those bodies Griffin helped bury."

More than one road seemed to be leading to city hall, but I wanted to figure out which one I needed to take to find Bailey at the other end.

———

AS I WAS about to pull out of my father's garage, my phone rang. I didn't recognize the number.

"Is this Ashe Cayne?" a woman's voice said.

"It is," I replied.

"My name is Evette Carson," she said. "I'm one of the supervisors at Calgary Arms. You left your name and number for someone to reach out to you about Mr. Griffin."

"Yes, I called a couple of days ago. Thanks for getting back to me."

"Sorry to call so late, but I just got the message. I've been on vacation the last few days. How can I help you?"

"I'm trying to get a better understanding of what happened during Walter Griffin's last visit to his mother. I know it's been a while, but do you remember that afternoon?"

"Like it was yesterday. Even to this day, every time I go into his mother's room, I can't stop thinking about him and how much he's missed. I've gone over the afternoon in my head a hundred times, trying to figure if any of us missed something that might've been a clue that he was in some kind of distress."

"Have you thought of anything?"

"Things were a little different, but nothing so abnormal that it might've been a sign he would kill himself a few hours after walking out our doors."

"What was different?"

"His mood. Mr. Griffin was always a happy man. He would always bring us food. Always had a joke to tell. That afternoon he seemed more serious, like his mind was somewhere else."

"Was he upset?"

"Not upset like he had been in an argument, but just distracted. He was kind and all, but he wasn't completely there, if you know what I mean."

"How long was he there for?"

"Not more than an hour. That was different too. He always stayed at least a couple of hours with his mother, but that afternoon it was only an hour."

"How do you remember that so well?"

"Because one of the nurses assigned to his mother mentioned it to me in passing. She thought it unusual that he only brought us one bucket of rib tips when he usually brought two. And then she wondered why he was in such a rush to leave."

"Did you ask him if everything was all right?"

"To be honest, I wish I had. But I didn't think about it like that at the time."

"Anything else happen that was out of the ordinary?"

"Yes, one more thing. He used his cell phone. Not once, but twice."

"It's normal to use a cell phone."

"Not Mr. Griffin. All the years I've seen him here, that was the first time I ever saw him leave his mother's room to take a call. He never let anything interrupt his visit with her."

"Where did he take the call?"

"Right outside her room."

"Was he close enough that anyone could hear what he said?"

"His mother's room is just a couple of doors down from the nursing station. I saw him take the first call, but he walked down the hall to talk where it was quieter. The second call, I was reviewing charts nearby. I didn't hear much of the conversation, but I did hear him say, 'That's exactly what I need.' Then he hung up and went back into his mother's room."

"How did he seem when he said that?"

"Best way I can describe it is content. Satisfied."

"Did it sound like he was on a personal or business call?"

"I have no idea, Mr. Cayne. I just heard him say those words, and the conversation was over."

15

AMY DONNEGAN EXITED CITY HALL on the east side of the building, earbuds plugged in, her long blonde hair flapping about her shoulders. A smidgen over six feet and a former captain of the DePaul volleyball team, she had every bit the stride of a capable athlete. I had placed a call to one of my friends, who was the admin for the deputy mayor of Public Safety. She'd placed several calls and discovered that Donnegan's father knew someone who'd called in a favor and got her the job as a mayoral aide. The Chicago way. She handled a lot of the education matters, serving as a liaison between the mayor's office and the CPS board as well as the CEO's office. She was the one who had called Griffin that Sunday afternoon after his round of golf.

I stepped in front of her. She was startled and tried to step around me. I moved in front of her again. She pulled out her earbuds.

"Amy Donnegan," I said.

"Is there a reason you're standing in my way?"

"Just trying to get your attention," I said. "I'm Ashe Cayne, private investigator."

"Okay. Nice to meet you. Now excuse me. I'm running late for an appointment." She put her earbuds back in and walked by me. I followed her to the corner, where she had to wait for the light.

I tapped her softly on the shoulder. She turned around and registered frustration when she discovered it was me again.

I mouthed the words, "Walter Griffin."

She took her earbuds out and looked around. There was a scrum of people in a rush to cross the street and get as far away from their offices as possible. No one was paying us any attention.

"I'm trying to find out what happened to Walter Griffin," I said. "I have a few questions I wanted to ask you."

She stepped closer, looked furtively over my shoulder, and said, "Not here."

"Then where? I have a CTA pass; will travel."

"Eli's Bagels," she said. "Corner of LaSalle and Calhoun. I'll meet your there in thirty minutes."

———

AMY DONNEGAN WAS SITTING THERE waiting for me when I walked in, banging away on her cell phone at a corner table. A few tourists trickled in for bagels and coffee, but the restaurant was otherwise empty. She put her phone down as I approached.

"What is it you want to ask me?" she said, not wasting time on pleasantries.

"So much for the light banter," I said.

"I'm very busy Mr. . . ."

"Cayne," I said. "But call me Ashe. And that's with an 'e' at the end."

She nodded. "Okay, Ashe. How can I help you?"

"What was your relationship with Walter Griffin?"

"Very professional," she said quickly. As if she was trying to convince me of something.

"In what way?"

"He was the president of the board, and I am the liaison from the mayor's office. But you already know this."

"I do. Did you get along?"

"Of course we did," she said. "He's one of the mayor's closest friends."

"Was," I corrected.

"Yes, was," she said. "It's very sad that he did what he did. We all liked him. He was a great guy. I enjoyed talking to him. He gave me a lot of good advice."

"If everyone liked him so much and he was such a great guy, then why did they want to squeeze him over a measly few hundred dollars on the city credit card?"

"I had nothing to do with that," she said. "I was just a messenger. My job as the liaison is to keep lines of communication open."

"Between whom?"

"Our office and CPS."

"And OIG?"

"I don't work for OIG. If they communicate something to me, my job is to make sure I report it back to the relevant parties."

"Do you know why OIG decided to do an investigation in the first place?"

"No clue," she said. "Above my pay grade."

"Do you know who makes the decision to investigate?"

"Above my pay grade," she repeated.

"You have any brothers or sisters?" I asked.

"I have two brothers."

"And both of your parents are still alive."

"They are."

"Have you ever met Walter's children?"

"Only at the funeral."

"How would you feel if your father was shot in cold blood and it was made to look like a suicide?"

"It was a suicide," she said, shifting in her chair. I knew she didn't believe it. Then she said, "The ME and CPD did independent investigations and came to the same conclusion."

"Did Walter strike you as someone who would take his own life?"

Donnegan shrugged. "I don't know all that Walter was dealing with. Whatever it was, I think it's sad he chose to handle things that way."

"You knew some of what he was dealing with," I said. "You called him that Sunday afternoon."

"Yes, in my official capacity as a liaison from the mayor's office."

"On a Sunday? So urgent it couldn't wait twenty-four hours?"

"Yes, it was that urgent," she said. "The business of the city doesn't take off on the weekends. OIG was calling him in, and I wanted to talk to him about the situation."

"What did the two of you talk about?"

"I'm not going to discuss that with you."

"Even if it can help me figure out what really happened to this great guy that everyone liked so much?"

"I appreciate what you're trying to do for the family, but I'm not at liberty to discuss internal city business."

"Even if it's off the record?"

Donnegan gathered her belongings and slid out of her chair. "Nothing is ever off the record, Ashe," she said. "Once it's said, it can't be taken back."

"Do you wish you could take back what you said to him on that call?"

Donnegan started walking away, stopped, and looked back at me. "I was just the messenger," she said. "I take orders. I don't give them. I wish what I said to him never had to be said."

"Who made you say it?"

Donnegan turned and walked through the door, and I didn't try to stop her. I knew more than I'd known when I walked in.

She was protecting someone. And I was getting too close to the fire.

16

PERNELL WATSON HAD A rap sheet longer than Lake Shore Drive and more guns circulating on the street than the entirety of the Chicago Police Department. He set up his front in a beauty supply store in one of the busiest intersections on the South Side of Chicago—Seventy-Ninth Street and Cottage Grove. At one o'clock in the afternoon the streets jumped like Rio in the middle of carnival. Music boomed from parked cars and out of open second-floor windows that sat atop an array of neon-lit storefronts selling everything from fried chicken to lace-front wigs. People were everywhere—fanning themselves at the bus stop, lining up to get into bodegas, walking and talking loudly on cell phones as they dodged panhandlers and offers of ice-cold dollar water. There were more people crammed into these four corners than the entire population of Maine. The heat index had to be somewhere north of a hundred. ComEd had already warned city residents to conserve on the use of electricity or face rolling blackouts.

I pulled up next to a fire hydrant, threw an old police placard in the windshield, then entered Coco's Beauty Supply. A security guard whose bald head and ample jowls made him look like a black

Buddha stood on the other side of the door. He gave me the once-over as I entered.

"Pernell here?" I asked.

"Who's asking?"

I looked around the store. "Since I'm the only one here, I guess that would be me."

"What's your business?"

"Proctology."

"What the fuck, man? Speak English."

"I give digital rectal exams."

"Digital? This ain't no computer store."

"You're forgetting the rectal part."

"Ain't no store about no ass either."

"Okay. Then let me talk to Pernell."

He took a step in my direction. "Once again, what's your business?"

"Cops and robbers."

"Man, can't you talk with some sense? Pernell don't just see anybody. If you ain't got no appointment, go back where yo smart-ass come from."

"Let him through," came a voice from the other side of the store. Pernell Watson stood at the end of the aisle, all six foot four of him, in a red silk shirt, white linen pants, and long red gators bending upward at the toes. His hair had been relaxed and combed back with a part in the middle big enough to fit a roll of quarters. A guy even bigger than Buddha stood at his side with a semiautomatic holstered at his hip. A patch covered his left eye.

"Don't ever go to London," I said as I passed him. "They drive on the right side of the road."

Buddha number two grunted and frowned. This was not an easy crowd. I followed Pernell through an aisle crammed with beauty supplies and packages of weave hair dyed every color of the rainbow. We went through a small door that Pernell had to duck to enter and into a spacious office that looked more like what you'd expect to find in a seventeenth-century Italian palazzo. The decor was intricate and elaborate, with lots of gold flowers and leaves. He must've spent a small fortune in this one room alone.

"Versace or Dolce & Gabbana?" I said, taking a seat in a leopard-print chair across from his gold desk.

"What the fuck that supposed to mean?" Watson asked.

"Your designer of choice."

"Neither one," Watson said. "It's all custom Italian fabric and woodwork that I personally picked out."

"You're a man of many talents."

"What can I help you with?"

"Walter Griffin," I said.

"I'm listening."

"Seems like the two of you had a disagreement about your taco franchises."

"Big fuckin' deal. I've had disagreements with lots of people. Way you comin' into my place, I might have a disagreement with you soon enough."

"I'm just trying to help the family," I said.

"I know who the fuck you are," Watson said. "You the one wouldn't let them sonsabitches get away with killin' Hazel McDaniels's little boy some years back. Lot of people grateful you stood up like that."

"My honor is my life; both grow in one. Take honor from me, and my life is done."

"The fuck? You recitin' poetry?"

"Shakespeare. *Richard II*."

"They said you could be a wiseass."

"That's what Buddha and I were discussing out there when you interrupted us."

"Man, I ain't got time for this shit," Watson said, shaking his head. "Listen, Walt and I grew up together. He was the big brother I never had. Course we had disagreements. Plenty of 'em. But what the fuck that supposed to mean?"

"Maybe the last one really pissed you off."

Watson smiled a set of perfect white teeth. "Ain't this some shit. You come into my place of business, trying to insinuate I killed one of my oldest friends because we had a couple of words?"

"There was a lot of money at stake," I said. "People have maimed and killed for much less."

"No argument from me on that," Watson said. "But you lookin' in the wrong place you think I'm behind Walt's killin'."

"So, you don't think he committed suicide either?"

"Ain't nobody with a quarter of a brain think Walt killed hisself. That's some shit downtown made up. Somebody put that bullet in him for damn sure."

"Any ideas?"

"Damn sure better believe if I knew, I would've put some lead in they ass just the same."

"So, nothing or no one comes to mind?"

"I got my ideas, but nuthin' I can prove."

"I'm listening."

Watson flicked his head quickly and Buddha 2 folded his enormous mass through the door and closed it behind him.

"Walt been in the ground going on two years," Watson said. "Sometimes it's best to let bygones be bygones. You stir up some old shit and it's still bad enough to stink."

"I have olfactory immunity."

He looked at me with a twisted face.

"My sense of smell can handle the shit."

Watson shook his head in resignation. "Walt was in all kind of stuff," he said. "Some good. Some bad."

"Why don't we take the bad."

"Walt and I did that taco business not because I needed the money but because *he* needed the money. See, Viola think this whole time he was doing me a favor. Well, it wasn't a one-sided thing. He needed the business to make some money and cover some of his shortfall. I needed the business to clean a little money. We both had our interests. But it wasn't making the kind of money he needed as fast as he needed it, so he wanted to get out of it altogether. I told him to hold on a little while longer. We could make things work."

"But he sold it anyway."

"He was under pressure. Big pressure."

"From whom?"

"I guess all your fancy detective work ain't taught you about the real Walt Griffin," Watson said.

"Not as fancy as your decor for sure," I said.

"My day what?"

"Your flair," I said, sweeping my arm. "Bold, vivid colors. Lots of neoclassical mixed in with rococo."

"You ever speak in just regular talk?" Watson said.

"Only when I'm tired."

"Then get real sleepy, muthafuckah, cuz I'm tired all these big words. I ain't got time for no English class."

"Fair enough. Back to what you were about to say before we got sidetracked by design talk."

"Walt liked ass," Watson said.

"Not exactly groundbreaking. I tend to share the same proclivity."

"Problem with Walt was, he liked really expensive ass. Always had, even when we was kids. He didn't want just anybody. He had to have the girl with the good hair and long nails and designer shit. Walt had women all over this town. They couldn't get enough of him and vice versa. One girl was his kryptonite, though."

"Care to expound?"

"High-yellow girl lives downtown. So pretty she stop traffic on Michigan Ave. And young. Can't be more than thirty."

"What is a thirty-year-old human stop sign doing with an almost sixty-year-old man?"

"Search as hard as you want, young blood, but ain't no pussy magnet greater than money and power. Walt had both."

"Her name?"

"Sophia Caballé."

"As in Montserrat Caballé."

"Who the fuck is that?"

"The greatest Spanish opera singer to ever grace the stage."

"What the fuck I care about some Spanish opera singer?"

"You should care a lot. She belted a mean Puccini. Would go perfect with this decor."

17

CAROLINA AND I SAT at a small center table at Momotaro in the trendy Fulton Market District. Dinner service was in full swing as the well heeled spent a month's worth of stock dividends to eat some of the best and most expensive sushi in the city. I had gotten news from my financial adviser that one of my investments would soon be making a sizable payout, so I decided to open my wallet a little. But Carolina looked more delectable than anything that could possibly come out of the kitchen.

"So, what are you gonna do next?" Carolina asked.

"Keep poking around until something jumps out," I said.

I had given her a full update on the investigation as we shared a plate of negitoro and momomaki rolls. Half of the rolls were gone, but Carolina was still working on finishing her first piece.

"Half a million dollars is a lot of money," she said.

"And Cephus paid it in cash."

"Do you think his wife knew about his financial struggles?"

"If she did, she didn't let on."

"And you believe this Watson character about the mistress?"

"Only one way to find out."

"Which is?"

"Talk to the alluring Sophia and see what she has to say for herself."

"If it's true, will you tell Griffin's wife about her?"

"Only if necessary."

"Have you found out where this Sophia works?"

"I have my suspicions."

"Which are?"

"The bedrooms of rich men."

"Sounds elegant."

"That's one way to describe it."

Carolina finally finished her first piece of the toro. She expertly picked up the momomaki with her chopsticks and managed to bite a perfect half.

"So, what exactly are we celebrating?" she asked.

"Probiotics."

"Probiotics as in the bacteria-you-eat-that's-good-for-your-stomach probiotics?"

"A bit lower in the gastrointestinal tract, but the stomach is close enough."

"Don't be a show-off because your father is a doctor."

"And a card-carrying member of Kappa Alpha Psi. Lest you forget that."

"Duly noted. So, back to celebrating bacteria."

"About two years ago I agreed to invest in a little start-up company that makes seasonal probiotics in the form of bars."

"Never knew probiotics were seasonal."

"Neither did I until Barzan, financial whiz kid, sent me over the company prospectus. There's all this research about probiotics and the gut and the connection to the brain and making you feel happier and younger. In all honesty, I wasn't totally convinced at the time. A lot of the science was way over my head. But Barzan being Barzan, he did all his research and called all his financial friends and recommended that I invest."

"In something you didn't fully understand?"

"That's why I have Barzan."

"So, we're celebrating because your gastrointestinal tract has all the right bacteria inside of it, and you now feel like a teenager again."

"We're celebrating because Barzan called me a few days ago and told me that the company was being bought out by a huge healthcare company out of the UK for hundreds of millions of dollars."

"Okay."

"And that means the tiny stake I own in the company is being bought along with it."

"You don't have any say-so? What if you don't want to sell your ownership stake?"

"Doesn't work that way. One sells, we all sell."

"So, what does that mean for you personally?"

"A long string of zeroes."

"Like how long?"

"Like long enough to keep you eating at places like this."

"But I don't always want a Michelin star. Sometimes I want simple Mexican street food at Chilango."

"In my book, they have Michelin stars too."

"You mind doing me a favor?"

"For you, anything."

"Don't let that Sophia woman know about your recent windfall. If she's as pretty and seductive as you say she is, she's gonna totally rearrange all the names on your romance list."

"Don't give it another thought," I said. "My list only has one name on it, and you're at the top."

18

SOHO HOUSE SAT in the Near West Side not far from Momotaro. This Chicago branch of an international private club had been built in an enormous old belt factory, making it larger than the clubs in New York and Los Angeles combined. Replete with a forty-bedroom hotel, fifteen-thousand-square-foot gymnasium, private movie room, three restaurants, and a rooftop pool, it was a hot ticket with the millennials and the arty crowd as well as moneyed older men who had to take off their ties and leave their briefcases with the coat check before they boarded the elevators to the private upper floors. The two ground-floor restaurants were open to the public, as was the bar and two spacious lounges. I had been here a couple of times, both late-night parties, both extremely rewarding.

I pulled up my '86 Porsche Turbo in front of a line of shiny Maseratis and Range Rovers and flicked the valet kid a twenty spot and told him to leave it up front. I walked through the heavy oak doors and took a left toward the membership check-in desk. A light-skinned Black girl who looked like she was two or three years into a graduate degree greeted me with a practiced smile. She wore a short, formfitting black skirt that wouldn't pass Sister Mary's ruler test and a white top that fell off her shoulders and conjured thoughts worthy of a confessional. MERCEDES was stamped across her name tag.

"Good afternoon," she said. Her voice sounded like two pieces of tissue paper being rubbed together. "Membership number?"

"I'm here to meet someone," I said, offering my most charming smile.

"Great. Let me check the list."

She started tapping the keys on the thin laptop sitting on the lectern in front of her. Her fingernails had been painted a joyous turquoise.

"I won't be on the list," I said. "It's a surprise."

"Who are you here to meet?"

"Sophia Caballé."

"Sophia is upstairs at the pool. You're here to surprise her?"

"As best I can."

She laughed softly, and I couldn't help but think how perfect a greeter she was for a place like this.

"I'm so sorry . . . what's your name?"

"Ashe."

"Spelled with an *e* like Arthur Ashe?"

I was impressed. "How do you even know who he is? Your parents hadn't even gone on their first date when he was alive."

"My father coaches men's tennis at Florida A&M." She smiled. "I've heard about him my entire life. One poster in the garage, another one in the family room."

"Do you play?"

"Not seriously anymore, but I can still hit the ball."

"Maybe we'll play sometime."

"I'm a bit rusty, so I'll have to practice a little first. I don't want to make a fool of myself."

"Impossible." I winked.

"You're a charmer." She leaned forward. "Okay, listen. Only members are allowed upstairs or guests accompanied by members or if your name is down here on the list. But I think I can make this one exception if you keep it between us."

I crossed my heart and bowed my head.

"You're funny," she said. "I like you. The pool is on the sixth floor. Take the elevators, and once you get off, the pool will be straight ahead. Sophia always lies out at the northwest corner. You can't miss her."

I nodded as I walked over to and entered the dark elevators. The doors opened to a sudden rush of light and the Jonas Brothers singing their hit "What a Man Gotta Do." Temperatures hovered somewhere in the low nineties. A long row of banquettes ran along a wall just across from the elevators. A collection of twentysomethings typed away on their laptops with their white earbuds plugged in. Beyond that sat an enormous pool crowded with young people in various stages of undress. I had to remind myself that it was only one o'clock in the afternoon.

Mercedes was right. Sophia Caballé couldn't be missed. She was stretched out on a padded chaise, partially shielded by an umbrella, a large pair of sunglasses protecting her eyes. Her legs were long and toned, her stomach flat but not too masculine, her full bosom likely the assist of an Oak Street plastic surgeon. Her curly sandy-blonde hair had been tied back from a face that God had created to prove only he was the master of perfection. Pernell Watson had said she could stop traffic on Michigan Avenue. That was selling her short. Sophia Caballé could stop traffic anywhere.

I made my way over and took a seat on an empty lawn chair next to her, facing the pool. A bottle of Pellegrino sat in an ice bucket on the table beside her.

"I'd expect you to be on a yacht somewhere in the Mediterranean," I said.

"You have the wrong girl," she said, never turning her head. "Too many boats over there this time of year. The water in the Persian Gulf is warmer."

We sat there, and I looked east toward the postcard skyline view of downtown Chicago. This view alone was worth the price of membership.

"Whatever you're selling, I'm not interested," she said. "I sun here alone."

"Just had a couple of questions," I said. "Won't take much of your time."

"Questions? About what?"

"You have a relative with the first name Montserrat?"

"As in the island in the West Indies?"

"You're very well traveled. It's also the first name of one of the greatest opera singers of all time. She has the same last name."

"Her name is Montserrat?"

"No, Montserrat Caballé."

Sophia shrugged her smoothly tanned shoulders. "Anything's possible, I guess. That's what you wanted to ask me?"

"That and whether you knew Walter Griffin."

Sophia turned and acknowledged me for the first time. "What's your name?" she said, none too pleased.

"Ashe Cayne."

"I'm not sure what game you think you're playing, but don't come over here and bother me with questions you already know the answers to."

"Then let me try something I don't know. How close of a relationship did you have with Griffin?"

Sophia turned back toward the pool and smiled. I didn't think it was possible for her to improve on perfection, but when she smiled, that was exactly what she did.

"Why are you here asking me all of these questions? I don't know who you are or what you're trying to do."

"I'm a private investigator, and the family has hired me to find some answers."

"What kind of answers?"

"Answers like why their husband and father ended up in a rat-infested, abandoned area on Lower Wacker Drive with a bullet in his head."

She didn't respond right away, but her inhalation was noticeable. Then she said, "It was a very difficult situation for all of us who knew Walter. And for it to happen the way it did. It didn't make sense."

"Did you know that Walter borrowed half a million dollars?" I said. "Maybe some of that money found its way to you."

"Walter and I were good friends," she said. "He was a very smart and successful man. I had nothing to do with his personal finances." She reached over and took a delicate sip of the iced water.

I looked down beside her chair. A red shiny crocodile bag with dual rolled-top handles and palladium-plated hardware sat next to her. I knew it was a Birkin bag. One of my former clients, Violet Gerrigan, had three of them that I was able to count.

"Must be nice being able to sit out here and get some sun in the middle of the day when everyone else has to trudge to work."

"It would be a lot nicer if I could do it quietly. I have a job just like everyone else. I can take care of myself."

"If catching sun by the pool is a well-paying job, then I'm definitely in the wrong business."

"You're starting to bore me," she said, turning her attention to the pool. Two girls had just slipped into the water and sidled up next to a guy who looked like he belonged in a Hollister ad.

I stood up to leave. "You never told me what you do," I said.

"PR for a very select clientele."

"They must pay you a lot of money. Your bag is worth more than what a teacher at CPS makes in an entire year."

"Money is always relative," Sophia said. "But I do what I need to do to get by."

———

I CALLED MECHANIC AS soon as I got into my car.

"Where are you?" I said.

"Where do you want me to be?" Mechanic asked.

"At Soho House on Green Street."

"You know that's not my scene."

"It's not a social call. I need you to do some reconnaissance."

"Details."

"Thirty-year-old Sophia Caballé, former mistress of Walter Griffin, alleged PR consultant and a conspicuous consumer for the extravagant. I just poked around a little. I want to see what she does well."

"Where does she live?"

"Not sure, but if you get here fast enough, you can follow her and see where the journey ends."

"You think she knows something?"

"A lot more than what she just told me."

"I'll be there in ten minutes once this traffic on Michigan breaks up. Text me a pic so I know what she looks like."

"Already on the way. You can't miss her. She's the second-prettiest thing walking the streets of Chicago."

"I don't need to guess who's the first."

19

PART OF THE REASON I had poured so much energy and focus into the Griffin case was that there was something else I had been trying to avoid. I now sat down on my patio thirty floors above the busy nightlife in Streeterville as a cool breeze swept in off the lake like some kind of apology for the day's fiery temperatures. I held an ice-cold Sam Adams with one hand and Julia's blue envelope in the other. Ed Sheeran working his way through "Photograph" played through the open sliding doors, perfect for my mood. It had been almost a year and a half since Julia had run away to Paris with some stockbroker guy she had never even mentioned she knew. We had been only six months away from the wedding, a lavish affair she and her mother had planned at some swanky hotel in the Rittenhouse Square neighborhood in Philadelphia. She had told me she was going to Paris with her girlfriends for the runway shows; then they were taking the Eurostar to London to visit another friend. Instead, she had been with him the whole time, and she'd never come back.

I'd lost my memory of the first five weeks after she left me. Where I went, who I talked to, what I ate, even how I felt—I couldn't remember anything. It was as if a big black hole had suddenly appeared, swallowed me for five weeks, then spit me out and returned me to the world. My therapist called it psychogenic amnesia. She said that it wasn't that I didn't have any memory, but that it was locked somewhere deep in my limbic system. At some point something would trigger my recall, and it would all come back to me. She advised me to be prepared, as the resurfacing of activities surrounding such a stressful event could be another traumatizing experience.

Julia's letter had been sitting in my apartment for two weeks, and not an hour had gone by that I hadn't thought about what it might contain. Fear and hope had waged a fierce battle in my head, and it was finally time to settle the score. I took a knife and slowly slit open the sealed flap. For some reason, I wanted the envelope to be neat and preserved. Sheeran scratched out those heart-wrenching lines of "Photograph." It was my favorite part of the song, where he talked about her keeping his picture inside the pocket of her ripped jeans so she would never be alone.

I took one last swallow of beer, but just as I reached into the envelope, my cell rang. It was Mechanic.

"Our pretty little Sophia is one busy lady," he said. "And very easy to look at."

"Where are you right now?"

"Parked across the street from the building she went into at 11 East Walton. She's been inside about an hour."

"I know the building," I said. "It's a private residential tower attached to the Waldorf Astoria Hotel. There's a big circular driveway out front."

"I'm in the wrong business."

"What makes you say that?"

"PR must pay a shitload of money. She went to four different designer stores, and each time she came out with at least three bags."

105

"Was that the first thing she did when she left Soho?"

"Nope. She left about an hour after you pulled off. Drives a black Range Rover. The Autobiography edition. She drove straight to a small office building way up north on Clark. I'll shoot you the address."

"How long was she there for?"

"About thirty-five minutes."

"Any idea what's in there?"

"A real estate broker, florist, travel agent, and some business called Brighter Horizons that I googled and couldn't find what they do."

"Did you see which office she went into?"

"Couldn't tell. From where I sat, it was impossible to see inside the building."

"Was she alone?"

"Yup. Then she pulls out and heads back downtown to Oak Street. She does all this shopping for a couple of hours; then she meets up with some tall blonde woman."

"What time was that?"

"A little after five."

"Where did they meet?"

"At a parking garage over on Division."

"A garage?"

"That's usually what the *P* on the outside of the building means."

"Was it attached to an office or apartment building?"

"Nope. It was a stand-alone garage. Entrance and exit on Division."

I wasn't sure what to make of it, but it seemed a little strange. There were plenty of places to meet. Why at a garage?

"The girl she met wasn't too bad herself. She was dressed like a businesswoman or a lawyer. She looked tall, but I didn't see her full body. I only saw her sitting in the car."

"Sophia's car?"

"No, the blonde's car. Sophia drove into the garage. Then about fifteen minutes later, a blue Tesla pulls out. I see Sophia in the passenger seat and the blonde sitting behind the wheel."

Now the garage meetup had gotten just a little more suspicious.

"You have a pic?"

"Sending it as we speak."

"Where did they go?"

"Straight here to 11 East Walton."

"Where's Sophia's car?"

"Still back at the garage where they met up."

My phone vibrated. I opened my text messages and almost dropped the Sam Adams in my hand. "What the hell is going on?"

"You got the pic?"

"Sure did. Are they still in the building?"

"Yup. Been here for just over an hour."

"Sit tight," I said. "I'm on my way. Sophia's friend is Amy Donnegan."

"Who the hell is that?"

"One of the last people to talk to Walter Griffin before he went missing."

———

I PULLED IN BEHIND Mechanic's silver Toyota Prius, then jumped into the passenger seat. Electronic dance music piped out softly through the speakers.

"A hybrid car," I said. "Never figured you as a greenie."

"Anything but," he said. "This car has less pickup than a tricycle. The Viper is in the shop. Besides, this helps me blend in better when on surveillance. No one expects an expert marksman to be tooling around in Grandma's car."

"You could've at least gotten leather seats."

"The girl at the dealership said it was possible but against the ethos of the car. Whatever the hell *ethos* means."

"And you listened to her?"

"After she slipped me her phone number."

"No better reason than that."

We sat there for the better part of an hour watching one luxury vehicle pull up after another, women draped in diamonds and designer handbags, men in starched polo shirts and pastel-colored pants in boat shoes and no socks. To pass the time, we decided to keep track of how many American cars pulled into the circular drive. So far, the Europeans were crushing us forty-five to one, but at least that one was a $150,000 ZR1 Corvette.

I was in the middle of typing a text message to Carolina when Mechanic said, "Beauty 1 and Beauty 2 on the move."

Sophia and Amy emerged from the tall glass doors, said something to the valet who almost broke his neck genuflecting as they approached him. His partner pulled up in Amy's blue Tesla, and with great pageantry they helped usher the women inside. Amy wasted no time pulling out of the driveway.

"A little bit of a rush," Mechanic said, waking up the Prius.

"I hope this damn thing can keep up," I said.

We followed them from a couple of cars behind, almost losing them at several yellow lights, which Mechanic had to blow through to avoid getting stuck with a red. They took a right near Ogden Elementary School, then headed north. Amy was giving Mechanic all he could handle as she wove effortlessly through the traffic. We followed them through Lincoln Park, then up into Lake

View East. She pulled into a one-story garage adjacent to a small office building.

"This is the building Sophia went into earlier," Mechanic said.

"That's strange," I said. "Now they're both going in. Why couldn't Sophia have stayed here and met Amy?"

We waited a few minutes across the street to see if they would emerge from the garage. They didn't.

"Plan B," I said to Mechanic. "You stay here so we can catch them when they come out. I'm gonna try the front door."

I casually walked over to the glass door and tried to open it. It was locked. There were four names stickered on the glass. Kleiman Realty Group, Tiffany the Florist, Brighter Horizons, and Oyster Travel. The lobby was dark, but looking through the window glass, I could see a single elevator door and a stairwell adjacent to it. There was one office door on the ground floor, but it was set too far in for me to see the name on it. I waited a few minutes, hoping I would see them coming down the stairs or out the elevator. No sign of either of them. I figured they must've been up on the second floor. I walked back to the car.

"Anything?" Mechanic asked as I got in.

"Our dynamic beauty duo is somewhere up on the second floor. Must be an entrance from the garage. Let's see how this plays out."

We waited another half hour as one electronic dance song popped and thumped and whined into another. I started wondering if they were all the same song, just with different movements. Mechanic sat there quietly, his head leaned back, his eyes open, motionless but fixed on the garage entrance.

After I explained to him who Amy Donnegan was and our conversation a week ago, he said, "So, what do you think they're doing up there?"

"Not a clue, but obviously it's something they don't want anyone else to know about. It's almost ten o'clock, and they're in an office building that doesn't have any businesses that should be officially open this time of night."

We waited out another ten minutes of no activity.

"We could always just drive into the garage and go in the same way they did," Mechanic said.

"And do what? Place them under citizen's arrest for being out past curfew?"

"Talk to them."

"And give away our leverage?"

"Which is?"

"The element of surprise. I have a better idea."

"Which would be?"

"We split up. They're gonna leave sooner or later. Assuming they all don't leave in the same car, I'll take whoever they're meeting. You take the beauties."

Mechanic almost smiled. "Only a fool would turn down following a pair of beautiful women."

Just as Mechanic said that, the blue Tesla stuck its nose out of the garage. Both ladies were in the car. The back seat was empty.

"Stay with them," I said. "Hit me when they land somewhere."

Whomever they were meeting was either still in the building or would be pulling out behind them. I jumped out of the car and walked across the street. Mechanic followed the Tesla down the street. I waited in the shadows between the front door and the entrance to the garage. I was perfectly positioned to see anything move from either direction. The traffic on Clark Street was brisk in the changeover, older couples leaving a late dinner and heading home to wind down for the evening, while the younger set was heading out to bars and late-night eateries that turned into clubs after the kitchen closed. I had spent little time in this far-north neighborhood, but I was struck by the diversity and energy of the people. This was definitely not the Chicago I'd grown up in. In this trendy neighborhood, interracial and same-sex couples unabashedly held hands, and English was most people's second or third language.

My cell rang.

"They drove back to the garage where Sophia's car was parked," Mechanic said. "A few minutes later, they pulled out separately. Donnegan turned west and Sophia turned east."

"Who did you follow?" I asked.

"Sophia."

"Why am I not surprised? Where did she go?"

"Back to her building at 11 East Walton."

"Good work. You can call it a night."

Just as I clicked off the phone, I caught headlights emerging from the garage. A black BMW sedan. The windows were too dark to fully see inside, but there was enough penetration from the streetlights that I could tell the driver was a man. He turned right and headed away from me going north. I was able to get a shot of his license plate as he pulled into traffic and disappeared. I texted the photo to Carolina. She called within seconds.

"Your ears must be burning," she said. "I'm lying here drifting off to sleep and just thought about you."

"Indecent thoughts?"

"Downright scandalous."

"Sans clothing?"

"And bedsheets too."

"You're teasing my manliness."

"I wish that manliness could find its way to 130 South Canal Street."

"I'm all the way up in Lake View. You'd be in your third dream by the time I got there."

"Pretty soon you're gonna run out of excuses."

"Just be careful what you ask for."

"Talk, talk, talk. Whose license plate did you send me?"

"I don't know. I think it's someone who just had an after-hours meeting with Sophia Caballé and Amy Donnegan."

"Amy Donnegan as in the mayoral aide?"

"The one and only."

"Did you know she and Sophia knew each other?"

"Not until about three hours ago."

"So, now what are you going to do?"

"Ask you to get me the call logs to Walter Griffin's phone and help me figure out who lives at 11 East Walton Street and knows Sophia Caballé."

"Aren't you making a big assumption?"

"What? That my irresistible charm will convince you to help me?"

"No, assuming this Sophia Caballé doesn't own a place there herself."

"I'll take the over-under that a thirty-year-old PR consultant can't afford a million-dollar apartment in the Gold Coast District."

"Never underestimate the power of good cha-cha."

"Now who's making an assumption?"

"Just a statement of fact based on solid evidence."

"Maybe I'll get a chance to see that evidence sooner rather than later."

20

THE HARBORSIDE INTERNATIONAL GOLF CENTER was located just fifteen minutes south of downtown and comprised two public eighteen-hole golf courses built in the old link-style tradition on what used to be a landfill. Both courses had been ranked as among the best to play in Illinois. The steep elevation and land dunes made them challenging even for the better players.

I was standing on the tee box at the practice range, warming up before a match with a friend who had played basketball at Stanford and another who worked the overnight shift at the Jackson Park Hospital. My cell rang as I was stretching.

"Where are you?" Burke said.

"Harborside."

"Since when did you start boating?"

"Never. Harborside as in the golf course over on one eleventh off the Bishop Ford."

"Have you started your game yet?"

"It's not called a game. That's basketball and football. It's called a match. And the answer is no. We tee off in fifty minutes."

"I'll be there in twenty."

———

WE SAT IN THE CLUBHOUSE at a small table against the window overlooking the eighteenth green of the Starboard Course. Lake Calumet rippled softly in the distance. Burke was not in uniform, but he still couldn't shake the look of a cop. He gazed out the window in bewilderment.

"I just can't figure out what it is," he said. "Why would people pay all this money to spend half of their day twisting the hell outa their backs and swinging metal sticks at something no bigger than a meatball at Maggiano's?"

"The same reason people pay a fortune to fly all over the world in subzero temperatures and put a fiberglass board under their feet and ski down the side of a mountain," I said. "It's the thrill of accomplishing."

"There's a lot of other accomplishing that makes a lot more sense, costs a fraction the price, and doesn't tear up your back like it did with Tiger."

A foursome stood in the middle of the fairway. A lanky player took a smooth swing, accelerated through the ball, and sent it flying onto the green about 170 yards away. An amazing approach shot, especially in the wind pushing off the water. The ball hit softly, rolled a little, and landed ten feet from the hole. The other players gave him fist bumps and pats on the back as they marched their way toward the green.

"The thrill of that one shot right there can erase the agony of a hundred bad ones," I said. "And that's why the game is so addictive. No matter how frustrated you get or how many bad scores you put up, you never give up the search for that one perfect hole and the adrenaline kick it gives you."

"Not bad," Burke said. "He made it look easy." He reached into his shirt pocket and pulled out a flash drive and slid it across the table. "Surveillance footage of the afternoon Griffin went missing. It's not the cleanest. They had to pull some from private cameras along the route in addition to our POD cameras. But they tracked him almost to Lower Wacker. Cameras there were down during an upgrade."

"I know. I've read the case file, including the supplementary report, several times."

"I'm not even gonna ask how you got your hands on it."

"I wouldn't tell you even if you did."

"Find anything?"

"That you were right and the cops moved the case through fast. No one formally interviewed anyone from Calgary Arms Nursing Home. That's where Griffin's mother is. He was visiting her before he went missing."

"Someone must've talked to someone."

"If they did, they didn't take the time to find the right person. The supervisor on duty that afternoon said Griffin took two phone calls. End of the second one, she heard him say, 'That's exactly what I need.'"

Burke thought for a moment, then said, "I found someone for you inside the Chicago field office. Daughter of the guy I told you retired. They moved her out here from San Diego about three years ago. Promoted to supervisory special agent. She's willing to talk to you about the FBI's interest in the Cabrini land. With limits."

"How soon?"

"When she gets back from Quantico in a couple of weeks. She's out there doing some type of counterterrorism intensive. My friend gave her your number. She'll reach out to you."

"She sounds tough."

"If she's anything like her dad, and I heard she is, then she's tough as galvanized steel."

Burke squeezed his eyes as he looked out the window. The foursome had made it to the green. The lanky guy stepped up to the ball and putted it into the hole with one stroke.

"Guy just got a birdie," Burke said.

"I thought you didn't know this stupid game," I said.

"I said I would never waste my time playing it, not that I didn't know it." He stood up to leave.

"We still have room for one more in our foursome," I said. "Tee off in twenty minutes."

"I'd sooner put a goddamn thirty-eight to my head." He marched out of the dining room like a bull getting released from a cattle squeeze chute.

21

AFTER FOUR HOURS OF some of the best and worst golf in my life, I turned onto the Bishop Ford Freeway, heading back north. My cell phone rang. Carolina's office number popped up on the screen.

"I have an early birthday gift for you," she said.

"Wow, that's two gifts in one day."

"What was the other?"

"An eagle on twelve."

"An eagle flew over you on Route 12?"

"No, the eagle was on the golf course. It means I scored two strokes better than par on the twelfth hole."

"That's it," she said. "I want you to create a cheat sheet so I can understand all this fancy golf lingo and not look like a fool."

"That can be arranged."

"How 'bout we start over empanadas at Chilango?"

"How about you just made me the happiest, hungriest golfer in all of Chicago?"

———

CHILANGO MEXICAN STREET FOOD operated out of a closet on Taylor Street squeezed between a boisterous Irish bar and a strip of grass where a building had been demolished and never rebuilt. The menu was the perfect size—enough choices to keep it interesting but small enough that the kitchen could master everything it cooked. Their empanadas and steak tacos were foods worthy of the gods. Carolina and I sat at one of the small Formica countertops in the window. I was making fast work of my third barbecue chicken empanada while Carolina forked a cube of steak out of her taco.

"Now that the growl in your stomach is quieted down, let's get to the gift," Carolina said. "First order of business, the tag you sent me is registered to a man by the name of Robert Kristly. He lives at 831 Diane Lane in Naperville. No priors. No moving violations in the last five years."

"A photo, by chance?"

"Already a step ahead. It's in your email."

"Now it's just a matter of figuring out which of the three second-floor businesses he works in."

"My guess is real estate, not the floral shop."

"What makes you say that?"

"Because he lives in a stone mansion with a long driveway. It would take a lot of roses and petunias to make that kind of money."

"Shouldn't be too hard to find out his business," I said.

"I'm working on it. Shouldn't take too long."

"What about the homeowner's list at 11 East Walton?"

"That took a little longer. I had to get one of my girlfriends at the clerk's office to run that for me." She opened her leather tote and handed me a manila folder. "There are fifty-one units in 11 East Walton but only forty-five names on the list. And your friend Sophia is not on the list."

I pulled the two sheets of paper from the folder. Of course, they had been arranged in alphabetical order. Not that I didn't believe her, but I looked at the *C*s. Carlington and Clement. No Caballé. She lived there but didn't own the apartment. Was she living with someone? Was she renting?

"If there are fifty-one units and only forty-five owners, what happened to the other six owners?"

"They never existed. Six of the forty-five names listed own a second unit that they combined with the first."

"Because a four-million-dollar three-bedroom condominium simply won't do."

"First world problems."

I went back to the top of the list. I recognized my first name midway through. Michael and Nancy Meinsdorf. They owned the Chicago Bulls and the White Sox. They had two unit numbers next to their names. I flipped to the second page and worked my way down. I stopped at the third name from the bottom and looked up. Carolina nodded as I met her eyes.

"Your gift." She smiled.

"Is it really him?" I asked.

"It is. I cross-checked it with other property records. He also owns a home in Bronzeville."

I looked back down at the list as Cephus Redmond's name stared back at me. Not only was he a resident in one of Chicago's most exclusive buildings. He was one of the six who owned two units.

22

MECHANIC AND I SAT in my office, feet on the desk, staring at the dry-erase board that ran almost the entire length of the north wall. I had created a timeline, then a list of the players and their connection to Walter Griffin and each other. By the time I was finished, the board looked like a spider's web hanging off a fishing pole. I had done all the writing and reasoning while Mechanic had done all the listening and grunting. It was common in cases to hit a point where either you seemed to have run out of new roads to turn down or there were so many roads forking off an intersection you weren't sure which one to take. When that happened, it helped to write everything out and try to look at it with fresh eyes. That made it easier to find something that might be hiding in plain sight.

"It's just not making sense," I said. "So many connections but not enough explanations."

"What bothers you?" Mechanic asked.

"Throw a dart anywhere up here and you'll hit a problem. How about Cephus Redmond owning two units in the same building where Sophia Caballé lives or visits often? Why is Griffin borrowing half a million dollars in cash when he's supposed to be worth millions of dollars himself? How about the OIG investigating one of the mayor's closest confidants over a couple of meaningless charges on a city credit card? How about no one interviewing the nursing home supervisor who could attest to Griffin's state of mind hours before he went missing? And you can't get anything from his mother because she has Alzheimer's."

"Lots of loose ends," he said. "Let's look at the video?"

I popped the flash drive Burke had given me into my computer. Mechanic pulled his chair around to face the monitor. A couple of taps with the mouse and the video played. A steady stream of cars headed toward the camera and passed out of frame. It was definitely State Street, where the traffic traveled both north and south. I could make out the Twenty-Sixth Street overpass, where the ramp entrance to 94 East passed underneath it.

"Okay," I said. "We know which direction is north and which is south. Now let's focus on his car."

I rewound the video to the beginning. Thirty seconds ticked away on the counter before Griffin's red Cadillac pulled into frame. I froze it.

"Can't see his face," Mechanic said.

"The focus is too bad. And we can't see if anyone else is in the car with him. But we can see the license plate: WMG."

I hit the "Play" button. In a few seconds, Griffin rolled out of frame at Twenty-Fifth Street. I could see the large field just east of the National Teachers Academy building. That camera's video came to an end; then another one started. I wrote down the start and stop time of the first camera in my notepad. The second camera picked him up in front of the Burger King at Twenty-Third and Michigan. This camera was much clearer. You could see him in the car. You could also see that he was alone. He drove out of frame, and the camera kept rolling another two seconds before it ended. I pushed the "Pause" button.

"So, we know he's heading north," I said. "He's by himself. And he made it all the way to Twenty-Third Street."

I hit "Play." It took me several attempts to get a location, but at the edge of the frame I caught the top half of the letters of the Old Navy store banner that hung above the entrance fronting State Street. I took this portion of the video back to the beginning and then focused on Griffin's car. Nothing different. He was still driving, and he was alone. Once that video ended, the next one started. Fifteen seconds in, the red Cadillac drove past the Wit Hotel, pulled up to the light, and stopped behind a blue pickup truck. A white BMW pulled up behind him, and a turquoise sports car with tinted windows and shiny rims pulled up behind that. They sat there for about forty-five seconds, then started moving. Griffin took a left on Upper Wacker and headed west. The BMW and turquoise car turned also. All three drove out of frame, and the video ended three seconds after they were gone. The time was 3:27 p.m.

"Nothing seems unusual," I said. "It took him about thirteen minutes to get from the nursing home to Upper Wacker. Sunday afternoon in November, not much traffic on the roads, everyone at home watching the Bears game. Seems normal."

"When did his wife first call him?"

"Five thirty-seven. She said it went straight to voice mail. Which could mean two things. Either his phone was off, or he swiped to decline the call. But that was two hours after he reached Upper Wacker."

"A lot of things can go wrong in two hours."

I pushed the "Play" button. This next clip had come from a camera positioned on Upper Wacker Drive, facing west. Twenty seconds in, Griffin's red Cadillac drove through the bend in front of Merchandise Mart. He drove out of frame, and the clip ended. Another clip started soon after. It showed him taking a left onto Lake Street and traveling east before he stopped at Franklin. The next camera caught him from behind and showed him going through the light, then taking another left. He pulled up to the light at the intersection of Post and Lower Wacker. Three cars pulled behind him, but only the first two were completely visible. The light turned, and he hung a right onto the access road that ran beside Lower Wacker. The clip played for another ten seconds, then went dead. That was the end of the video: 3:39 p.m.

"Movie over, lights up," Mechanic said.

"I didn't even get a chance to finish my popcorn."

"Hard to believe the country's third-largest city didn't have working cameras on a street as big as Lower Wacker."

"And you wonder what they do with a one-and-a-half-billion-dollar CPD budget."

"Probably a third of that in overtime. Cops sitting in their cars at construction sites or in the middle lane of Michigan Avenue, keeping an eye on Biffy and her friends store hopping with Daddy's credit card."

"So it goes."

"What are your thoughts about the tape?"

"Nothing remarkable. But I'll need to look at it again. I might see something I missed."

"Something's bothering you."

"I can't stop thinking about how Griffin's final hour might've played out and what the cameras missed between the time the tape ended and the first time his wife called and got his voice mail. They found his body at almost four o'clock in the morning. The ME had an estimated time of death of five o'clock the previous afternoon, but I have a feeling he had been in trouble a long time before then."

"I gotta go," Mechanic said, standing up.

"And desert me before the encore?"

"I have an encore of my own, and she's expecting me in thirty minutes."

"Someone new?"

"That girl from the dealership who sold me the Prius."

"Does she know yet how lethal you are with a gun?"

"Which one?"

"I figured you'd say that."

———

I TOOK ANOTHER LOOK at the video, made a few more notes, then called it quits. I went home, pulled out some leftover layered meat lasagna, put it in the oven on low, then made a fresh salad. I took Stryker for a quick walk to the lake and back, then fixed my plate and popped the flash drive in my computer. I watched the video again, but this time assuming Griffin's mindset. I often found that when working with a hypothesis that you believed, sometimes you could gain new perspective by assuming the opposite. I didn't believe for one second that Griffin had committed suicide, but for the sake of the exercise, I assumed he had. I started the tape from the beginning and kept thinking to myself, *My life has become too much to bear; I need to end it today.* I watched closely, stopping the tape and checking my notes, rewinding it where I thought there might be something. But the five minutes of video didn't give me anything. Maybe I needed to get away from it. Sometimes when you looked at the same evidence too much, things started to slip into the subconscious. I got up from the computer, went to my room, and climbed underneath the covers.

Two hours later, I was still awake. Something about the video was bothering me, but I couldn't pinpoint exactly what it was. I knew my mind was too busy to fall asleep, so I got dressed and headed to the garage. Minutes later I was sitting outside the Calgary Arms Nursing Home. I shifted the car into gear and started to follow the route Griffin had taken that afternoon.

I reached Twenty-Second Street, also called Cermak Road, a nineteen-mile stretch of road named in honor of Anton Cermak, a Czech immigrant who had been Chicago's forty-fourth mayor. The camera had caught the Sharks Fish & Chicken fast-food restaurant in the northeast corner of the intersection and the cluster of cylindrical mixed-income housing buildings across the street. I continued heading north on State. I passed the first district police station, then stopped at the light at Roosevelt. The video had grabbed the Mattress Firm store just in frame at the southeast corner of the intersection. There weren't many cars on the road this late, so I was able to eat up a big chunk of State when the light turned green. I made it all the way down to the Old Navy at the northwest corner where Randolph cut across State. Rolling a couple of blocks north, I stopped at the same light where Griffin had stopped at State and Lake. I looked down at my notes. He had gone straight through the light and hung a left on Upper Wacker along with the BMW and the turquoise car. I looked up to get my bearings and saw theWit Hotel on the right. I tried to channel Griffin's thoughts at the time. What was he thinking as he searched for a place to end it all? Someplace quiet where no one would be able to intervene and stop him?

I continued on Wacker, running west along the Chicago River underneath me. I drove until Wacker turned south, then hung a left on Lake Street. Griffin had decided the best place to do it was on Lower Wacker, where it was always dark and desolate. There were lots of places you could hide a car and not be found for hours, maybe days. I drove onto a small road called North Post Place that led to Lower Wacker. Griffin had gotten stopped at the light here. He had waited for the light to turn green before making a right turn. There were two choices. A sharp right would have put him on the access road, while the other right turn would have put him on the main Lower Wacker Drive. He had chosen a sharp right, so I did the same. That was where the cameras had lost him.

I drove down the access road lit by the hazy orange glow of streetlights stuck underneath an overpass. There wasn't much to see except a series of loading docks and cars parked diagonally against the drab delivery basement entrances of these spectacular skyscrapers that shot above Upper Wacker Drive but were impossible to see down here in the underbelly of Lower Wacker. This was a perfect place to disappear. Cars raced up and down the main road, but the access road was largely forgotten save for the occasional noisy truck dropping off its load before continuing to its next stop. Then it struck me as I saw a sign for Clark Street. This was completely the wrong direction. Griffin had been heading east, but his body had been found partially submerged in the river at Wolf Point, which was due west and on the other side of the river. I quickly pulled a U-turn and headed west. I drove past where I had originally taken a right, onto the access road; then I saw the sign for Randolph. I had three options: take the ramp leading to Upper Wacker above; continue going west on Lower Wacker, where I could eventually take a ramp heading up to the expressways; or take a right onto a sketchy-looking access road where a couple of abandoned cars sat on their rims and a homeless man with a shopping cart sat rubbing his bare chest.

This was all wrong. There weren't any cameras where Griffin eventually settled at Wolf Point, but the route to get there was full of cameras—in fact, one posted every ten yards that I could see. They couldn't all have been out of commission. Could they? How was it possible there wasn't more tape?

I took the access road because, thirty yards in, this was where Griffin's car had been found and his body discovered only feet away down in the river. I pulled over and dialed Burke. He answered on the second ring and sounded fully awake.

"This better be good," he said.

"It's good, but it's bad."

"What the hell does that mean?"

"Either someone was being really sloppy, or someone conveniently erased surveillance footage. Take your pick, but both are bad."

"I'm listening."

I explained to him the video and the last point it caught Griffin and the wrong turn. He listened carefully, then said, "Who have you told about this?"

"No one. I just figured it out."

"Keep a lid on it for now," he said. "Let me do some digging around and get back to you. I don't want to make any waves before I know what's going on."

23

CAMILLIA OBRECHT STOOD ABOUT as tall and wide as a fire hydrant, but she was like no other force I had ever seen in the real estate business. A smile always at the ready and absolutely inexhaustible when it came to doing what she loved best—buying and selling real estate. She had sold me my apartment after I called her office to speak to the listing agent and was told they were too busy. I asked the receptionist to connect me with whomever she thought was the best agent they had. In thirty seconds, Camillia was on the phone.

"You ready to buy that penthouse in the Gold Coast?" she said now in her husky voice. "Inventory is high right now. Lots of good deals out there."

"Let me rob Wells Fargo first; then we can talk."

"Stop it. I know Barzan is making you money hand over fist."

"When I'm ready, you know you're my first call," I said.

"I'll hold you to it."

"I need to ask you a question about 11 East Walton."

"The Waldorf condominiums. One of the most expensive buildings in the city. Robbing Wells Fargo won't be enough. You need to hit Bank of America too."

"Not asking for me." I laughed. "I'm working on a case, and I need to understand how the ownership in the building works."

"In what way?"

"Is it normal for people to buy two units in the same building?"

"Depends on what you mean by normal. When you're dealing with clients who have that kind of wealth and usually have three or four other homes, it's not unusual at all. Sometimes they decide the place is too small, so they take another unit, tear down the walls, and combine them. Thus the expression 'mansion in the sky.' They do it a lot in those buildings."

I looked at the list Carolina had given me. Four of the six multiunit owners had purchased units on the same floor as their original unit. Cephus and the Meinsdorfs had purchased units on separate floors.

"I get the concept of buying units next to each other," I said. "But why would they buy units on different floors?"

"That's not uncommon. They're trying to make a duplex or triplex, so they buy the unit underneath them, rip out the floor, and add stairs."

That made sense in the case of the Meinsdorfs, because their second unit was directly underneath the first. But Cephus had purchased two units that were separated by seven floors. I'd never heard of a septex.

"So, you would be suspicious if you heard that someone bought two units that were separated by four or more floors?"

"Not at all. People buy another unit to house their staff—maid's quarters, if you will. They don't want them living in the house, but they want them close by. Or they want the extra space for guests who visit."

Cephus Redmond didn't strike me as someone who had staff he needed close by. But I had a feeling I knew who he was keeping in the second unit.

———

CAROLINA AND I SAT on a bench in Grant Park looking at Buckingham Fountain shoot water into the hot air.

"I haven't been here in a long time," Carolina said. "It's interesting how many little pleasures we Chicagoans miss out on because we don't want to get stampeded by tourists."

"I love this fountain for all its extravagance and wastefulness," I mused. "Everyone thinks it's named after Buckingham Palace over in England."

"It isn't?"

"Nope. Named after a guy called Clarence Buckingham. His sister donated it to the city. Cost three-quarters of a million dollars to build it, all Georgia pink marble. Then she set up a three-hundred-thousand-dollar investment fund to pay for continual maintenance."

"Doesn't sound like a lot of money for all that," Carolina said.

"Nineteen twenty-seven. It was a fortune back then. Still the most photographed landmark in the city."

A cluster of tourists stood with the fountain at their backs, vamping with their selfie sticks. The wind blew a slight mist in our direction some thirty yards away. It was a welcome relief from the sweltering heat. The fountain had just undergone a year-long renovation, and it was stronger and more glorious than ever.

"How do you know so much about it?" Carolina asked.

"Had to do a school report on it in fifth grade. Mrs. Tahan gave me an A minus."

"I can't imagine what the water bill would be."

"The fountain basin holds one point five million gallons. When the water show goes on at the top of the hour, fourteen thousand gallons per minute are pushed through a hundred and ninety jets."

"You're very sexy when you do that."

"Do what?"

"Spit out data like a computer."

"You're trying to make me blush, but it's not gonna work."

"Why?"

"The melanin advantage."

"Speaking of advantage, one of my girlfriends thinks you're taking advantage of me."

"Moi?"

"Yes, you. She said a dinner at a fancy restaurant isn't enough for all the goodies I bring you."

"What does she suggest?"

"Maybe a weekend getaway to an exotic island in the middle of winter when this fountain is frozen."

"That could be negotiated," I said.

"Let the negotiations begin." She handed me a large manila envelope.

I pulled out five pages with a running list of phone numbers.

"All calls made to and from Griffin's cell phone twenty-four hours before they found his body," she said. "I saw some patterns and made some notes in the margins."

"There must be close to a hundred calls," I said. "In just the span of twenty-four hours."

"He was a busy man."

"In more ways than one."

I studied the list. Carolina had created a table that showed the ten most frequent numbers and listed them in descending order. The length of each call had been listed next to the phone number.

"I didn't know what I should be looking for, but I randomly called some of the numbers listed on Sunday," Carolina said.

"And?"

"A couple of people answered, and I pretended I had the wrong number. He called places people usually call, like Walgreens, South Shore Country Club, a car wash. Nothing out of the usual."

"If he did commit suicide, kind of strange he would go get his car washed that morning, then blow his brains out later that afternoon."

"Stranger things have happened," Carolina said. "Never know what makes a person finally snap."

She had a point. I quickly turned my attention to the hour he had been at Calgary. There were two calls placed to his phone during that time, which matched Evette Carson's recollection. I focused on the second number. That's the call where she had heard him say, "That's exactly what I need."

I pulled out my phone.

"What are you doing?" Carolina asked.

"Calling that number," I said, pointing to the sheet. "That was the second call he received before he left the nursing home."

I dialed the number.

"Hello," a man answered in a gruff voice.

"I'm not sure I have the right number," I said.

"Jesus Christ! When will this stop? When are you people gonna realize Bryce doesn't have this number anymore?"

I went along. "Sorry to bother you, sir, but do you know how I can reach Bryce?"

"Not a damn clue," he growled. "I wouldn't know him if he walked up and punched me in the face."

"So, why do you have his phone?"

"I don't have *his* phone," he said in an angrier voice. "This was his old number. It's been my number for the last ten months. If you guys are his friends, I don't know why you don't have his new number. I'm tired of answering his calls."

"Who's been calling you?"

"How the hell should I know? Friends like you. I don't know. Then every few months it's a bill collector calling about his student debt. I tell them this isn't Bryce's number anymore; then two months later another person calls looking for him, and I have to go through the same thing all over again. I'm sick of it."

"Do you know Bryce's last name?" I asked.

"What the hell kind of question is that?" he said. "You're his friend, and you're asking *me* what his last name is? Is this some kind of joke?"

"Just making sure we were talking about the same Bryce. That's all."

"I don't remember. One of those bill collectors might've said it, but I forget. I just know everyone keeps asking for Bryce."

"Once again, I'm very sorry to bother you, sir. I'll make sure to spread the word that this isn't Bryce's number anymore."

"I'd appreciate that."

Just as the line disconnected, the top of the hour hit, and the fountain shot fourteen thousand gallons fifteen stories toward the pale-blue sky. No Bryce had been mentioned in the investigative supplementary report, but I was going to find him. I wanted him to tell me what exactly it was that Walter Griffin said he needed just hours before his death.

———

"ANY PROGRESS YOU CAN REPORT?" Junior Griffin asked me. He sat on the other side of my desk as rush hour traffic started building up a head of steam beneath us on Michigan Avenue. He had declined anything to drink. I was content with a frosty bottle of root beer.

"I'm still trying to connect a lot of dots," I said.

"It's been three weeks," he said. "I just figured you might have some answers."

"More questions than I do answers right now."

His face dropped in disappointment.

"Sometimes these things can take months just to even get going," I said. "I just want to be honest with you."

"Do you think this is gonna take months?"

"I don't."

"Do you still think my father was killed?"

"Even more than I did when you and your sister first came through that door."

"Do you think you'll be able to prove he was killed?"

"I won't stop tinkering under the hood until the problem is fixed."

Junior looked out the window pensively. The sun hit his hazel eyes just so, and he looked even more like his father. He had something to say, but he was figuring out when or how to say it. I decided to help him along.

"Your father was a very complicated man," I said.

Junior nodded his agreement.

"He had some very complicated relationships."

Junior nodded again, still looking out the window.

"Sophia Caballé seems to be one of them."

He never stopped looking out the window. He also didn't nod. But I could tell he already knew.

"He was a great father," Junior finally said. "He wasn't a perfect man, but he did his best to do what he thought was right."

"Did your mother know?" I asked.

"About Sophia?"

It was my turn to nod.

"I never asked her, and she never mentioned it. It hurt me to think what knowing about it might do to her."

"Adult relationships can be complex," I said. "How long did your father know Sophia?"

"I'm not sure. But Sophia is my age. In fact, we're two days apart. We have mutual friends."

"Did they know too?"

"Not about my father, but everyone knows about her."

"Knows what?"

"That she leads a much more extravagant life than a twentysomething public relations girl can afford. Sophia has that *it* factor. Men have a hard time staying away."

"When I talked to her last week, she was lying at the pool at Soho," I said. "The handbag sitting next to her was worth around forty thousand dollars."

"That's my point. Unless your clients are Brad Pitt and Leo DiCaprio, you're not making that kind of money."

"When was the last time you saw her?"

"It's been well over a year. Right after she got back."

"Got back from where?"

"Rumor was she had gotten married to some oil magnate in Dubai and moved over there to live in some palace. She was gone for about ten months; then she came back. No one knew what happened. She just started showing up again, going out and being seen."

"Do you know Cephus Redmond?"

"Of course I do. He and Dad were friends. They've known each other since they were kids."

"You think Sophia knows Cephus?"

Junior wrinkled his brow. "I wouldn't think so. Cephus runs in much different circles than Sophia. He's all South Side."

"With a lot of money."

"I know his car washes are successful, but I don't know what kind of money he makes."

"Enough to own two units in one of the most exclusive addresses downtown."

"Cephus lives out in Harvey. I've been to his house a couple of times with my father. I can't see Cephus living in some swanky apartment building. That's not who he is."

I decided not to get into the half-a-million-dollar loan that his father never paid back or the land deal with the Russians that went bad. I wanted to understand all of it better and the full context before presenting it to him. Junior stood up to leave.

"We know you're gonna find out who did this," he said. "And whatever answers you find, we're prepared to deal with them." He extended the envelope he had been carrying. "Here's the autopsy report from the medical examiner's office. We can't make much of it, but maybe you can."

After he walked out the door, I sat there looking out at Buckingham Fountain and those arching fourteen thousand gallons of water. Dark clouds had moved in toward the lake. Soon the rain would fall, and people would start frantically scattering to beat the downpour. I opened the envelope and took out three folded pieces of paper. I had read many autopsy reports in my cop life, but most of them were written in such medicalese that I often had to call one of our staff physicians to explain some of the subtleties that I didn't understand. I spent the better part of an hour reading through the report, but nothing seemed unusual or contradictory to what the investigative report had found. Gun residue had been found between Griffin's thumb and index finger and the index and middle finger of his right hand. The report described the entry and exit wounds. The rest of the internal and external examinations seemed straightforward. Then I looked at Griffin's name on the front sheet and just stared at it.

I had seen hundreds of names on reports like this, and each time it sent a jolt through me, knowing this name had been a person who once was full of life and hope. They watched sports and had dinner with their family and danced to music. Now they were a footnote in history, reduced to a name on a page. No more weddings or birthday parties or kissing their loved ones in the morning. I always believed that if people really thought about and respected the finality of death, they would find less extreme ways to vent their anger and exact revenge, catch themselves before that snap during a moment of rage.

My cell vibrated and chirped with a text message. I didn't recognize the sender's number.

Meet tomorrow at 2 o'clock at the Art Institute. The bench on other side of "Nighthawks." Important WG info. Come alone.

I tried texting back but got an error message that it was a landline. I dialed the number and got an automated recording that said the call couldn't be completed as dialed.

24

IT HAD BEEN A WHILE since I last visited the Art Institute of Chicago. I had stayed away, mostly because Julia liked to meet me there, and we'd walk through the galleries, traveling back in time through the works of the artists. She liked the impressionists. I liked the Ancient Egypt rooms. Often, we would compromise and choose something altogether different. We'd spend a couple of hours "exploring," as she liked to call it, then walk down Michigan Avenue and find a café where we would talk about the artwork we liked most.

The massive museum sat prominently on Michigan Avenue, with its rear parked at the northern border of Grant Park. After several additions since 1893, it now occupied almost a million square feet, making it second in size only to New York's Metropolitan Museum of Art. Rather than entering through the lion-guarded entrance on Michigan, I slipped through the less frequently used doors on East Monroe Street.

I didn't need directions to *Nighthawks*. Edward Hopper's 1942 masterpiece was one of the crown jewels of the museum. I had seen it at least a couple of dozen times, and each time I discovered something new. There were those iconic paintings scattered throughout the world that, regardless of how many times you saw them, you felt like it was the first time—the *Mona Lisa* at the Louvre, van Gogh's *Starry Night* at MoMA in New York, David's *Death of Socrates* at the Met. The Art Institute laid claim to Grant Wood's *American Gothic* and *Nighthawks*.

I walked through the new glass-roofed court, where several counselors were having a difficult time corralling a large group of elementary school children. The bright courtyard gave way to the entrance of the modern wing and a glass-encased space filled with sculptures. Immediately, I could see the queue of visitors excitedly making their way to the wide limestone staircase in the southern portion of the wing. Just like the *Mona Lisa*, you know where *Nighthawks* is by seeing the crowds first.

I joined them and turned into the Ivan Albright Gallery. A chorus of collective gasps punctured the silence as visitors immediately encountered *Nighthawks* upon stepping into the room. The painting hung alone on the center wall, hidden behind glass that the museum controversially claimed better protected it against potential damage from the ultraviolet wavelengths in camera flashes. Scientists had debunked this idea, but museum curators around the world continued to shield their most popular paintings and, in some cases, ban flashes altogether.

I waited my turn with the rest of the crowd, then, when there was an opening, slid in front of the painting to take it in. Three customers, two men and a raven-haired woman, sat at a wooden countertop in an otherwise empty diner as a waiter behind the counter busied himself with work. They were all in the same place but at that captured moment were strangers of the night, lost in their own thoughts, as separate from each other as they were the viewer. This late-night scene had been inspired by a restaurant Hopper had seen on New York City's Greenwich Avenue. Hopper had been questioned incessantly about his motivation, and eventually he relented and admitted that, unconsciously, he was probably painting the loneliness of a large city.

I was about to relinquish my position when I saw something I hadn't seen before. It wasn't easy to make out with the glare of the protective glass, but it was the coffee cup sitting in front of the woman, who was examining something in her hands. I had never noticed it before. I felt a sense of accomplishment that after all these times observing the details of the painting, I had discovered something new.

I finally stepped away, the tourists quickly filling in the small gap I had left. I walked around to the other side of the wall. The crowd had thinned, but traffic was still brisk. A large single oil hung on this wall, one I had never seen before. A heavily bearded man wearing some type of robe had his hand on the head of a Greek bust. Green American currency had been placed throughout the painting, clipped to the front of the bust, hung from the wood-planked wall against which the painting had been hung, and suspended from the man's chest and over his heart. The bright, bold colors of the money and two playing cards, which were kings of diamonds, stood in sharp contrast to the muted tones of the man resting his hand on the bust.

I spotted the bench some ten feet in front of the painting. A couple listening to an audio guide stood to leave, and I took a seat in the center of it. I looked around, trying to identify who might be the mysterious informant, but everyone looked busy, quietly studying the various paintings on the walls. I directed my attention back to the painting. I didn't want to read the title of it or the inscription until I had a chance to take it in and form my own idea of what the artist was trying to express. I was just about to go and read the exhibit label when a short man in round glasses and a rumpled gray suit sat next to me. For some reason, my eyes were drawn to his black wingtip shoes. They were extremely shiny and miniature, like the first pair of real dress shoes a boy is given when he must attend an important event. He smelled faintly of cigars.

"What do you make of it?" he said, looking straight ahead.

"Different," I said.

"That's one way to describe it."

"Interesting, but not exactly my kind of art."

"You don't like American art?" he asked.

"I do, but there's too much going on here. The colors, the money, scissors, playing cards—it almost feels like a collage."

"You didn't get a chance to read the story behind it."

"Not yet. I looked at *Nighthawks* first, then was working my way through this."

"This oil was done by a guy named Otis Kaye. He lost all his savings in the stock market crash of 1929. Totally disillusioned by his experience and virtually bankrupt, he begins to make currency the focus of his very detailed paintings."

"Hard to miss the money," I said. "He put it all over the place."

"Decades later, in the early sixties, Kaye was still scarred from the crash and paints this piece. He called it *Heart of the Matter*. It all had to do with what happened in 1961. The Metropolitan Museum of Art purchased Rembrandt's famous 1653 *Aristotle with a Bust of Homer* for two point three million dollars—at that time, the highest amount ever paid for any picture at a public or private sale. Many art enthusiasts were critical of the purchase. They feared that deep-pocketed individuals and organizations would hoard all the great art, because the common man couldn't afford to buy it. Kaye was one of the more vocal critics, so he decides to paint this in protest."

"So, that explains the heart cut out and the money hanging in its place," I said.

"And the Rembrandt painting ripped up and the edges curling. Kaye destroys Rembrandt's masterpiece, then litters it with money, sticking it in the background and weaving it into the Homer bust and Aristotle's clothing. His message is clear. The connection between art and commerce is too close—so close that the commerce is destroying the purity of the art."

We sat there for a moment as I now saw the painting through a different lens. It was still too busy for my liking, but I had a greater appreciation for why the artist had put the disharmonious images together and how loudly he expressed his thoughts. The money looked completely out of place, but it was the first thing that caught your attention, and that was exactly what he wanted to convey.

Without turning toward me, the man said, "Walter was a good person. He was fiercely loyal. He tried to do what he thought was most honorable in this cesspool of city government. He helped a lot of people he didn't have to, including me."

"How's that?" I said.

"I had a cousin who had moved here from Poland. She didn't have any health insurance. She had a complicated problem with her intestines. She needed a surgery, or she would die. Every hospital turned her away. Somehow, Walter heard about it. He called me. Within twenty-four hours she was in the operating room at Northwestern. That's the kind of man he was."

"He had a lot of friends," I said.

"But many of those friends were also his enemies."

"Friendship is constant in all things, save in the office and affairs of love."

The man smiled. "One of my favorite Shakespeare plays, *Much Ado About Nothing*. But Walter was a smart man and very tough. He let them think that he had been lulled by their friendship, but he knew they were enemies behind his back."

"Care to share any names?"

"Money really is the engine of corruption," he said, looking at the painting.

"Which is why you wanted to meet me here. To drive home the point."

"And sometimes one can feel the loneliest in the biggest of cities."

"Which is what Hopper signals to us in *Nighthawks* on the other side of the wall."

"Do you know how the city's Office of Inspector General works?" the man asked.

"Rudimentary understanding. They investigate misconduct and illegal behavior by city employees."

"That's part of their mission. They also address inefficiency and waste within the programs and operations of city government."

"Then they must never sleep. Our city government is one big twisted heap of inefficiency."

The man nodded. "OIG is a very powerful office. They have the authority to conduct both criminal and administrative investigations. They can even issue their own subpoenas in furtherance of such investigations. The office, by charter, is supposed to be independent and nonpartisan."

"Independent and nonpartisan in Chicago?" I said. "Good luck with that."

"Walter was being investigated by OIG."

"So I've gathered."

"But the investigation should've never happened. Or at least not through OIG."

"Why not? The personal credit charges on the city card were small, but technically they could be considered misconduct."

"Ah, but CPS is such a massive and complex system, it has its own inspector general separate from the city's. He's specifically charged with investigating all acts of malfeasance anyone in the school system is alleged to have committed. Remember the Barbara Henson case?"

Barbara Henson was the former CEO of the Chicago Public Schools. She had been a major ally in Bailey's never-ending feud with Shawna Simpson, the president of the teachers union. Henson had steered a combined $23 million of contracts to close business associates and her former employer, who was in the business of training educators, all for a few hundred thousand dollars in kickbacks. She'd finally resigned when the pressure and scrutiny became insurmountable and the reporters started putting the Fifth Floor in their crosshairs. Henson pleaded guilty and received a four-and-a-half-year federal prison sentence. The city moved on, and her case became just another footnote in Chicago's long history of rampant corruption.

"Henson was a convicted felon," I said. "I wouldn't compare a few hundred dollars in Griffin's case to the twenty million plus she shoveled out."

"Agreed. My point is that the OIG for CPS handled the initial Henson investigation; then, when it got really good, the Feds stepped in and finished the job."

"What's your point?"

"Paul Shulman is the OIG for CPS. Tough as nails and about as honest as they come. If Paul found a dollar on the bathroom floor, he'd turn it in to lost and found. He's always kept an objective distance from the Fifth Floor. He rarely speaks with Bailey, and when he does, he either takes notes of the conversation or makes sure there's someone else in the room with him. Paul's office should've been the one handling the investigation into Walter's credit card charges. Instead, Pete Dent, the city's OIG, handled the case."

"Who made the decision that Dent would handle it?"

"I don't know, but I know it came from high up."

"Why would someone want Dent to handle it when Shulman could be trusted to do everything by the book?"

"That's exactly why they didn't want Shulman to handle it. He would've done his investigation, filed a report, and disposed of the case. That's obviously not the outcome someone wanted. Everyone knew Walter wasn't trying to take the city for a few hundred dollars, but Dent mysteriously gets the case and is hell-bent on squeezing Walter. There was all kinds of talk about looking into his personal finances and his other businesses and prior deals with the city. Dent was giving Walter a really hard time."

"Why would Bailey let them do this to one of his closest confidants? He could've had the plug pulled anytime he wanted."

"Friendship is constant in all things, save in the office and affairs of love."

"Therefore all hearts in love use their own tongues."

"You're as well read as they say you are. Walter had been an insider for a long time. There was no city department where he didn't have friends or a connection. From Streets and Sanitation to the Fifth Floor, he knew everyone from the security guards to the men in the corner office. But sometimes you can know too much, and that makes you a liability, because you know where all the skeletons are hidden, the deals that were made behind closed doors. Walter was loyal, but he also wasn't anyone's fool. He wanted to get his share just like everyone else."

I considered his words before saying, "How did you know I was working on this case?"

"Everyone knows."

"Who's everyone?"

"The people that matter over on LaSalle. All of Walter's friends around the city. Everyone is watching you."

"That sounds scary."

"It is. I wouldn't have the courage to take on a case like this."

"But you had the courage to reach out to me."

"I wouldn't call it courage," he said, gazing back up at the painting. "It's about fatigue. I should've spoken up a long time ago. When you see so much bad shit for so long, you just reach a point where you have to do something. You're the one who can finally bring Walter some justice. He didn't deserve to die that way."

"You think he was killed."

The man smiled slightly. "Think? I know."

"Why are you so sure?"

"Because if Walter had problems, he was not one to run away from them. I also know that a lot of people weren't sad he was out of the picture."

"Any names you want to share?"

"Start with Pete Dent. His investigation was motivated by more than a few hundred dollars on a credit card. Then look at a company called Sunrise Holdings."

"What can you tell me about Sunrise?"

"Not a lot, other than they were connected to seventy million in CPS contracts last year. You have to follow the money."

The man got up and casually walked out of the gallery. It wasn't until he was gone that I realized I didn't even know his name.

25

MIKEY LESTEAU HAD BEEN AT&T's chief state lobbyist for more than thirty years. When he wasn't at the capitol in Springfield twisting the arms of legislators, he was at some boozy golf tournament presenting a sizable company check to the pet project of the very legislators he was asking to pass favorable legislation. He and my father had been friends for as long as I could remember. When I called, he was walking up to the first green on Cog Hill's championship course Dubsdread.

"I need a favor, Mikey."

"Can it wait? My third shot just landed in a green-side bunker. Everybody else made it to the green."

"I'm going to text you a phone number and the first name of the person who had that number. I need the person's last name."

"Easy enough. This got anything to do with Walt? Wendell told me you were working on something for his family."

"Yes and yes."

"Walt was an old friend of mine," he said. "We did a lot of business together through the years. We all know he didn't shoot himself. He was a good man."

"And a helluva golfer from what I hear."

"His second office."

"Good luck on that bunker shot," I said.

"I'm gonna need it. My sand game has been in the toilet these days. I'll have something for you by this afternoon."

While I waited for news about Bryce, I went to work on my computer, looking to find anything I could on the company my anonymous informant had mentioned. My initial search for Sunrise Holdings turned up nothing, no website linked to the company, nor any press mentions. I spent over an hour looking at databases that held corporate information. How could a company that held $70 million in city contracts not be mentioned somewhere? I then remembered a database my younger cousin from New York had introduced me to last year. Offshore Leaks was a database, compiled by the International Consortium of Investigative Journalists, that tracked corporate offshore accounts. I typed in the company name and immediately got a hit.

Sunrise Holdings had one listed officer, the Bearer, and it was connected to one intermediary, a company called Roseland Monaco SAM. It had been incorporated in 2010 and registered in Panama. The data on the company had been collected from the Panama Papers, a famous leak of eleven and a half million files from the database of the world's fourth-biggest offshore law firm, Mossack Fonseca. I clicked on Roseland Monaco SAM, and that took me to another page, which showed a diagram that looked like a spider's web. Roseland Monaco SAM was at the center, and the spokes connected it to eleven other companies that it served as an intermediary. I pulled up another search to better understand what that role was. Basically, an intermediary agency was registered to do business in foreign countries and had undergone all the checks and documentation to give it the legitimate rights to conduct business activities. That meant Sunrise Holdings didn't have to bother with any paperwork with foreign governments, could pay fewer taxes, and could be largely hidden from the tax authorities of its native country. Roseland Monaco made deals on behalf of Sunrise and its clients, collected money, paid the requisite taxes, took a fee for its service, and deposited the rest of the money in Sunrise's bank account.

I scrolled back to the first page of the search and clicked the hyperlink to the Bearer. It wasn't an individual but a company that had one unlisted address in Ukraine. The company was connected to twenty-three other entities and thirty-seven officers. For the next couple of hours, I kept following the links and the intermediaries and all the connections. They had all kinds of names that didn't give any indication about the nature of their business. Names like Babylonshia, GEM, Sheephead, and many more, but I couldn't detect any pattern. Tracking them was like playing a shell game with fifty coconut halves and ten balls and five guys behind the table moving everything at once. It was dizzying just trying to keep up.

The names of the officers were hidden, but I wrote down the names of the twenty-three entities in alphabetical order. I then turned to a Google search and started with the first company. A few results came back, but nothing caught my eye. It wasn't until I searched for Belvedere Technologies that I got a hit. Belvedere was a Frankfort, Illinois–based company that managed and developed creative IT solutions. It had a fancy website with a lot of tech jargon describing what they did but no mention of the ownership or officers by name. It did, however, list their clients, and sitting at the top was CPS. The dots connected. Belvedere had the contract with CPS, but Sunrise Holdings, through a complicated structure that most probably didn't know, actually owned Belvedere. The whistleblower hadn't told me to look at Belvedere. He wanted me to look at Sunrise. He knew the connection. What was he really trying to tell me?

———

THE CHICAGO TEACHERS UNION occupied an enormous brick building prominently situated in an industrial area in the Near West Side. Shawna Simpson helmed the more than twenty-five thousand union members representing teachers, paraprofessionals, and clinicians working within CPS. The fiery Simpson, a former high school physics teacher, had become a sort of national union celebrity when she'd pulled her teachers out of classrooms for a week last year to demand a contract that increased teacher compensation, reduced classroom size, and eliminated merit pay based on teacher evaluations.

Simpson sat behind an enormous glass desk in a corner office that out of one window had views of the United Center, where the Chicago Bulls and Blackhawks played, and out of another row of windows the formidable Chicago skyline. She got up from behind her desk and met me as I made my way into the office. She was much taller than she appeared on television. Her large frame moved easily underneath a flowing powder-blue silk pantsuit. She ushered me to a long glass conference table underneath the east window.

"If you don't look like a young Dr. Cayne," she said, shaking her head. "I mean a carbon copy of what he looked like when he was at Columbia Med and I was at Teachers College."

"Hopefully a more handsome version," I said.

"And got his sense of humor too." She laughed. "I remember your mother bringing you to the Delta Sigma Theta meetings in diapers, and just look at you now."

I smiled. "Pretty spiffy offices," I said, getting comfortable in a soft leather swivel chair that felt like I was sitting on cotton.

"You say that with surprise," she said. "As if teachers and leadership should live by some vow of poverty."

"No offense intended," I said, raising my hands. "Just admiring the view."

"It's even nicer at night when darkness falls and you can see the lights of all the buildings. If it's not too cloudy, you can see the planes flying across the lake."

"And you have an almost direct sight line to city hall."

"I have a sight on city hall no matter where I am," she said, turning down her lips. "We're in a fight for our lives and the students we serve."

"Another walkout on the way?" They had called a strike just last year over a better contract. It was the first time a strike had been called in twenty-five years. This one lasted for seven long, contentious days.

"If Bailey and Milton continue to play their bullshit games, absolutely we're gonna walk out. We don't have a choice. Too much at stake."

Andrew Milton was the newly appointed CEO of CPS. The CEO, just like a corporate CEO, had the unilateral ability to make all the decisions—unlike in the old structure that left decisions to be shared between a superintendent and the local school boards. Like everything else in Chicago, the creation of the CEO position had been politically charged, and the union viewed it as yet another attempt to curb their power.

"How did Walter Griffin factor into all of this?" I asked.

Simpson shook her head. "We would've had a contract by now had Walter not died," she said. "His death was a great personal loss to me and the CPS family. He was Bailey's man, but only to a point. He knew Bailey and Milton were being unreasonable. He was doing his best to move them closer to the middle so we could get some kind of deal done without having to strike. They were being hard-asses and wouldn't budge."

"But Bailey put him on the board and made him chairman," I said. "He was still on Bailey's team."

"He was, but Bailey didn't own him like he does the other board members. Walter obviously had an allegiance to Bailey. They had been friends for over forty years, and Bailey was the one who appointed him. But that didn't stop Walter from standing up for what he believed in."

"Was there tension between Griffin and Bailey?"

"When it comes to that egocentric, unethical little dictator sitting on the Fifth Floor, there's always tension whenever someone dares to think for themselves and not as they're told."

"It's clear he's not your favorite person."

"The only way he knows how to govern is through intimidation and vindictiveness. He's a spoiled little man whose father and his cronies handed him the mayor's office. He doesn't understand the concept of compromise. It's either his way or no way. Well, those days are over, at least when it comes to what we're willing to accept as professional educators. We're not gonna sit back and let a man who has not an ounce of educational experience in his body tell us how to teach and what's best for the almost four hundred thousand students we serve."

"Did Griffin feel the same way?"

"Behind closed doors, he absolutely did. Walter was a product of CPS. His mother was an elementary school teacher over in Homan Square not too far from here. He knew the challenges we face as educators trying to do what's right for the children under exceedingly difficult circumstances. He was not afraid to fight."

"Who else was he fighting besides Bailey?"

"Andrew Milton, the CEO."

"But wasn't Griffin the chairman of the board that elected Milton to that position?"

"He was, but you have to take a closer look at the vote. Of the seven board members, six of them voted in favor of Milton. One board member abstained from the voting."

"Let me take a guess."

"Exactly. Walter never thought Milton should get the job. He didn't say as much publicly on account of it was Bailey's pick, but we all knew where Walter stood. He knew Milton would ultimately be voted in by the rest of Bailey's lieutenants, but he wanted the record to show he was not part of that decision."

"Did Griffin and Milton get along?"

"Publicly? They were a united front. Privately? They hated each other."

"Why was Griffin never on board with Milton?"

"The same reason the rest of us who really care about the issues weren't on board. Milton has no business running the country's third-largest school district. He helped run a midsize insurance company in Philly. He grew up somewhere in Pennsylvania and had never set foot inside a CPS school before he was appointed. He couldn't tell you the difference between a selective enrollment school and a charter school. Then all of a sudden we're supposed to accept this complete outsider with no previous experience in education coming in telling us what to do when we've been in the struggle for years trying to get things back on track. Hell to the no."

"In all fairness, I've lived here my entire life, except for a college stint in Boston, and I can't tell the difference between those schools either."

"But you're not running the entire school system. Bailey put Milton there as a pawn to carry out his work. First, he wanted to take away our pension increases that he had already agreed to. Second, he wanted to close and consolidate lots of schools he said were underperforming."

"Kinda makes sense to me," I said. "If a school and its students are constantly not doing well and not hitting the mark, who does it really serve keeping it open?"

"That's where he's slick. That's what he wants people to think. Those schools have needed help for years. Everyone knew that, including previous administrations. The answer was not to close the schools but give them more resources like improved infrastructure, new computers, more teachers. No, there were two real reasons he wanted to close the schools. First, his little bean counters figured that was an easy way to trim the budget. Second, a lot of those schools sat on very valuable land that had developers' mouths watering for years. Who do you think many of those developers were?"

I shrugged.

"His rich donors. And many of them were children of donors whose parents had similar relationships with his father, Old Man Bailey, when he was in office."

"What was Griffin's position on all this?"

"Publicly he had to side with Bailey. Privately, he knew it was unfair and wanted to help us without seeming like he was crossing the boss. He knew Milton was nothing more than a hired gun put in charge to do Bailey's bidding."

"But Griffin and the rest of the board went along with fifty schools across the city getting closed under his watch."

"They had Walter in a trick box," Simpson said. "The political optics were in Bailey's favor. The city is practically bankrupt. They're throwing a city tax on everything from soda to gas. Any proposal that looks like money is being saved and taxes might be reduced is a political victory. They announced to the city that almost half a billion dollars could be saved by closing those schools and taking away over two thousand jobs. They only saw the money in the deal. They didn't think about all the people impacted. Not just teachers but janitorial staff, security, administrative positions—hardworking people throughout the system who suddenly found themselves jobless. Then look at what it would do to the impoverished neighborhoods already depressed and struggling. They now had no local schools, and children were forced to travel sometimes thirty minutes or longer each way on public transportation to find the nearest school. It's been a complete disaster and total disruption to our communities, and Walter knew this."

"But?"

"Get out of the way of the swinging ax or get cut down yourself. There's only so much one person can do. He did his best to stop it, but the train was moving too fast, and too many people stood to make a lot of money with those school buildings and their land."

Simpson's secretary knocked on the door and dropped off a thick folder of papers. She made a not-so-subtle mention that the next appointment was already in the lobby waiting.

"Do you think Griffin committed suicide?" I asked.

"Not in a million years. He sat in the same chair you're sitting in now, dozens of times, as we tried to figure out how we both could feed our own beasts yet at the same time not get our hands eaten in the process."

"Any ideas who might've killed him?"

"We all have our own ideas. Everyone's heard the rumors."

"Such as?"

Simpson looked out the windows toward downtown and city hall. "Walter had a complex existence. Poor kid from Lawndale who scratched and climbed his way up to the city's elite corridors of power. He was behind a lot of closed doors and witness to a lot of things that many people wanted to keep quiet. Backroom deals that would never pass an ethics review, city vendor contracts handed out to Bailey's cronies like pieces of Halloween candy. Walter had seen and heard it all. That OIG investigation? A complete sham. That wasn't about personal charges on a city credit card. That was their way of tightening the noose around his neck and reminding him that at any minute they could easily take away all they had given him. That was a clear message. What the boss has given, he can just as easily take away."

"Every action has an equal and opposite reaction."

Simpson smiled. "Good old Newton's third law."

"That was one of the few days I was awake in physics."

"You really are your father's son."

———

I HAD JUST COME IN from a long run around the lake and was in the process of heating up a generous portion of layered meat lasagna when my cell phone vibrated and twirped. I opened it and read the text message from Mikey Lesteau.

Bryce Horner. Line disconnected two years ago on November 18th. Last billing address on file was 1335 North Wells apt. 2L. Let me know when you want to play a round. I get three strokes a side.

I replied, Thanks for the help. Let's play soon. Stop sandbagging me. I'm only giving up two a side.

I took the lasagna out of the oven as well as the baguette slices I had spread with garlic butter. I poured myself a generous glass of Caymus Napa Valley Cabernet Sauvignon and turned on my computer. I typed *Bryce Horner* into my search engine. Within seconds I had several pages of results. I had an auto body repair technician, a detective in Toronto, an actor who had played in a zombie movie, and a varsity football player from Youngsville, Pennsylvania. None of them seemed to have a natural connection to Walter Griffin. I narrowed the search to *Bryce Horner Chicago* and got many of the same hits. This was going to take a while. A pop-up ad with a picture of the Eiffel Tower jumped across my screen. A travel site promoted its once-in-a-lifetime package deal for a trip to Paris. My mind instantly thought of Julia and her letter.

I got up from the computer, grabbed her blue envelope from where I'd stashed it back underneath the wine cooler, poured myself another glass of wine, then took a seat on the patio. A light wind moved the warm night air around.

I pulled the stationery out of the envelope and opened its neat folds. Just seeing her handwriting made my breathing uneven. She began like she always did when writing me notes, calling me DC, a joke that had to do with the first time she'd heard one of my friends call me AC, and for some reason it had made her think of alternating current and direct current. She'd thought it would be funny to call me DC since my friends called me AC, so the nickname had stuck. Her letters were soft and feminine and perfectly aligned.

I have started this letter many times, only to put it away when the right words escaped me. I've never been as good as you with words. I mean seriously, how many people can quote both Shakespeare and Biggie Smalls? So I'll just cut to the chase. I'm sorry. I'm sorry for all the pain I've caused you. I'm sorry for never being honest about how I felt like I was often in your shadow and the angst it caused me. I know you've always loved my confidence, but it's that confidence that wouldn't let me share how vulnerable and inadequate I sometimes felt around you. You always know who you are and what you want to do and be damned with others who might think differently or can't understand your motivations.

I know this sounds cliché, but I needed to find myself and regain my confidence. I thought a new relationship would be the fix, but eventually I realized that only allowed me to hide from the truth. I can admire who you are and still feel the same way about myself. I completely understand if you hate me and never want to talk to me again, but I would not have been the wife and partner you deserve had we gotten married before I found those answers. It was a process, and I had to work through it, but I never stopped loving you for one second. I'm sure you've moved on, but I want to wish you all the happiness in the world.

Love,
Jules

The pain and the sadness and the anxiety all came rushing back in strong, unrelenting waves. I was angry and relieved at the same time. It had been almost two long years of nothing but my agonizing thoughts, believing there was something I had done or said that had chased her away.

I never stopped loving you for one second.

But she was also right that I'd moved on. I hadn't even kissed Carolina yet, and I was already falling in love. I didn't want to admit it to anyone for fear of being vulnerable again.

I reached to pour another glass of red wine, then thought better of it. I grabbed my keys instead. I didn't want to be alone tonight, at least not while sober. I needed noise and people and a full complement of drinks, as many distractions as I could summon—anything to squeeze the thoughts of Julia out of my mind.

26

TAO, LIKE ITS OTHER locations in New York and Las Vegas, was a nightclub-and-restaurant hybrid housed in a large stone mansion in the trendy River North neighborhood. This landmark building at the corner of North Dearborn and Ontario had once been home to the Chicago Historical Society and later the popular Excalibur Nightclub with its purple floodlights that ran up the building's front entrance. Tao had come to Chicago with great fanfare given its reputation of impossible-to-get dinner reservations and a club that could hold hundreds of people and still have enough room for a soccer game. I flashed my shield and got past the beefy doormen wearing black suits a couple of sizes too small. I followed a group of girls up the steps and into a massive hall decorated with Asian art, strobe lights, and a two-story painting of a Japanese woman that occupied one entire wall. It was a Thursday night, and the place was packed. The music echoed off the cavernous ceilings, and waitresses walked around in skimpy outfits, carrying thirty-six-dollar bottles of vodka for which they charged an even $500 to some idiot who wanted to sit on a banquette and impress his friends. I worked my way through the layers of bodies crammed against the bar and put in an order for a shot of Grey Goose. It was the only vodka I found smooth enough to drink straight up.

I threw the shot back and asked the bartender to bring another. The DJ started playing hip-hop, and the crowd—mostly North Siders and kids who had driven in from the suburbs in their parents' cars—started knocking into each other while yelling lyrics that most of them didn't even understand. I was about to throw back the second shot when I felt a hand on my shoulder and someone say into my ear, "You're not gonna drink that alone, are you?"

I turned into the smiling face of Mercedes, the greeter at Soho House from when I'd gone looking for Sophia Caballé. She had just a hint of makeup on and had wrapped herself in a tight striped dress that demanded all kinds of attention.

I motioned for the bartender to bring me another shot. Mercedes slid beside me. She placed her left hand on my shoulder and leaned into my ear.

"You don't even remember my name," she said.

"I never forget a pretty face," I said. "And I definitely don't forget a name attached to that pretty face."

"Nice line, Mr. Charmer," she said. "What's my name?"

"BMW."

She laughed. "I like you."

The bartender brought the second shot over, and we tipped our glasses back in unison and jointly slammed them on the countertop.

"Let's go," she said.

"Where?"

"To my table. We're celebrating my birthday."

"Happy birthday!"

"It was last week, but I had to work. So, we're celebrating tonight."

"You're finally able to drink legally."

"And do a lot more than that."

She grabbed my hand firmly and with purpose. Her skin was smooth and her fingers long and slender. It felt good to touch her.

"My table is up by the DJ's booth," she yelled above the music. "It's a lot better up there."

We wove and elbowed and pushed our way to the other side of the dance hall. She kept her grasp firm. We made it to an area about ten feet in front of the DJ's booth before hitting a blockade of people who weren't making any forward progress. Mercedes stood on her toes and started waving her hand. I wasn't sure who she was waving at, but then I saw two enormous bouncers scanning the crowd before recognizing her and flashing a light in our direction. One of them plowed through the crowd like a freight train without brakes, sending bodies in every direction until he reached us. We fell in behind him as he marched his way back. Once we were inside the ropes, Mercedes walked me to her table. Five bottles sat chilled in metal ice buckets, and about eight people lounged on the top of the banquette. Three models stood on the other side of the table, dancing together, the two blonde girls sandwiching an Ethiopian girl. All three were stunning.

"That's Melissa, Malaka, and Morgan," she said to me. "They call us the M&M's. They're my party friends." She pointed to two guys sitting on the other side of the banquette. "The white guy is Harry, and the Black guy is Edsel. We all went to school together. Edsel's brother is one of the party promoters here."

A short guy with moussed blond hair and a tight shirt with rock-hard biceps walked in our direction.

"Neils, this is Ashe," she said. "His father named him after Arthur Ashe."

"Who the fuck is that?" Neils said.

"One of the greatest tennis players of all time," she said. "He helped break the color barrier. My father idolizes him."

Neils looked me up and down. "You're cute," he said. "Where the hell did Merc pick you up?"

"On the street corner selling bean pies," I said.

"And you have a wicked sense of humor." He smiled. "I love bean pies." He rolled his tongue around his lips.

"Leave him alone, you predator," Mercedes said, slapping his shoulder. "He's completely mine and I'm not sharing."

"Fine," Neils said, pouting. "But only because it's your birthday." He twirled around and joined the other gyrating M&M's.

"Let's have some champagne," Mercedes said, pulling a bottle of Cristal out of the bucket. She picked up two glasses and filled them until the bubbles spilled onto the table. I wasn't a big fan of champagne and definitely not a fan of mixing drinks, but it was her birthday, and I was just happy to not be alone with Julia's letter. We toasted, drank a few sips; then she pulled me toward the banquette. The spinning disco ball scattered light across her soft caramel skin.

As I stepped up to sit on the cushions, I looked to my left and could barely believe what I saw. Antoine Nelson walked right in front of me with two tall, skinny girls, one blonde, the other a redhead. He wore a colorful T-shirt that looked like someone had thrown several cans of paint at him. A large diamond chain hung from his neck and matched the pair of links stuck in his ears. He carried a magnum of champagne in one hand, while the girls wrapped their hands around his shoulders.

They walked several tables over and disappeared into a sea of spinning bodies. Demetrius Jackson was lying in the ground somewhere, and Nelson was here, life of the party. My muscles tightened. I needed to get further along in the Griffin case, but I still had my sights on Nelson. It was just a matter of time before I dealt with him.

Mercedes pulled close to me. She rested her hand innocently on my upper leg. It felt good. I wasn't drunk yet, but I had a good buzz working. I turned away from Antoine and looked at Mercedes. I had the sudden urge to kiss her, but I didn't. "Why are you here alone?" she asked.

"Better than being alone in my apartment," I said.

"Why would you be alone? You're too cute to be by yourself."

"It's a long story, and it's your birthday celebration. Another time. Another place."

"You have a girlfriend?"

"That's part of the alone thing."

"What? You have more than one?"

"I'm not seeing anyone." And I wasn't. Not formally.

She winked. "Do you dance?"

"Only if I have to."

"Well, you have to, because it's my birthday and I want to dance with you."

She grabbed my hand and pulled me from the banquette. The M&M's had disappeared, so we had the floor space to ourselves in front of the table. It had been a while since I'd last danced. In fact, it had been over two years. Julia and I had gone to a friend's wedding. They had the best cover band I had ever heard. Julia was an excellent dancer. We'd barely sat down the entire night.

Mercedes pulled me tightly against her body and slid her leg between mine. She wrapped her hands around the back of my head and leaned back. I grabbed her by the waist. I could feel the flatness of her stomach. Her hips moved rhythmically, and we were no longer dancing as two people, rather moving as one. I looked at the long arch of her neck and the fullness of her lips. It had been a long time since I had held a woman, but it all came back so fast. As the music grew faster and louder and the alcohol worked its way through my system, I felt free and uninhibited.

She leaned her face into me and put her lips so close to my ear I could feel their wetness as she spoke. "You're an excellent dancer," she said. "What else are you holding out on?" She ran her hand across my stomach and up my shirt. "And you go to the gym."

She rested her head on my shoulder; then she softly kissed my neck, opening her mouth and making slow tiny circles with her tongue. I explored her hips with my hands, and when I stopped, she took them in her own and encouraged me to continue. She kissed me softly underneath the bend of my jaw as her cheek brushed mine ever so gently. I closed my eyes as she moved along my face until the corner of her mouth rested against mine. I don't remember who made the first move or if it had been simultaneous, but the next thing I felt was the wet warmth of her tongue tracing the curves of my lips. Then she separated my lips and explored my mouth slowly before grabbing the back of my head and opening her mouth fully, hungrily. She suddenly stopped, then pulled me back to the banquette. Two of the M&M's were kissing each other on the seat next to us. Mercedes pushed me down on the seat, then straddled me. Nothing else mattered to me at that point. There must've been more than five hundred people around us, but it felt like we were all alone.

I wasn't sure how long we were sitting there like that, but I heard someone yell above the noise, "You two need a room." I looked up and found Neils standing over us.

Mercedes whispered in my ear, "He's so right." She grabbed a glass of champagne, finished off what was left, then pulled me to my feet. Before I knew it, we were out on Dearborn, climbing into the back of an Uber.

27

"YOU LOOK LIKE SHIT."

Mechanic and I were sitting in my office with the blinds drawn and lights off. My head felt like someone was trying to hammer a nail into the back of my skull but kept missing.

"I look about ten times better than I feel," I said. "It was a long night."

"You stayed out too late."

"There was too much of everything."

Mechanic raised his eyebrows.

"Well, almost everything," I said.

"Her place or yours?"

"Hers. I don't remember exactly how we got there, but I remember waking up knowing that I wasn't in my bed."

"You need more of that in your life."

"Some of it. Not all of it. My head feels like there's a tiny jackhammer trapped inside."

I took a long swallow of coffee. The caffeine seemed to be helping. I still didn't have an appetite, and it was almost noon.

"I took some liberties and did a little digging around," Mechanic said.

"So, you were out enterprising?"

"One way to put it. Turns out my cousin's girlfriend works at OIG."

"What does she do?"

"Administrative assistant. She helps sort out the complaints coming into the office and makes sure they get seen by the right people."

"Have you talked to her yet?"

"No, but my cousin said her friend would be willing to sit down with you. She remembers the Griffin investigation."

"When is she available?"

"Anytime we want. She has the day off."

———

LILIANA PAZLOVSKI MET US at Argot Tea at the triangular intersection of Rush and East Chestnut. The entire shop sat right across the street from the Sofitel Hotel and had been constituted entirely out of glass. She sat alone at an outside table. Mechanic made the introductions; then we got right down to business.

"I don't want my name to be involved in any of this," she said. "I like my job. I have two small kids. I need my job."

"Ashe is family," Mechanic said. "You have nothing to worry about."

"I give you my word; it will never come back to you," I said. "I just want to understand a few things about how OIG ended up investigating someone as high ranking as Griffin."

Liliana looked at Mechanic, then back at me. "I don't know all the details, but I know the case didn't come into the office through regular channels," she said.

"Which are?"

"Our website, where you can fill out an online form, or through the hotline, where you can call it in."

"How did the complaint come in?"

"Not through the website or phone. It was handled directly by Mr. Dent and his staff."

"Is that normal?"

"Not at all. There's a very organized system in place to handle the complaints. There are five of us who divide up the hotline calls and the online reports. We process and document when they come in, then pass the report up to the investigative teams. Once the teams have it, they do the follow-up and open a preliminary investigation to see if the case has merit and if it should be pursued."

"But Griffin's case went directly upstairs?"

"It must've, because none of us took it in."

"Do you know who brought it to the IG?"

Liliana nodded. "Andrew Milton."

"Didn't you find it strange that the city OIG was conducting an investigation of the chairman of the board of education, rather than the OIG at CPS?"

"Of course. So did the other girls. Samantha, who sits in the cubicle next to me, asked about that. Not to cause any trouble or be critical, but to just understand what was going on."

"And what was she told?"

"It was a decision made upstairs and not to concern herself with it."

"Basically, mind your own business."

"Pretty much."

"And did she do that?"

"Of course not. We asked Mr. Dent's admin, Ramona, and she told Samantha this had been a special request. Andrew Milton had directly arranged with Mr. Dent to handle the investigation. Ramona heard the call. Mr. Dent said he didn't think his involvement was necessary, but Milton insisted."

"Did you have access to the investigative file?"

"Not at all. The file stayed in Mr. Dent's office. None of us had a reason to access it, nor did we have the authority to do so."

———

MECHANIC AND I DECIDED to drive by Bryce Horner's last known address that Mikey had provided, since Old Town was only a few minutes away. I didn't have any real plan, which didn't bother me, as sometimes the best approach was to have no approach and simply play the hand as it was dealt. We pulled down North Wells Street and found his small apartment building sitting on top of the Village Cycle Center, which billed itself as the nation's largest bike store, with factory closeout sales up to 20 percent off. We slipped into a spot across the street and walked over to the entrance to Horner's building. The exterior door was unlocked and gave us access to a panel of buzzers on the right wall just as we stepped in. The name Ripley had been written next to the buzzer marked 2L.

"Now what?" Mechanic said. "Ripley ain't exactly Horner."

"When you come to a fork in the road and you're in doubt, go straight," I said. I pushed the buzzer. We waited a few seconds for a response through the intercom. There was none, so I pushed it again. Another fifteen seconds and still no response. I looked at the other names taped alongside the buzzers. The superintendent lived in apartment 1L. I rang his buzzer. No answer from him either.

"Plan B?" Mechanic said.

"We could go bike shopping," I said.

"I don't even know how to ride a bike."

"You're kidding, right?"

"Not kidding," Mechanic said. "Never learned. My parents couldn't afford to buy me one, and I was too proud to learn on someone else's. So, I just didn't bother with it."

"So, you started with guns instead."

"Much easier to come by where I grew up. And more practical for protection."

"Never too old to learn how to ride."

"I'm good," he said.

We walked back to the car.

"Let's wait a little while longer and see if there's any activity," I said. We turned on the radio softly, then opened the windows to let the wind blow in. The heat wave had snapped, and the temperature had precipitously dropped to the midseventies. I had forgotten what it felt like to be outside without melting.

After a few minutes of watching the slow traffic pass, Mechanic said, "How do you feel about last night?"

"Guilty."

"Guilty about what?"

"Guilty that I was with someone else."

"When you should've been with Carolina?"

"Well, I was guilty that it wasn't Jules. But I'm also feeling guilty that it wasn't Carolina. My head is still spinning."

"You should feel guilty about Carolina. You guys are meant for each other, and she really likes you. But this guilt about Julia is crazy. She's the one who ran away to Paris with that stockbroker. Why the hell should you feel guilty about moving on? She went and did her thing. You need to do the same."

"Can't explain it," I said. "Doesn't really make sense to me. Maybe it's because I've only been pretending that I've moved on, when really

I hadn't. Maybe deep inside I was hoping it wasn't over and eventually she would come back, and we would be together again. The mind can try to lie to the heart, but it rarely gets away with it."

"That's still no reason for you to feel guilty," Mechanic said. "She's over there living her life, probably eating fresh croissants every day on that big fancy street with that giant arch."

"It's called the Champs-Élysées, and that arch is the Arc de Triomphe."

"Yeah, that. Anyway, what are you supposed to do? Sit here and waste your life away by yourself? It's been almost two years. That's a long time. You deserve to have fun and get back in the game. Life is way too fuckin' short to sit around and lick old wounds."

"My therapist said the same thing. Just not with such eloquence."

We sat in silence for the next few minutes. I thought about the letter but wasn't ready to talk about it with anyone. Then I thought about Mercedes and the M&M's and Neils. I definitely had a good time last night. Large chunks of the night escaped my memory, but the parts that had stuck made me smile, even if I felt a little guilty because of my feelings toward Carolina. I wanted Carolina, and I knew she wanted me, but I just wasn't ready. Mercedes would never be anything serious, and I was completely fine with that. It was better that Carolina and I remained friends for now.

"We have activity at three o'clock," Mechanic said.

I looked across the street. An old woman wearing a thick cardigan sweater and wheeling a foldable shopping cart had stopped in front of 1335. She was digging in her purse. Mechanic turned off the car; then we quickly jumped out and dodged the passing cars as we crossed the street.

"Can I help you gentlemen with something?" she said as we approached. She had a small black cat propped up in the cart next to a bundle of fresh flowers and a container of skim milk. The cat opened its eyes momentarily, then got bored and peacefully fell back to sleep.

"We're looking for Bryce Horner in 2L," I said. "No one's answering his buzzer, and the super's not home either."

"Is there a problem?" she asked.

"Not at all," I said. "We just wanted to ask him a couple of questions."

The old woman looked at Mechanic, then at me, as if trying to assess whether we were a danger. I smiled my most charming smile.

"Bryce has been gone for a couple of years," she said.

"Do you know where he moved to?"

"He didn't move anywhere. He died."

"Died? Was he sick?"

"Not that I know of. Bryce was a wonderful, healthy young man. He was such a pleasure to have in the building. Helped me with my flowers and even helped me decorate my apartment. I miss him dearly."

"What happened to him?"

"I don't do any of that computer stuff like the young people do these days," she said. "But one of the girls who lives above me on the third floor said she had read a story on the internet where they found his body in the lake. For the life of me, I can't make sense of it. Bryce was an excellent swimmer. He went out in the water at least twice a week and swam for hours. I don't understand how he could just drown one day."

"That's very sad," I said. "Sorry for your loss."

"I'm still not over it. He was like the grandson I never had. My daughter never had children."

I wasn't sure why, but an idea popped into my head. I pulled out my phone and brought up a picture of Walter Griffin.

"Have you ever seen this man before?" I asked.

The old woman lifted her glasses, which had been hanging around her neck, and pushed them up her nose. She tilted her head back slightly and looked down at the phone before taking her glasses off.

"Sure," she said. "He's been here before. He was walking out one night when I was coming home from the store."

"Are you certain?"

"My memory slips now and again, but I'm certain about seeing him. He had beautiful light hazel eyes, something I had never seen on a Black man before."

28

"JESUS FUCKIN' CHRIST!" Burke roared. We were sitting in his car, parked in front of Buddy Guy's blues joint on the corner of Wabash and Balbo. Burke sat in the front passenger seat, while I sat in the back. He had sent his driver, Bibbens, around the corner to Peet's Coffee so we could have some time alone. The air conditioner quietly pumped in cool air.

"There's a lot of inside work going on," I said. "One of the last phone calls Griffin made was to some thirty-one-year-old guy who suddenly washes up in the lake. And somehow this guy doesn't appear anywhere in the investigator's supplementary report."

"This is exactly what I was worried about," Burke said. "You're not opening a can of worms; you're prying the lid off a dumpster full of shit."

"Not exactly the visual I prefer on a full stomach," I said. "But yes, there's a lot of shit in this case, and someone or multiple people on the inside worked really hard to cover it up."

"One day people are gonna learn that cover-ups always make what's being covered up seem worse than it actually is."

"Bravo," I said. "You might suggest that be part of the curriculum at the Academy. Catch 'em young when they're impressionable."

"Don't be a wiseass."

We sat there watching packs of college students walking by with tall coffee cups and half-eaten muffins. I was always amazed at how the vast majority of Chicagoans operated so freely and were oblivious to the darkness that existed just below the surface. Some of them would inevitably become innocent victims of the harsh realities of urban life.

"So, what do you have so far?" Burke said. "Off the record."

I gave him an update on the OIG investigation and the suspicions of Shawna Simpson. I told him about Sophia Caballé knowing Amy Donnegan. I left out the part about my trip to the Art Institute and the tip from my informant. Then I brought him up to date on Bryce Horner, the main purpose of our meeting privately outside of Buddy Guy's place.

"Griffin has two phone calls while at the nursing home," I said. "The first call came in from Amy Donnegan in Bailey's office. The second call was from Bryce Horner. They talked for about thirty seconds. The nursing supervisor, who was just feet away, heard Griffin say, 'That's exactly what I need.' Two weeks and one day after Griffin's death, Horner, a great swimmer who's been in the lake probably hundreds of times, mysteriously washes up dead on North Avenue Beach at the age of thirty-one. I have a witness who puts Griffin at Horner's apartment building at least once. Your turn."

"Bryce Horner was a thirty-one-year-old man living alone in Old Town for the last five years after previously living in San Francisco," Burke said, looking straight ahead. "He had gone to design school in New York and was doing a few odds-and-ends jobs here while he searched for his big break. He had one sister who lives in California and a mother and father who were both high school teachers. Never married. No children on record.

Never in trouble. He liked to party in Boystown but at the time of his death didn't have a partner. He split from his last boyfriend about a year and a half before he drowned, but they remained on good terms. He was pulled from the water after being spotted by a jogger early on Sunday morning. No marks found on the body. No defensive wounds. He was alive when his body hit the water, because they found a considerable amount of water in his lungs. No suspects. No surveillance video. Which, by the way, was very similar to Griffin."

"So, no known motives for why someone would kill him. No video surveillance, though he had to go through some of the busiest streets along the lake to get there. ME ruled it an accidental death. Case closed."

"So, what are you thinking?" Burke asked.

"That it's mighty suspicious one of the last persons to speak to Griffin, a guy who's completely healthy and an excellent swimmer, suddenly drowns two weeks after Griffin dies. Coincidental? Possible. But I have that tingling in my gut."

"I saw the report," Burke said. "There was a really powerful riptide that morning."

"Bullshit."

"I'm just telling you what was in the official report," Burke said. "No findings at autopsy to suggest foul play. He was overcome by the current. Accidental drowning."

"And you're buying that?"

"Of course not. But it wasn't my case then, and it's not my case now. I can't dig into it. Officially." He reached a yellow inter-office county envelope back to me. "I agree with your assessment. The sudden death of a last-known contact who happens to be an extremely healthy man is definitely suspicious. You can read what the detectives found. Nothing jumped out at me, but someone should've done more follow-up. I thought the investigation was thin."

"As it was with Griffin's case. I believe in coincidences, but this is becoming a stretch, even for me."

———

I DECIDED TO WALK back to my office just ten minutes away. A gentle breeze blew off the lake. I planned on going to the driving range to work on my swing path and clear my head a little. I had just turned the corner when my phone rang.

"I'm surprised you're not on the golf course," Carolina said. "It's so gorgeous out."

"I was on my way to the driving range."

"Well, I don't want to hold you up, but I have something for you. I got that info you wanted on those businesses in that building on North Clark where Sophia visited. Sorry it took so long."

"Patience is bitter, but its fruit is sweet."

"Shakespeare?"

"Not a bad guess. Aristotle."

"Show-off," she laughed. "I was wrong about Robert Kristly likely owning the travel agency or real estate company. Brighter Horizons is your match. It's owned by Amygdala Care LLC, which is registered to the same address in Naperville as the one that came back from Kristly's plate."

"Did you find out what type of business it is?"

"It just says family services. That's all I could find."

"And it might be by design. It's possible that's all Kristly wants anyone to find."

"But why would Sophia and Amy Donnegan visit a family services office that late at night?"

"That's what I'm about to find out."

"What are you gonna do?"

"Pay a friendly visit to our friend Mr. Kristly. See if I can find out what was so important he needed to burn the midnight oil."

———

I FOUND A PARKING SPOT about a half a block south of the entrance to 2954 North Clark Street. I opened the door to a small vacant lobby. I took the elevator to the second floor and followed the sign to Brighter Horizons. There was only one other door farther down the hallway. It belonged to Oyster Travel. I entered the Brighter Horizons office. A nervous-looking woman in a white silk blouse and large misshapen glasses sat behind a black metal desk. She was reading something on her computer screen with great concentration.

"I was hoping I could speak with Robert Kristly," I said.

"Do you have an appointment?"

"Not yet."

"Meaning?"

"I will make one if I need to."

"May I ask what it is in reference to?"

"Sophia Caballé."

I looked carefully at her face when I said Sophia's name. I knew she recognized the name when her eyes tightened slightly.

"We are an adoption agency," the woman said. "Privacy rules prohibit me from confirming the identity of any of our clients."

"So, she is a client?"

"I didn't say that."

"How about Amy Donnegan? Is she a client?"

"Sir, I've explained to you our policy. There's not much—"

She was interrupted by the opening of the office door about ten feet behind her. A man with neatly trimmed red hair with touches of gray coming in at the temples stood in the doorway. He had the body of an ex–football player who had turned a little soft over the years. He didn't seem the least bit put off by my presence.

"Let him come back, Elena," he said.

I smiled at Elena, who seemed totally outdone by the situation. The man closed the office door behind us.

"Robert Kristly," he said, shaking my hand firmly. I could feel the remnants of calluses.

"Ashe Cayne," I said.

Kristly walked around an ornate cherrywood desk, a small hitch in his left hip. Probably an old football injury. He took a seat in a high-backed leather chair. The office was sparsely but expensively decorated. A couple of oils on one wall, a couple of potted plants strategically located, and an autographed jersey of Scottie Pippen behind his desk. I took a seat in a black leather tufted chair that proved to be a lot more comfortable than it looked.

"Pippen instead of Jordan," I said, nodding at the framed jersey.

"All day long," Kristly said. "Don't get me wrong. Michael is the greatest human to ever bounce a basketball, but without Scottie, they never would've won all six of those championships in the nineties. Maybe two or three, but definitely not six."

"You won't get an argument from me," I said. "And don't forget about Horace Grant. He was another critical piece to the puzzle. Hardworking. Reliable. Always came through with a rebound or shot in the clutch."

"What a time that was for the city," he said. "Six championships in the span of eight years."

"Makes you wonder what it was like for Boston. Eleven championships in thirteen years. That dominance will never be repeated. At least in our lifetime."

"All those championships won just by a handful of guys; then you think of all the great Hall of Famers who never even won a single ring their entire career."

"Barkley and Karl Malone lead the list," I said.

"Ironically, both had chances, and the Bulls beat them during that great run. Took down Barkley and the Phoenix Suns for championship number three. Beat Malone and the Utah Jazz for numbers five and six."

"I appreciate a man who knows his sports," I said.

"But I'm sure you didn't come here to talk sports," he said. "How can I help you?"

"I came to talk women."

Kristly leaned back in his chair and arched his heavy eyebrows.

"Well, in this case, just one woman. Sophia Caballé."

Kristly shrugged.

"I'm a private investigator," I said. "I've been hired to find some answers. Sophia Caballé has blipped across the radar screen."

"I'm sorry, Mr. Cayne, but I can neither deny nor confirm the identity of our clients. As you can imagine, given the business we're in, privacy is our currency."

"I got that speech already from Elena," I said. "But I thought we might have an off-the-record conversation."

"With all due respect, we are a boutique adoption agency. We place children with families, and we do it very discreetly. People come to us because of our reputation. Discretion is the stamp of our credibility."

"Do you know Amy Donnegan?"

Kristly smiled. "You are quite persistent," he said.

"Sort of a necessary evil of detective work."

"Understood. But I must be persistent as well. I really can't confirm or deny clients."

"Of course not." I looked around the office a little more. A pad and pen sat on his desk next to a large monitor. The bookcase against the window had a couple of vases and a large dictionary. The small conference table looked like it hadn't been used since it was installed. No phone ringing or stacks of mail that needed sorting. Everything was so quiet.

"What time do you guys close up shop around here?" I asked.

"We typically wrap up around five. If we're busy, we might still be here till six, but not much later."

"You have a big staff?"

"Just Elena and me and a part-time consultant here and there."

"The three of you must be very productive to run an entire adoption agency. I hear it's a big business."

"We don't do the run-of-the-mill adoption work," Kristly said. "We're more specialized. Very select clientele."

"Deep pocketed, I'm sure."

"Adoptions, unfortunately, are an expensive proposition. But well worth it. Children are matched with loving families that will provide a life for them they otherwise might never have."

"Thus the name Brighter Horizons."

"Not the most original, I have to admit. But it embodies the work we do and what we hope to accomplish for children and families."

"What does an adoption cost?"

"We only deal with private adoptions, of course. But there's a wide range. Anywhere from ten to forty thousand. In some cases, could be a little more. But it's not really about the dollar amount. It's about needs being met and matched. Everyone wins."

Including you, I thought to myself. His $2.5 million house sat on two lush acres in one of Chicago's wealthiest suburbs.

"Tens of thousands of dollars is a pretty big commitment for working families," I said. "Insurance cover any of that?"

"Unfortunately not. The adoptive parents are responsible for all the related expenses and fees."

"And what about the parents who give up their children? Are they paid?"

"That's basically selling children. Absolutely against the law. I would never participate in that kind of arrangement. I can't speak to what others do, but that's not how we run our business."

I nodded as if he had disclosed a tightly guarded piece of national intelligence. Then I said, "Your clients must like you. Sounds like you run a first-rate operation. Very attentive."

"I'd like to think we try our best," Kristly said. "The stakes are very high for both families, those giving up their child and those adopting. This can be very emotional for all involved."

"The hours must be brutal."

"How's that?"

"Well, I imagine you're like a doctor on call. Things can happen anytime, and you need to be available to handle it."

"It's nothing like a doctor," he said. "There's rarely a reason for us to work outside of our normal hours of operation."

"So, that means the visit from Sophia and Amy to your office at ten the other night was more personal in nature."

I paid attention to his body language. It was like watching a guy just before he took a punch. His first instinct was to tighten up. It was a reflex. Part of the body's innate defense system. It was almost impossible to override it.

"I have no idea what you're talking about, Mr. Cayne."

I stood to leave. I had gotten all the information I was going to get. Plus, I kind of liked the guy. He was trying to feed his family like anyone else, though he was definitely buying the better cut of steak. But I wouldn't hold that against him.

"You forgot about the Human Highlight Reel," I said.

Kristly stood with a puzzled look.

"Going back to the greatest players who retired before winning a championship."

Kristly smiled. "Yes, Dominique Wilkins. Atlanta Hawks. Saw him play once in person. Man could he jump through the roof. TV didn't do his raw athleticism justice."

The man definitely knew his basketball. He also knew something about Sophia Caballé and Amy Donnegan.

29

MY INTEL HAD BEEN spot on, which was why I found Amy Donnegan sitting alone at a back table in Randolph Tavern, a busy pub just a couple of blocks away from city hall. She tore into a mountain of greens while tapping furiously on her phone. She didn't notice me as I approached.

"This chair taken?" I asked.

She looked up. The disappointment registered immediately on her face. I took a seat.

"It's been a while," I said.

"Are you following me?" she said.

"What makes you say that?"

"I don't think it's a coincidence that of all the restaurants in Chicago you just happen to choose the one where I'm eating lunch."

"I like salads," I said. "I read a study where the average American eats only a third of the recommended amount of daily fiber. Leafy greens are loaded with fiber, but those chia seeds you have sprinkled on top . . . now that's where the gold is. They are probably the single best food source of fiber on the planet."

"Thanks for that nutritional tidbit," she said. "But I'm sure you're not here to talk about fiber."

"No, I was wondering about Andrew Milton."

"What about him?"

"Why did he have it in for Walter Griffin?"

"What makes you say that?"

"How about he persuaded Pete Dent to open a major investigation into a complaint about a measly few hundred dollars being spent on a city credit card?"

"That doesn't mean he had it in for him."

"I see it differently."

"Okay."

"Walter Griffin, a man who has made millions of dollars in his career, mistakenly charges a few hundred dollars on a credit card. Everyone knows he's one of the mayor's best friends. So, the bean counter who discovers these charges doesn't go to Griffin and tell him he's made a mistake. They don't even go to the OIG for CPS. Instead, they go to the city OIG and file a complaint?"

Donnegan looked at me. I looked at her.

"This is the part where you formulate some type of response," I said.

"I can't explain why other people behave the way they do," she finally said.

I shrugged. "Maybe there never was an official complaint filed. Maybe someone was looking for a way to squeeze him, and out of thousands of charges they found a few that looked suspicious. So, they go after him under the pretense he had fraudulently used the city card for personal expenses. That means whoever's doing the squeezing has to be powerful enough and have the resources or authority to do so. I thought you might offer a name."

"You really overestimate my job," she said. "I'm just a liaison between the mayor's office and the board of education. I have nothing to do with OIG or investigations. If any of these issues come up, all I do is communicate them between the respective parties."

"But you know that the investigation of improper behavior carried out on the part of anyone connected with CPS falls under the jurisdiction of the IG for CPS, Paul Shulman. Why wasn't Shulman's team in charge of this investigation? This was strictly a CPS-related matter."

"I can't answer that."

"You can't because you don't know, or you can't because you don't want me to know?"

"I don't sit in meetings at that level of decision-making," she said. "I'm just a messenger. That's it."

"You don't find it strange that Shulman's office wasn't investigating?"

"My opinion doesn't matter."

"It does to me. You said you liked Walter. You said he gave you great advice. You called him the day he died to talk about the upcoming meeting he had with Pete Dent. I'd like to know what you think."

Donnegan sighed, dropped her fork, then said, "I think Walter was getting a raw deal, okay? It was pretty obvious to all of us that he didn't need the city's money to eat a lunch and fill his car up with gas. We all know it was an honest mistake. But someone felt the need to press him about it. I was given the job to tell him about the meeting with Dent. That's it."

"Did you know about the meeting before that Sunday afternoon when you called him?"

"I knew a meeting was possible. There were talks about it happening, but nothing was definitive until that afternoon.

When I found out, I called him and told him what was about to happen."

"Just seems a little strange that the liaison between the mayor's office and CPS would be communicating about a meeting with OIG."

"I was asked to give him the heads-up. The OIG has their own process and methods of alerting those they are investigating. Walter was a friend. We wanted him to hear it from us first."

"Are you planning on starting a family soon?" I asked.

"That's a strange question," she said. "Not that it's any of your business, but the answer is no. I haven't even thought about it."

"I just figured since you were visiting an adoption agency, you might be thinking of giving some needy child a brighter horizon."

Donnegan gathered her things to leave. "What I do on my own time is my business," she said. "And you following me and checking on me is an invasion of my privacy."

"Did you know that Sophia Caballé was Walter's girlfriend?"

"And that's relevant why?"

"I don't know yet," I said. "But it stretches the imagination that Walter's much younger girlfriend was visiting an adoption agency with a friend who has never even thought about starting a family and was also the friend who let Walter know he needed to attend a shakedown by OIG."

"Those weren't my words," she said.

"But they were your thoughts."

"You're in over your head," she said, standing. "I know you want some closure for the family, but it might be best for everyone to let the past stay where it is. Unfortunately, nothing you do or the answers you find will bring Walter back."

"That's true. But those answers might bring him some justice and his family some amount of closure about who really put that bullet in his head and why."

———

ONE OF THE BASIC RULES of detective work was you could never look at the same information too many times. Even the sharpest minds can miss something staring right at them. That was why I sat in my office digging again into Griffin's postmortem examination report. I had a gut feeling something was there, but I just hadn't seen it the first time. I started with the external examination portion of the report. X-rays showed fractures where the bullet had entered and exited. I went to the internal examination next. I focused on the gastrointestinal section. It said there was twenty milliliters of tan-colored food mixed with mucus. Then I read the diagnoses section. The ME listed two—number one, gunshot wound to the head, and number two, extensive craniocerebral injuries due to number one. I kept staring at the three sentences in the opinion section. *This fifty-eight-year-old Black male, Walter Griffin, died as a result of a gunshot wound to the head that fractured the skull and lacerated the brain. The wound coursed from left to right. The entrance wound showed evidence of contact-range firing.*

I picked up the phone and called my father.

"This is a surprise," he answered.

"Why is it when I call you, it's always some type of surprise?" I asked.

"Because you never call me."

"I call you at least once a week."

"That's my equivalent of never."

"Your fingers aren't broken," I said.

"Don't get smart with me," he said.

"I'm just saying it's a two-way street. It would be nice if sometimes you reached out to me."

"Every time I call, you're on a damn golf course somewhere. Or at the range working with one of your irons."

"Just like when I call, you're always on a tennis court or about to get on one."

"I'm not on one right now."

"Okay, fine. Point made. I will call you more often."

"And I, you."

"Now that we've gotten that settled, how are you?"

"Icing my knees. We decided to play an extra set today. Seemed like a good idea at the time. I'm paying for it now."

"Are you busy?"

"Packing my bags for Paris. Henry Mulligan got us on at Roland-Garros through one of his contacts, so four of us are heading over."

"This is the first I'm hearing of this."

"That's why it would be nice if you called me more often. You would know more about what's going on in my life."

"I'm sure you'll have a blast."

"You're more than welcome to come," he said. "It's about time you got back on the tennis court. The red clay is a fun surface."

"I can't go anywhere right now. I'm in the middle of this case."

"How's it going?"

"That's why I'm calling. I need some help with this autopsy report. I have a feeling there's something in there, but I don't have the medical knowledge to make sense of it. I don't know what I should be seeing or if what I'm seeing should be given more attention."

"And I probably don't either," my dad said. "Forensic pathology is extremely specialized. It couldn't be further away from the field of psychiatry. But I know someone who can help. Barry Ellison. We went to med school together. He retired a few years ago from over at Rush. He was the head of their pathology department for twenty years. He probably could've gone for another twenty, but he got prostate cancer, caught it early before it spread, and decided he wanted to do more with the rest of his life than stain specimen slides and keep his eye glued to a microscope. So, he volunteers twice a week teaching science to kids over in Chatham."

"Please text me his number."

"I have it somewhere on my desk. I'll fetch it once I get to my study."

"When do you leave for Paris?"

"Day after tomorrow."

"How about we grab lunch before you go?"

"I'd like that very much. Come to the house at noon tomorrow. I'll have Pearline fix your favorite."

The next text I got, however, was not from my father but from Mercedes inviting me to join her for sushi that night. I didn't have any other plans, and I thought it sounded more fun than sitting at home eating leftovers and watching the Golf Channel, so I accepted. Carolina texted me thirty minutes later, and I felt guilty as hell. She, too, asked about my plans that evening. I told her that I was going to make it a quiet night, but I would be thinking about her and looked forward to our dinner in a couple of nights. Just as I finished her text, my phone rang. I didn't recognize the number.

"This is Dr. Barry Ellison," the caller said in a raspy voice. "Wendell said you were looking for some help."

"I appreciate the call, Dr. Ellison," I said. "I could definitely use your expertise."

"Wendell said something about the Griffin case."

"Yes, I'm trying to help the family figure out if it really was a suicide, and if it wasn't, what actually happened."

"I remember reading about the case," Ellison said. "Very tragic indeed. Caught all of us by surprise."

"Did you ever see the autopsy report?"

"No, but Fred Skinner handled the case. He's one of the best forensic pathologists in the business. Rather, he was."

"He died?"

"No, he retired not long after the case was closed. A small group of us retired pathologists hold two meetings a year here in Chicago. He hasn't come for several years. Last I heard he was up in Wisconsin running his own dairy farm."

"Could I get you to take a look at the report?"

"Not a problem. But I don't want to get your hopes up too much. It's very unlikely I'll find something that Fred missed. He was a meticulous pathologist."

"You might be right, but it's worth a shot," I said. "I've read it several times, and there are things I simply can't understand with my limited knowledge of medicine. You'll bring a fresh set of eyes to it. Maybe you can help see something I'm missing."

———

THE UNION SUSHI + BARBECUE BAR occupied the first two stories of an otherwise drab-looking building. I had once met a client there to tell him that his wife was having an affair with their ostensibly gay nanny. I found the decor of the place to be thrown together and without thought, but the sushi was delicious and a tenth the price of Momotaro.

Mercedes was talking to the hostess as I entered. She turned and, before I could say anything, planted a soft wet kiss full on my lips. Her lipstick had the faint smell of sweetened vanilla. The hostess led us to our table against the window and in full view of the bar. I took my time admiring Mercedes as she gracefully swiveled in a black miniskirt with an exposed zipper down the front and a black off-the-shoulder top with ties across the chest. As soon as we sat, she rested her hand on mine underneath the table.

"I'm very tactile," she said. "I hope that doesn't bother you."

"Not so much as being projectile." I smiled.

"Does your brain ever stop working?"

"Depends on which one you're referring to."

She squeezed my hand softly. "I really like you. You have a great attitude about life."

"I try not to take things too seriously," I said. "Until I need to take them seriously."

"Have you been here before?"

"Only once. I had their beef filet and the duck fried rice. It was good."

"I like it here," she said. "It never feels crowded, and if you get the right bartender, they're very generous with the drinks."

Someone came over and quietly filled our water glasses.

"So, how's business?" I asked.

"Which business?"

"Soho House."

"Very busy. Summer is high season, especially with the pool and rooftop bar open. Everyone wants to be outside."

"And what do you do when you're not working there?"

"Work on my real career."

"Which is?"

"I want to be a novelist."

"Sounds like fun," I said. "And a lot of work."

"Yes and no," she said. "It's a lot of time alone, but I love writing and creating stories, so it doesn't feel like work. Soho House is work. That's what pays the bills."

"What's your genre?"

"Romance."

"Like that Nicholas Sparks guy?"

"Look at you trying to know your romance writers." She laughed. "I write more literary romance."

"What's the difference?"

"Think about it like the difference between playing a real round of eighteen-hole golf and minigolf. Both can be fun, but they cater to a different audience and have a different purpose."

The waitress came, and we placed our order: calamari and a tempura plate to start, then an assortment of rolls.

"So, why did you decide to be a private investigator?" she asked. "Why not a police officer? You would look really cute in a uniform."

"I was a police officer," I said. "But I didn't wear a uniform very long. I was a detective."

"You went from detective to PI?"

"I left the department a while ago. Politics didn't work for me. Among other things."

"You carry a gun?"

"Only when I need to."

"You ever shoot anyone?"

"Only when they tried to shoot me first."

Her eyes widened as she brought her hand to her mouth.

"It's a dangerous world outside of those club doors." I smiled.

"I've never held a gun before," she said.

"They're heavier than most people think."

"So, why were you going to see Sophia?" she asked. "You are so not her type."

"What is her type?"

"Really rich and kinda old."

"Well, then I strike out on both fronts."

She leaned forward and whispered, "Is she part of a case you're working on?"

"I can't really say," I whispered back.

"Which means you just did, or you would've said no."

"Quite perceptive for a romance writer."

"Did she do something bad?"

"I plead the Fifth."

"Tell me. No, let me guess. She stole a ton of money from some rich old guy just before he died, and the family wants the money back."

"Sounds like a bad ending to what could've been a good romance plot."

"I'm serious. Did she do something like that?"

"Does she have a lot of money?"

"Well, not hers technically, but what's the difference when you can ask for whatever you want, and guys just give it to you?"

"I imagine you could find similar success in that department. Every guy who's walked in here tonight has stopped and looked at you."

"Not passing any judgments, but that's not how I roll," Mercedes said. "I'd rather sleep in a studio apartment and eat ramen for the rest of my life if my only way of making it is on my back."

"Which you would be very good at too." I smiled.

"From anyone else that would sound vulgar." She laughed.

"It's my poetic license."

We finished off the tuna and salmon rolls, then went to work on the asparagus.

"You ever hear of a woman named Amy Donnegan?" I asked.

She shook her head. "Should I know who she is?"

"A friend of Sophia's. Just wondering if you've ever seen them hanging out together by the pool."

"Sophia only hung out with one person at the pool. But not anymore."

"What happened?"

"They died."

"What was her name?"

"It wasn't a she. It was a he. His name was Bryce Horner."

30

I COULDN'T SLEEP THAT NIGHT. It wasn't a nightmare or anything, but several times I woke up and stared into the darkness of my bedroom. I kept replaying the afternoon's events, specifically Mechanic and me sitting in the car across from Horner's old apartment building. I kept seeing the cars passing us by and the people walking in and out of the Village Cycle Center. Something had happened that caught my attention before we got out of the car and talked to the old woman. What was it?

I got out of bed, gave Stryker a piece of jerky, then stood in the window staring at the Ferris wheel on Navy Pier. Its lights had been turned off for the night, which made it look creepy against the black sky. Something had happened before we got out of the car. We'd been listening to the music; then Mechanic had spotted the old woman. That was when it came to me. Mechanic had taken the key out of the ignition before we'd left the car. He'd slid it in his jacket before he'd opened the door.

I turned on the lights and found the autopsy report. The ME had mentioned Griffin's key. I quickly found the line on the first page. A single car key had been found in his left outside jacket pocket. Then my mind went back to Mechanic before we'd left the car and crossed the street at Horner's apartment building. He'd taken the key out of the ignition with his right hand and slipped it in his right pants pocket. I didn't know why that moment had caught my attention when he'd done it, but something had registered in my subconscious that made me think of Griffin. This line in the report was what had bothered me. Maybe it was purely coincidental, but why had Griffin put the key in his left pocket when he'd left the car? If he'd gotten out of the car under his own power, it was most likely he would've opened the door with his left hand and put the key in his right jacket pocket, not the left.

———

I HAD JUST GOTTEN into my car after having lunch with my father. He'd been in a great mood, full of excitement about his upcoming trip to the red clay of Roland-Garros. After Paris, he and his friends were taking the Eurostar to London, where they had been given a chance to play on one of the outer grass courts at Wimbledon. It would be his first time playing on grass, and he wanted to make sure he was in his best form. I didn't have the heart to tell him that no one would be paying much attention to a sixty-eight-year-old man from the South Side of Chicago. But Pearline had gone out of her way to make the lunch as delicious and pleasant as possible, and I didn't want to ruin it.

My cell phone rang. It was Dr. Ellison.

"How was your round?" I asked.

"Not bad until I got to the back nine."

"Let me guess. The twelfth hole."

"How did you know? I four-putted the damn green."

"Because it makes no sense putting the flag in the middle of a slope. It's impossible to land the ball on the approach shot, and putting to the hole once you're on the green is like putting down a seesaw. Impossible to stop."

"I lost a two-dollar skin on that hole."

"Last of the big-time spenders."

"That's a lot of money when you're on a fixed income and playing for a quarter a skin."

I laughed.

"Anyway, I've read the report."

"And?"

"If you're not too busy, why don't you come by the apartment? It's better if I show you what I found."

"Where do you live?"

"Corner of Elm and State. Apartment 24H. I'll leave your name downstairs."

"I'm fifteen minutes away."

———

DR. BARRY ELLISON LOOKED EXACTLY as I'd expected from the gravelly sound of his voice. He stood broad at the shoulders and sported a heavy gray beard that hid his lips until he spoke. His large black rectangular glasses appeared even more prominent with his bald dome. He wore a white polo shirt, linen shorts, and a pair of velvet house slippers. He asked me to leave my shoes at the door with the others. All his outer walls were floor-to-ceiling windows with views east overlooking the lake, south to Soldier Field, and west to the United Center. The furniture was ornate, the oil paintings large and modern. He led me to a sitting room with fluffy chairs and a TV screen the size of Jupiter.

"My father should've chosen pathology instead of psychiatry," I said. "Your fixed income seems to be doing a lot better than his."

"Nonsense," Ellison bellowed. "Wendell is doing quite well for himself. It wasn't the specialty that mattered, rather hiring a real professional to oversee my investments. I was a lot humbler than my peers who thought just because they mastered the very difficult discipline of medicine, they could also master the world of finance. Most of them lost almost everything they'd earned in the market or on silly start-ups before they realized it was time to hire professionals."

He reached over to a Chinese lacquer coffee table and picked up a stack of papers.

"Am I the only one you've shown this report?" he said.

"My one and only," I said.

"How did you get it?"

"The family gave it to me."

"Who gave it to them?"

"I assume the county medical examiner's office."

"Did they get a second opinion on the findings?"

"I'm not sure, but I can ask."

"I found some small things that are a little odd," he said. "They don't feel right, especially coming from someone as good as Fred."

"Like what?"

"Second paragraph, first line. 'Recovered from the left jacket pocket is a single car key.' Just seems a bit odd to me. A man is so depressed and upset that he wants to kill himself. Why does he leave his car and take his car key? Why doesn't he leave the key in the ignition?"

"I thought the same thing," I said. "But what also bothered me is where they found the key. In his left pocket. I can't seem to get that out of my mind. In that year and model of Cadillac, the ignition is located on the right side of the steering wheel. And it was not a push-button ignition. That was in the next year's design. This model, you still had to insert the key. When you take your key out of the ignition, what do you normally do? In most cases, you'd put it in the right pocket of your pants or jacket. Yet his key was found in his left pocket. Doesn't make sense."

Dr. Ellison flipped over the first page. I could see where he had circled certain words in red marker and had written in the margins.

"Have you read the report from the actual crime scene?"

"I have."

"Can you tell me exactly how they found the body?"

"He was on his right side on a ledge just above the water. His left hand, face, and part of his upper torso were submerged in the water. His right hand was partially pinned underneath his body on the ledge."

"Was his right hand dry?"

"Yes, it never touched the water."

"And what was the orientation of his face?"

"Facedown. Resting partially on the ledge and partially on his forearm."

Dr. Ellison looked closely at the report and shook his head. "Doesn't make sense," he said, thinking aloud. "No external facial abrasions. If someone shoots himself and falls to the ground, then into the water, there should be some type of facial skin abrasions. But there are none noted here in the external examination section."

"Couldn't it be possible he fell to the ground, landed on his arm, then fell into the water? That would've protected his face from injury."

"Possible, but extremely unlikely," Ellison said. "When a self-inflicted gunshot wound to the head occurs, the body doesn't stagger and fall slowly to the ground. It crumples. Very unlikely it fell in such a perfect way that the face was protected."

"But there were cuts on the lips," I said. "That could be from the fall."

"Not the manner in which these are described. These cuts and abrasions are inside the mouth. If he had fallen on his face, there would be external abrasions as well as internal. None of his teeth were missing, nor were they loose. He did not fall on his face."

Ellison flipped the page and reread his notes carefully.

"I have a couple of questions about the evidence of injury section," he said. "They clearly state the entrance wound is on the left side of the head measuring zero point five inches in diameter. They note the muzzle imprint on his skin being manifested by a round abrasion surrounding the entrance wound, which measures zero point nine inches in diameter. I'm okay with that so far. On the right side of his head they found a slit-shaped exit wound three inches below the top of the head and five inches to the right of the anterior midline. The wound was a through and through. I'm okay with that also. The right upper eyelid is swollen due to the damage the bullet caused. They mention that his left hand was submerged in the river, but his right hand was dry. How was that?"

I stood up in the middle of the floor and reenacted what could've happened. Griffin was left handed, so I put my left fingers in a gun formation, then held the index finger to the left side of my head. I pulled the trigger, then tried to fall so that my body landed the same way his body was found. It was extremely difficult to land in the exact position and took me three times to do it. I got up and sat back in my chair, a little winded.

"Now you see what's concerning me," Ellison said. "A very unnatural position." He turned the page. "Then they go on with the internal examination where they look at the different physiologic systems."

"I barely understood any of it except for the food in the stomach," I said.

"That was a question I had for you," Ellison said. "Not a pathologic question but an investigative question. What's known about his activities before he died?"

I went through the timeline I had pieced together so far. He had purchased food at Lem's, but that was for the nursing home staff. No one said he had eaten any of it, but maybe he had. And he never picked up the food he was supposed to bring home for dinner.

"This food business interests me," Ellison said. "They recorded fifteen milliliters of tan-colored food mixed with mucus inside the stomach. No food was located anywhere else in the gastrointestinal tract."

"What does that say to you?"

"From a pathology perspective, he must've eaten something within two to six hours before he died."

"Can you tighten that range?"

"Only if I had more information about what he ate and when exactly he ate it. Under most conditions, the stomach will empty its contents and pass them through to the upper duodenum or the small intestines within two to six hours. How fast the food travels depends on lots of variables, such as amount of food eaten, ratio of solid to liquid in the meal, hormonal factors, how much of the macronutrients were in the food. There's a lot that impacts digestion and food transit, thus the broad time range."

"Fifteen milliliters seem like such a small amount of food."

"It is. It's more like a snack. The fully distended stomach can hold anywhere from two to four liters of food, which is about fifty times the volume when it's empty. Fifteen milliliters might be a chocolate bar or some beef jerky, but it definitely wouldn't be a big meal, like a steak or big salad."

I made a mental note to go back over the timeline and check to see if anyone remembered him eating that day. Maybe he'd had something at the golf course.

"The cardiovascular system was my next concern," Ellison said, turning the page. "He had about sixty percent occlusion of the left anterior descending coronary artery due to calcific atherosclerotic plaques."

"Translation?"

"He ate too much fatty food, didn't exercise enough, and probably had some degree of high blood pressure. The coronary arteries are the special vessels that feed the heart. The heart pumps out blood to the rest of the body, but it needs to be fed also. The coronaries crawl over the heart like a spiderweb and deliver oxygen-rich blood and all the nutrients it contains to the heart muscles so they remain healthy and function properly. The left anterior descending artery, or LAD, is a branch off the left main coronary artery, and it supplies the front left side of the heart. This is a very important blood vessel, and if it has too much blockage, it can cause a heart attack and, in many cases, death."

"So, he had heart disease?"

"Technically, yes. But it's possible neither he nor his doctors knew it, because his blockage was only sixty percent. A lot of people won't experience symptoms at that level, and it's likely he didn't experience any symptoms. But when you start getting above the seventy percent range, then it can start becoming a problem."

"Is that what's bothering you about the heart section?"

"Not really. You open the chests of most men his age, and there's going to be some blockage in that artery. It's the second line. 'The epicardium demonstrates diffuse pinpoint petechiae.'"

"What does that mean?"

"Petechiae are tiny circular red marks that appear on the skin or in a mucous or serous membrane. They are the result of hemorrhage or bleeding. They can occur anywhere in the body, but when you see them in the mouth or eyelids or heart, then you have to consider them the result of some kind of trauma."

"Like blunt force trauma, where someone gets whacked in the chest or the face?"

"Not that type of trauma. You typically see these petechiae as a sign of asphyxia where the flow of oxygen has been suddenly cut off. We see them often in cases where some external means has caused obstruction of the airways."

"What would be common?"

"Strangulation by the hands or some type of ligature like a rope or cord. We see them in cases of a hanging. You can also see them in cases of manual suffocation."

"But why does the bleeding happen?"

"Because of the increased venous pressure. When the veins don't have any way to release the blood, pressure builds up, and the tiny capillaries rupture. There are all kinds of situations when you get them. Straining for prolonged periods of time like you do when weightlifting, certain medications can cause it, or other kinds of illnesses like low platelet count, where your body has problems forming blood clots. Numerous infectious diseases like mononucleosis and cytomegalovirus can cause it too. But you see it a lot in strangulation cases. The eyes will have lots of petechiae in the conjunctiva underneath the lower eyelid." Ellison pulled the skin underneath his eye. "Down in here. Sometimes you can also see them in the membrane of the upper eyelid."

"But they reported that his eyes were clean. No findings."

"That's what's puzzling me. His eyes are clean, but he has these petechiae of the heart. Heart petechiae are less common than those found in the eye, and fewer things cause them."

"Such as?"

"Not too long a list. Mostly sudden infant death syndrome, SIDS; blunt trauma like the chest hitting the steering wheel during a car accident; asphyxiation; or CPR."

"We can rule out two of them right away. He wasn't an infant, so that's gone. And if there was some type of blunt trauma, we would see other injuries to his chest. There weren't any. So, that leaves us with asphyxiation and CPR. Why does CPR cause them?"

"One of the main goals of CPR is to manually compress the heart so that you push the blood out of the chambers and to the rest of the body. This is critical when the heart stops beating, and you have to basically do the beating for it. But depending on how hard you press and how long you try the CPR, you can cause these minihemorrhages on the surface of the heart. Did they perform CPR on him? There's no mention of it in the narrative section of the report."

"I don't remember. I'll have to check the investigator's report."

"If it was believed his body had been there for some time, then they wouldn't have tried CPR, so you'll have to read what they did and what their thinking was in the report."

"What about the asphyxiation as a possibility?"

"It can occur through strangulation or suffocation."

"Suffocation how?"

"A plastic bag wrapped around the head. Smothering with a pillow or some other type of method that stops the person from breathing in or out, like someone lying on top of the mouth and nose or having them taped up."

"But if someone smothered him, wouldn't you see some type of injury to the face due to the pressure?"

"Yes, you would, especially if someone is trying to hold down a man of this size. He would be thrashing and punching about, trying to free himself and get air. But there are no wounds here in the report that suggest there was any type of struggle."

"What if they bagged him?"

"Same idea. He would be fighting like crazy before or after they put on the bag. His nails are clean. No abrasions or lacerations on his hands or arms. The one thing I did notice, however, were those minor cuts on the interior of his lower lip. But the report doesn't go into much detail about their appearance."

"What do you think they could be?"

"Not sure, but I feel like something is missing."

"Like what?"

"This is just a hunch, but the petechiae on the heart and no pete-chiae on the face or under the eyelids—possible. But doesn't match the evidence of injury or the diagnoses. If they were found on the heart, I'd expect them under the eyelids also."

"What would you do next?"

"Try to find Fred Skinner and see if he can explain the inconsis-tencies a little better."

"If you were me, what would you ask him?"

"First, if there were petechiae anywhere else on the body, and second, if Griffin had any history of blood-clotting disorders."

THAT NIGHT I COULDN'T shake a yearning for a brussels sprouts and bacon pizza. Robert's Pizza and Dough Company occupied a large kitchen and dining room hidden in the basement of a long brick building whose entire back wall of windows fronted the main stem of the Chicago River that flowed west from the lake. I had just turned the corner off the Riverwalk about two blocks away from the restaurant when two guys the size of water buffalo stepped in front of me. The streetlight showed their patchy red skin and long knotted veins popping out the side of their necks. Their arms stuck out from their wide trunks as if they were borrowed from a couple of guys several inches shorter. They both wore black baseball caps and flexed biceps the size of footballs.

"We need to have a little talk," the taller one said as he stepped in front of me. He had to be at least six four and one good steak shy of three hundred pounds.

"You prefer English or French?" I said. "But I must warn you, my French accent is a little rusty."

"Fuckin' wise guy," the shorter one said. "I should pop you right in your fuckin' mouth and then see what language you speak."

"Please don't talk that way," I said. "I scare easily."

The short one looked at me like he wanted to take my head off; then he looked at his partner, who said, "Consider this your friendly and only warning. Leave it alone."

"I might consider it if I knew what the antecedent for the *it* is."

"What the fuck!" the shorter guy said. "Enough with the SAT words. Talk regular."

"Leave this Griffin shit alone," the taller guy said. "That simple."

"Or what?"

"You won't know your ass from your face."

"Then I'll be in good company, because looking at you right now, I can't tell the difference."

I knew the shorter guy would blow his fuse first. His right shoulder was the tell. He dipped it back a little to give the punch more power. It was just enough time for me to step left and deliver a blow flush to his nose. He turned to the left as I expected, which exposed his entire flank. I squatted and loaded my legs to generate as much power as possible and kicked him with my full two hundred pounds to the side of his lower back and into his kidney. He dropped immediately. There was no doubt he would be peeing blood tonight.

I made the rookie mistake of admiring my work too long, though, and the taller guy already had a punch en route. I didn't have any time to block it, so I threw my body back to lessen the blow. It still felt like a sledgehammer when it grazed my shoulder. I stumbled back a couple of steps but kept my feet. He closed in on me quickly. Too quickly. He left his midsection completely unprotected. I had a perfect line to his sweet spot, just beneath where his last pair of ribs connected to the breastbone. This was going to be the only way to take him down, given how big he was and the fact that he was already in motion. I got as low as I could in the short amount of time and sprung forward to meet his charge. He raised his right fist to clobber me, and I threw mine along with the rest of my body into that small, unprotected opening just beneath the ribs, smashing into his diaphragm. I made contact first. The air rushed out of his mouth like a balloon whose knot suddenly got untied. His fist landed on the back of my head, but at that point it was ineffectual. He doubled over, gasping for breath, and I stood and kneed him as hard as I could underneath his rib cage. I felt the crunching of bones against my kneecap.

The shorter guy was already on his feet and running toward the river. The taller guy hit the ground, moaning and gasping, then rolled for a few seconds, scrambled to his feet, and ran in the opposite direction. I let them go. They had delivered their message, and I had sent one back. I just wasn't sure who would receive it.

31

"IT SCARES ME THAT you're not scared," Carolina said. We were sitting down at the new dog park a block from my building, watching Stryker bounce and flip in the dog scrum that was getting bigger by the minute. Carolina nursed a coffee. I took my time with a freshly squeezed OJ and a sore shoulder.

"The only thing we have to fear is fear itself," I said.

"Stop joking," she said. "I'm serious. You really could've gotten hurt."

"Impossible."

"Why?"

"Because there were only two of them, and they only outweighed me by about half a ton."

"Will you take this seriously, please? You don't know what kind of people you're messing around with. What if they had guns?"

"They wouldn't've used them. I made the calculation. We were in too public an area. The most they'd try to do was rough me up a bit."

"Well, look at what happened to your shoulder."

"Not as bad as what happened to the short guy's kidney."

"Now what are you gonna do?"

"The only thing I know how to do."

"Which is?"

"Keep moving forward."

"And what if they have guns next time?"

"I'll make sure I have a bigger one."

Carolina shook her head in frustration and took a sip of coffee. I considered telling her about Mercedes but decided not to. Mercedes would be a limited engagement, and I didn't really need Carolina's analysis about something that had no impact on what our future plans might become if we ever arrived at the time in our lives when we both were available and ready.

"Maybe you should go play golf today so that you can relax a little," she said.

"Golf on a Saturday is anything but relaxing."

"Why?"

"Because all the working stiffs who can't play during the week load up the courses. Getting a tee time is impossible, and what is normally a three-hour round can take up to five hours. Besides, I have a really busy day."

"What's going on?"

"First I need to speak to the alluring Sophia Caballé. I'm not sure it'll get me anywhere, but I can't stop trying."

"Maybe you just like looking at her."

"Not too hard to do, but I've been told very clearly that I'm not her type."

"Which is?"

"Really rich and kinda old."

"I deplore it when women are so predictable."

"That part of her might be, but I think there's another side that's very unpredictable."

"You think she killed Griffin or knows who killed him?"

"I don't think she would do it herself, but I think she might know why someone killed him. She comes across very cold and calculating. And she was besties with Bryce Horner, who was one of the last people Griffin talked to before he was killed. Which leads me to my second appointment. Dryhop Brewers."

"What's that?"

"A brewery up in Boystown that serves dishes like bacon poutine and Scottish eggs and frites with a tangy dragon sauce. Horner was wearing a wet suit when he washed up on North Beach. But they found a receipt from Dryhop when they searched his pants left on the nearby rocks."

"What's your plan once you get up there?"

"See if I can find out if anyone knows him. Maybe he was a regular. Maybe he worked there. Maybe someone knows how he mysteriously ended up floating in the lake."

"If you go to Boystown alone, they might think you're on the market."

"That's kind of the plan." I smiled. "Maybe a little bit of leg might arouse somebody's memory, and they'll start talking."

"God forbid you show up in those black jeans I like. They just might fall over and die."

———

MERCEDES HAD THE DAY off, but I found Sophia Caballé on the sixth floor of Soho House, sitting at one of the indoor banquettes by herself, facing the pool. All the sliding doors had been opened, so the jagged Chicago skyline and all its glory sat there in full view, as if daring you to reach out and touch it. She had a small salad and tall glass of Perrier in front of her. Her sunglasses were different than the ones she had been wearing last time I was here. These were octagonal with gold bars running along the frames. Her bikini top revealed a well-cultivated tan.

"Another busy day at the office," I said, sliding onto the cushioned bench.

"Another busy day of harassing me," she said without looking at me.

"*Harass* is a bit strong, don't you think? Just doing my job as the intrepid investigator."

"You think highly of yourself."

"Sometimes. But in this case, I just wanted to use a little alliteration."

"I'm having lunch," she said. "I prefer you let me eat in peace."

"Not much peace in Padenga," I said.

"Where the hell is that?"

"Zimbabwe."

"What's that got to do with me?"

I nodded toward the silver crocodile bag sitting on the bench next to her. "Takes the belly skins of three crocs from a Padenga farm in Zimbabwe to make that one bag," I said.

"You're doing investigations for PETA now?"

"I'm just saying."

"Well, this isn't a Birkin bag," she said. "That's what I had when you bothered me the first time. This is an Hermès Kelly bag. And it's not made from African crocodile. This skin is Himalayan."

"Ah, of course. Much more eco-friendly."

"Is there something you want from me?"

"How about the truth?"

"The truth about what?"

"You and Walter."

Sophia took a small sip of water, then turned to me. "What's this obsession you have with my relationship to Walter?"

"I wouldn't call it an obsession. More like an inkling."

"Inkling? Who even uses words like that these days?"

"I do when I'm trying to impress."

"Well, try again."

I shrugged. "Were you and Walter copulating?"

She frowned. "It's none of your damn business what we were doing."

"Did his wife know?"

"That's a ridiculous question to ask me. What went on between him and his wife was none of my business, and I kept it that way."

"Did he pay for the apartment?"

"It's none of your business how my apartment was purchased."

"Or are you staying in Cephus Redmond's second apartment?"

"Why are you so interested in my living arrangements?"

She didn't flinch or hesitate when I mentioned Redmond's second apartment. She knew about it.

"Everything about you intrigues me," I said. "For some reason almost every road I turn down leads back to you."

"Such as?"

"Bryce Horner, for one."

"Bryce was one of my best friends. That was no mystery. Everyone knew that."

"Was he Walter's friend too?"

"How would I know? I didn't keep a running list of Walter's friends."

"Did you introduce them?"

"I'm sure there was a time all of us were in the same room together. Walter was very social. I don't know if I introduced them to each other or they introduced themselves."

"Did Bryce know you were pregnant with Walter's child?"

"Excuse me?"

I decided to go for it. "You were pregnant with Walter's child. You thought about aborting the baby but couldn't bring yourself to do it, or you realized the baby could be a strategic asset. Monetized. So, you left the city before the baby bump started to show and didn't return until you had the baby and your body was back to its splendid self. You couldn't keep the baby for all kinds of reasons; maybe it would cut into your social calendar, or you had convinced Walter that it had been aborted, so Amy Donnegan, who you met through Walter, puts you in touch with Robert Kristly at Brighter Horizons. Amy knew Kristly because he was her father's roommate at UC Berkeley. Kristly specializes in extremely discreet adoptions, so he places the baby into a loving home and the adoptive parents pay him a small fortune, which bankrolls another guest room in his two-and-a-half-million-dollar mansion in Naperville. You go on sunning and yachting with the half a million dollars in cash that Walter provided when you told him you would make sure his problem would go away."

"Are you done yet?" she said calmly.

"Just a little more. Bryce knows that you're pregnant with Walter's child, because the two of you are besties. For some reason, which I haven't figured out yet, someone decides to put a bullet in the left side of Walter's head. Bryce's body washes up a couple of weeks later without any signs of struggle or trauma. Now the coast is basically clear, except for Amy Donnegan, who's beholden to you for reasons I can't yet explain. All threats of revealing the identity of your secret baby have now been conveniently eliminated."

"So, that's your summary?"

"Three may keep a secret, if two of them are dead."

"You have a very creative imagination," she said. "How much time do you spend coming up with this stuff?"

"Unfortunately, I didn't make that one up. Ben Franklin gets the credit."

"You should try writing fiction. You're a natural."

"Or maybe go into PR. It seems to pay really well."

"Wasn't the settlement from the police department enough?" she said. "I heard it was somewhere in the millions."

"Exaggeration is the truth that has lost its temper," I said.

"I'll trust my sources on this."

I stood to leave. "Enjoy the rest of your salad. I'm sure we'll be running into each other again."

Sophia took her sunglasses off for the first time and stared those cold beautiful eyes at me. "You should be very careful messing around in other people's business. You aren't the only one who knows things."

I squeezed my eyes slightly and did my best to return the stare. "Having the knowledge is only half the battle. It's what you do with it that wins the war."

32

DRYHOP BREWERS OCCUPIED THE bottom floor of a newly renovated building on the busy block of 3100 North Broadway. Several square wood tables with red metal chairs filled up an outdoor space that had been barricaded by large wood planters. The clientele was mostly men, most dressed fashionably, some carrying small dogs inside designer leather tote bags. The handsome young waiters moved hurriedly, cozying up to tables and darting in and out the door.

Inside, large shiny metal brewery tanks lined the back wall behind the long bar. A middle-aged man in tight jeans and equally tight shirt unbuttoned to his stomach was standing at the host stand when I approached.

"Dining alone?" he said, brow raised.

"I'm not here to eat," I said. "Though the food looks great. I just had a couple of questions."

"Questions?"

"I'm trying to find some information on a customer who might've eaten here a couple of years ago."

"Are you serious right now?" he asked. Those eyebrows went up again. They'd been bleached to match his bottle-blond hair. "We are in the middle of our rush, and you wanna play detective."

"I'm not playing a detective," I said. "I *am* a detective."

He stood back and straightened his neck. "A detective like with the police and a real gun?"

"I used to be with CPD; now I'm private."

Someone called the name Gabby from the bar. The host turned and held up his hand. "Give me a minute," he said to me. "Let me deal with those two. They've already had way too much to drink."

I looked around the restaurant as he scuttled off to the bar. Breweries had become all the rage in Chicago, popping up on every corner in the North Side like pimples on a teenager's face. There was a culture and an attitude that came with these places, almost like personalities. Dryhop's carefully crafted slogan had been stamped across the front of its menu: *Hop-centric ales & fresh brewery-inspired fare at the source in Chicago.*

"My God," Gabby said as he returned. "So lecherous, those two."

"What's wrong?"

"They want to know if you would have a drink with them."

I looked in their direction. They both were wearing tight tank tops and diamond studs in their ears. I smiled my most charming smile. They winked back.

"The short one, Connor, is totally loaded," Gabby said. "His family owns some kind of factory in Rhode Island. The tall one is Magnus—doesn't have any money, doubt that's the name his parents gave him, but he's fine as hell, and everyone in this restaurant wants to fuck him. Including me. Forgive me, I'm being so rude. What's your name?"

"My name is Ashe. I'm a private investigator." We shook hands.

"Not being judgmental or nothing, but you look too cute to be a real private investigator. I could see you playing one on TV."

"I'll tell my agent that."

"See, I knew you were an actor."

"I'm only kidding." I took out my phone. "I'm a real private investigator, and I want to know if you've ever seen this guy before." I showed him a photo of Bryce Horner. His eyes widened.

"I take it you knew him."

"Of course I did. Bryce was the sweetest. He came in often."

"Did he come alone?"

"Not really. He usually had a really pretty Judy with him. She was so gorgeous even I thought about switching teams."

"Do you know Judy's last name?"

"You are so hetero." He laughed. "Judy is what we call a heterosexual woman who likes to be around gay men."

I scrolled through the gallery on my phone and brought up a picture of Sophia Caballé and showed it to him.

"That's her," he said. "Drop-dead gorgeous. I haven't seen her since Bryce died. She just stopped coming in."

"I'm trying to find out if he was with her the last time he came in."

"Honey, my memory is good, but not that good. She wasn't the only one he came with. Sometimes he brought along some candy."

"Candy?"

"Good-looking men." He sighed.

I brought up a picture of Walter Griffin and showed it to him.

"Dear God, no," Gabby said. "He has straight written all over him. I've never seen him before. Wait, let me see that picture again."

I showed it to him. He thought hard.

"Those eyes," he said. "I've seen him before."

"He's been here?"

"No, a woman came in here just before Bryce died and showed me a picture of that man and asked me if I had seen him here."

"What did you tell her?"

"That I hadn't. I was sure of it. How could anyone forget those eyes?"

"Do you know who this woman was?"

"She didn't say. She asked me about that man; then she wanted to know if I had seen her husband."

"Did she show you a picture of her husband?"

"Yes."

"Do you remember what he looked like?"

"Most definitely. Tall, dark hair, almost Cuban looking. Very beautiful with those dark eyebrows and wavy hair. I remember he was kind of serious. He came in with Bryce a couple of times."

"Were he and Bryce together?"

"As in?" He made a copulation motion with his index finger and a circle he made with his other hand.

"That's one way to put it," I said.

"It kinda felt that way, but I wasn't sure. I remember thinking he was nervous. Like it was a first date or something. I can't remember exactly what made me feel that way, but that was the vibe."

"The woman who was looking for her husband. Do you remember what she looked like?"

"Average height. Bright-blue eyes and flame-red hair. I remember thinking how funny it was her hair matched the hot little Lexus sports car she rolled up in."

"Did you tell her that you saw her husband?"

"Well, I didn't want to lie."

"Did you tell her that you saw him with Bryce?"

"I didn't have to. Once I said her husband had been here, she already knew he was with Bryce."

I handed him my card. "Call me if you think of anything else," I said.

"Personal or professional?"

"Let's keep it professional." I smiled. "My girlfriend exhibits dangerous behavior when she's jealous."

33

I STOOD OVER THE golf ball on my office floor trying to imagine a straight line from the face of my putter to the makeshift hole seven feet away. I lifted the edge of the carpet a little so that it would give the path some slope and a greater degree of difficulty to the putt. I had just figured out the line I wanted the ball to follow to the hole when my cell rang. I didn't recognize the number.

"Ashe Cayne," I said in a slightly irritated tone.

"Delroy Thomas," the caller said. "Am I interrupting something?"

"An eight-foot putt with a little right-to-left break at the hole."

"What the hell you talkin' about, man?"

"Never mind," I said. "How can I help you?"

"It's more like how I can help you," he said.

"I'm listening."

"I was with one of my constituents at church yesterday, and since everybody knows you tryna find justice for Griff and his family, she wanted to share something with me that might or might not help with your investigation."

"Why come to you and not your nephew? Isn't he the alderman now?"

"I gave him the office and title," Thomas said. "But this is still my ward, and these are my people, and I can barely get any rest, cuz they still come to me all hours of the day and night with all their problems to solve."

"Uneasy lies the head that wears a crown," I said.

"You make up all this shit yoself?"

"If I could only be so eloquent. That shit, as you call it, was the work of Shakespeare in *Henry IV, Part Two*."

"Well, I don't know nothing about Henry the Fourth and what the fuck his deal was, but I should be wearing a crown, all the shit I been through trying to help my people."

"Self-praise is half scandal."

"That Shakespeare too?"

"No, something my grandmother used to say a lot to my father."

"Well, at least you get it honestly. Anyway, I'm calling because of my constituent. Her name is Luella Wright. She works as a secretary in the CPS administrative offices over on Madison. She can tell you about the OIG investigation they was doing on Griff."

"You have a number where I can reach her?"

"She can't take personal calls at work. Plus, she don't wanna talk about this at the office. She said she'll call you on her way home."

"I appreciate the help, Delroy."

"Anything for Griff. And next time we talk, I'm gonna have something to quote too. You ain't the only muthafuckah can read some Shakespeare."

I smiled at the thought of him grinding his way through *Othello*. I dialed Viola Griffin, who happened to be downtown running errands. She agreed to stop by my office before she went back home. That meant I had about thirty minutes to see if I could get my putting percentage up to about 40 percent, a respectable number considering the pros made 50 percent of their putts from eight feet and 20 percent from sixteen feet. I was consistently knocking in about 30 percent when Mercedes texted me about grabbing drinks once she got off work. I had never heard of the bar, but I agreed to meet her.

Viola Griffin knocked on my door just as I had missed the last putt that would've notched the 40 percent mark. She wore a powder-blue summer dress and a double strand of pearls that made her appear even more regal. She took a seat across from my desk.

"Walter used to do the same thing for hours on end in our basement," she said, nodding toward my makeshift green and putter. "He said it relaxed him. But I could never understand that, because all I ever heard coming from down there was a bunch of screaming and cursing."

"Golf is like that," I said. "It can be the most frustrating and satisfying game at the same time."

"You would've liked playing with Walter. He was the kind of man that other men enjoyed."

"So I gather," I said. "Speaking of which, have you ever heard of the name Bryce Horner?"

Viola shook her head softly.

"He never mentioned him to you?"

"No. The only Horner I know was my English literature professor in college. Derek Horner. He helped me fall in love with literature."

"I know you've gone over that afternoon and evening a thousand times, but I want to take you back for a moment, if you don't mind."

"Okay."

"Take me through your last conversation again."

"He was just leaving the golf course. He told me about the match."

"What did he say about the match?"

"That he had played well. He and Clarence had won thirty dollars apiece. They were happy because they had lost the last two matches. He said his right hip was bothering him, and I told him he needed to get it checked out or stop playing so much. He then said he was going to see his mother. He was going to stop by Lem's and bring some food to the nursing home staff like he always did."

I put up my hand to stop her as I looked down at my notes.

"Did he say he had anything to eat at the golf course?"

"They wanted him to stay and have drinks and lunch, but he told them he wanted to get going. He told me he wasn't really in the mood."

"What was bothering him?"

"The OIG thing. He couldn't stop thinking about it. After all he had done for so many, he felt betrayed. No one was standing up for him."

"I know we went over this before, but bear with me. What else did he say?"

"He was going to stop by Capital Grille on the way home. He liked the citrus-glazed salmon they have there. I always got the lobster. He told me he loved me, and he hung up."

"Is there anything else you remember? Even the smallest of things that seemed out of the ordinary or caught your attention."

"I'm sorry, but I just don't remember anything else."

"I understand. Did your husband have any medical problems?"

"Not really. He had that sore hip. He had a little high blood pressure, but he didn't need any medications for it."

"What about blood-clotting disorders?"

"Never."

"Are you certain?"

"Very. Did someone say he did?"

"Not at all," I said, thinking of my conversation with Dr. Ellison. "Just checking off all the boxes. Do you remember what they reported to you when they found your husband's body?"

"I was very distraught," she said. "To be honest, my memory is a little fuzzy. They told me his car had been found near Wolf Point, across from the Mart. They said he was alone. He had a gunshot wound to his head, and he was partially submerged in the river."

"Did they mention anything about trying to perform CPR?"

"They said he had been dead for a while, so there was no attempt at CPR."

"Are you certain?"

"That detail I'm certain of," she said. "I asked the officer who called me if they tried to save him, and he said that unfortunately it was too late. He was already dead by the time they got there."

———

LUELLA WRIGHT CALLED about an hour after Viola Griffin left. She felt uncomfortable talking on the phone, so we agreed to meet in person at Shawn Michelle's Homemade Ice Cream shop on the corner of Forty-Seventh and South Wabash, an entire planet away from the business of downtown. A steady stream of customers lined up in front of the freezer full of every floor combination imaginable. I had chosen the peach cobbler ice cream. Luella had two scoops of the banana pudding ice cream, a flavor I had seen only on the South Side.

"Delroy said you knew something that might help," I said after we had gotten comfortable.

"I can't afford to get my name caught up in anything," she said.

"I will never mention your name."

"Mr. Griffin was a good man," she said. "He was so sweet. All the girls in the office loved when he came in."

"Did he come in often?"

"He used to when Mr. Buchanan was the CEO, but then he left or got fired, and Mr. Milton took over. Mr. Griffin stopped coming around as much as he used to."

"I've heard they didn't get along."

"That's the biggest understatement of the year," she said, rolling her eyes. "They hated each other. Well, it was more on the side of Mr. Milton. He really didn't like Mr. Griffin."

"Do you know why?"

"There was always talk."

"Like?"

"Mr. Griffin didn't really want him to get the job. He felt like the CEO of CPS should be someone who was born and raised in Chicago and a product of CPS. Someone who understands the system from the inside."

"Sounds like you agreed."

"We all did, but we don't get a vote. They chose Mr. Milton because of the politics. He had the support of the mayor, so once that happened, it didn't matter what anyone else thought. There was also talk about Milton doing some favors for Bailey. But I don't know the specifics. You hear lots of rumors. What I liked about Mr. Griffin was how he spoke his mind. He wasn't afraid of them with all their big titles. He had his principles, and he stood up for them."

"Others have said the same thing."

"Mr. Griffin was a straight shooter, God rest his soul. Some people didn't like that. But I had the utmost respect for him. He never forgot where he came from, and he was the same way with everyone. He didn't change who he was to fit in. That's why they did that investigation."

"The OIG?"

"Yes. I was in the office that day when Dent came over for a meeting."

"Pete Dent, the IG?"

"That nasty little man," she said. "Always with a scowl on his face and marching around like a little dictator."

"You're not a big fan."

"I had a run-in with him a few years back, and we ain't been right since. I told him that he can bark at the girls in his office any way he wants to, but I don't work for him, and he's not gonna talk to me any old kinda way. I got grown kids of my own. I ain't his child. Straightened him right up. He hasn't had much to say to me since."

"What happened that day he came to the office?"

"I remember like it was yesterday. Mr. Milton keeps a very tight schedule. He's particular about his calendar. He likes all meetings and conference calls and anything else he has to do to be clearly spelled out in his calendar. He doesn't like last-minute situations."

"Sounds a little anal retentive," I said.

Luella frowned.

"Someone who's obsessed with details."

"Yes, he's that for sure. So, Mr. Dent's assistant called that day and said that he was on his way to meet with Mr. Milton. I told her that she must be confused. We didn't have any meeting on the calendar for Mr. Dent. She insisted that Mr. Milton had personally called Mr. Dent and scheduled the meeting. That was strange because I schedule all of his meetings. Anyway, Mr. Dent's secretary said Mr. Dent would be arriving in fifteen minutes. I told Mr. Milton that Mr. Dent was on his way. We assumed he was gonna have a heart attack. But he didn't. He was very calm, like he expected it. He said to show him in the second he arrives. Mr. Dent arrives, and we take him back right away. I went to get some water and coffee to take in, because Mr. Milton always likes to make sure his guests have something to drink. That's when I caught a piece of the conversation. They were going back and forth. I heard Mr. Milton say this would be a personal favor and that he didn't want Shulman at CPS to handle it."

"How did Dent respond?"

"Said he wasn't sure it was his jurisdiction, and Mr. Milton said he would see to it that Shulman's office was kept out of the loop." Luella shrugged. "That's all I heard. I left the office and closed the door behind me."

"How much longer did Dent stay in their meeting?"

"Another five minutes; then he left."

"Did Dent ever come back for more meetings?"

"Not that I know of."

"Did Milton ever mention the OIG investigation again?"

"After that meeting with Mr. Dent, none of us ever heard him say a word."

34

THE FOURTH OF JULY WEEKEND IN Chicago was always the busiest weekend of the year for CPD. Illegal fireworks lit up the night sky, and gun violence spiked at its predictable yearly high. Carolina and I had settled in to watch the pyrotechnics from my apartment balcony, sipping martinis and snacking on a robust cheese plate.

"You have that look on your face," Carolina said.

"What look?"

"Like you're here, but your mind is a million miles away."

"I can't stop thinking about Sophia," I said. "She's at the center of it all."

"You decided not to tell Griffin's wife about Sophia?"

"It didn't make sense to do it. What would I gain? What would she gain?"

"I bet she already knew."

"About Sophia or the baby or both?"

"Sophia."

"Probably, but Junior claims he doesn't know if she knew."

"You don't believe him."

"Nope. I think he's saying that to save her embarrassment."

"It's not an embarrassment when your spouse cheats on you and you remain strong and confident enough to find a way to make it work. Sometimes even difficult love is better than having none at all."

"'Tis better to have loved and lost than never to have loved at all."

"Shakespeare again?"

"No, the British poet Tennyson."

We sat there quietly as a gentle wind blew off the lake and the boats slowly slid by each other. The first firework off the pier exploded into the sky. Our view couldn't have been more perfect.

"I went on a date last week," she said.

I pretended like what she said hadn't stung. But it did. She had every right to be on a date, since we were just friends. "Hopefully not the pompous ass with the fifty-car collection," I said.

"Disgusting," she said. "I would never go out with him again. And he only had something like twenty cars."

"Most people lose count after ten."

"I like this new guy," she said.

I pretended to be unfazed by her revelation, though my heart dropped about a foot in my chest. I could feel her measuring my reaction.

"What does he do?"

"He's a surgeon."

"What kind?"

"He replaces joints in old people."

"Orthopedic. How did you meet?"

"One of my girlfriends is dating his neighbor."

"Be careful."

"Why?"

"I thought my father was bad," I said. "He's junior league compared to surgeons."

"In what way?"

"They rarely have a low opinion of themselves."

"Herbert doesn't seem that type."

"Herbert?"

"You know him?"

"No, I just can't imagine someone in the last century being cruel enough to name their child Herbert. Please don't tell me his friends call him Herbie."

"In fact, they do. And I find that cute."

"Maybe you should call him Herbie Berbie. Has a ring to it."

"Now you're being facetious."

"So much for romance."

The conversation trailed off again while the fireworks and their brilliant colors painted the sky. When the sky was really bright, we could see the thousands of people crammed onto Navy Pier, taking in the show.

"What are you thinking about?" Carolina asked.

"That I should come clean too."

"About what?"

I wanted to tell her that Julia had written me, but I wasn't even sure how I really felt about her letter or what I wanted to happen next. Carolina would ask me questions, but I simply didn't have the answers. There was no question, however, that she did have a right to know about Mercedes.

"I've been seeing someone too," I said.

Carolina's eyes widened as she leaned back. "Didn't see that coming," she said.

"Trust me, it's no big deal," I said. "Just having fun. Nothing remotely serious."

"You wanna tell me about her?"

"Not really. You wanna know?"

"Not really."

"Then let's talk about something different."

"Good idea."

I pointed toward the lake. "I'm looking at those expensive yachts down there, and I can't help but imagine Sophia being on one of them with one of her yearly-salary bags, sipping champagne, while Walter Griffin is buried under some dirt about ten miles away in various states of decomposition."

"Do you really think you'll ever find out what happened?"

"For sure."

"Do you think she knows more than she's telling?"

"For sure."

"Do you feel like you're close?"

"It's all within the grasp of my hands."

"So, what will you do next?"

"Keep squeezing until something pops."

———

I COULDN'T STOP THINKING there was something more Sophia was hiding. Two of the people who knew her best were dead, and Amy Donnegan was holding her cards tightly, so I decided to circle back to Cephus Redmond to see if maybe he knew anything about Sophia and Griffin and the mysterious baby. Mechanic and I stopped by Redmond's car wash on State Street. They told us he was never in at that time on a Saturday. His weekly poker game was already underway in the back of Almuflihi Food & Liquor, so we headed deeper into the hood.

"There's probably a lot of metal over there," I said to Mechanic, who had his eyes half-closed, sitting in the passenger seat. He lifted up the hem of his shirt and flashed Silver Betty, as he liked to call her—a Smith & Wesson .500 Magnum with an eight-inch barrel, the most powerful commercially available handgun in the world. I knew on his other hip he had Black Betty, a custom-made Bowen Ruger Blackhawk with a wood-handle grip and black six-inch barrel. She shot .500 Linebaugh Maximum cartridges traveling more than a thousand feet per second and was capable of knocking down a twelve-hundred-pound brown bear a mile away. He enjoyed sharing the tiniest of details when describing his potency.

Almuflihi Food & Liquor sat by itself on a deserted block in a crumbling white-brick building on the edge of Englewood, one of the city's toughest neighborhoods and an area that had become the enduring symbol of Chicago's gang violence. The front windows had been entirely covered by discount paper advertisements faded badly in the sun, offering everything from toilet paper to imported whiskey. Several cars sat in the store's back lot. I parked in front, so they knew we were coming. Surprising people in this neighborhood dramatically increased one's chances of being welcomed by a stream of hot lead.

Mechanic walked closely behind me. I quickly spotted three cameras along the roofline of the building. We stepped in through the rickety doors, and it felt like we had gone back in time fifty years. Merchandise was crammed on shelves in no particular order. Three ceiling fans knocked and wobbled as they moved around the hot, musty air. A small counter and cash register stood just to the right of the entrance, with several live monitors behind it flashing video of various sections of the store. A short man about as wide as the counter and with a mustache heavy enough to build a nest in leaned toward us.

"Help you?" he said, sizing up Mechanic. It had probably been years since a white person had stepped foot in the store, and that would've been a cop or someone from the water department looking to change the city meters.

"Looking for Cephus," I said.

"He know you looking for him?"

"You know if the Royals really like Meghan Markle?"

"Royals?"

"Queen Elizabeth and clan."

"Oh, the British and that Black girl they made a princess."

"That would be the one. The Duchess of Sussex."

"I thought she was married to the prince."

"She is. She's both a duchess and a princess. Duchess is her working title. Higher rank."

"Didn't they run her and the prince out of Britain?"

"They left on their own accord, but clearly she wasn't being treated well over there."

He shook his head. "Black people got it hard anywhere they go. Married into the goddamn royal family and still got it tough."

I couldn't disagree. "Back to Cephus," I said. "We need to talk to him."

The man looked by me and studied Mechanic. He reached under the counter and picked up a phone and told whoever answered that two guys were looking for Cephus. Next I heard him say, "One of us and one of them."

He hung up the phone and nodded toward the back of the store. A man the size of a garbage truck and the color of hot engine oil stood there staring at us. We walked through one of the narrow aisles to reach him. He didn't say anything once we got there. Instead, he jerked his bald head for us to follow him, which we did through a small door and down a dark narrow hallway that he had to turn sideways to fit in. We reached another door, and he said, "Stay right here." When he opened the door, I could see a small dark room with a circular table in the middle and a light hovering above it. Several men sat around stacks of money and cards. It was difficult to make out their faces behind the heavy clouds of smoke.

A couple of minutes later the door opened, and Cephus Redmond stood before us with a wide smile parting his meaty face, a half-smoked cigar jammed into the corner of his mouth. He was dressed in a completely lavender linen suit, including a Kangol cap to match. A thick braided gold chain glistened against his wet skin.

"How can I help you boys?" Cephus asked.

"Dressed for the derby?" I asked.

"I don't bet horses," Cephus said. "I'm a cards and dice man."

"By the looks of all that money on the table, you're pretty damn serious about it too."

"What is it you want to talk about?" Cephus said, not bothering to hide his irritation. He looked at Mechanic. "And who's this?"

"My driver."

"Fuck outa here," Cephus said. "You talk a lotta shit. What's so urgent you come trackin' me down?"

"Just trying to tie some things together," I said.

"Already told you what I know," he said. "Not much more I can give you."

"You can give me Sophia Caballé," I said.

Cephus looked at Mechanic, then at me. He rotated the cigar from one corner of his mouth to the other.

"I respect what you're trying to do," Cephus said. "But why you need to poke around in a dead man's business like this?"

"I'm just trying to get to the truth."

"Sometimes the truth is better when it's left alone. People need to heal and move on with their lives. Can't nuthin' and nobody bring Walt back."

"The family wants answers. They deserve them."

"They don't need these kinds of answers. Some things are better left unknown."

"They're adults. How about we let them decide what they can and can't handle?"

Cephus shrugged and rolled the cigar around his mouth a little more. "What you wanna know?" he said.

"Who bought her the apartment?"

"I did. I bought the apartment for Walt for her."

"Sounds like a game of three-card Molly."

"You always got somethin' smart-ass to say."

"Reflex."

"Well, cut the shit, cuz I ain't got no time for it. I got a hundred thousand dollars on the table in there, and you out here tryna be the next Chris Rock."

I shrugged. Point made. Point taken. "A two-million-dollar apartment is a lot of cash to spend on a side chick," I said.

"I don't get involved in another man's business."

"Did Walter pay for it all?"

"I helped a little till he could come up with the rest."

"Did he know she was pregnant?"

"Who said she was pregnant?"

"Just a hunch."

"Maybe you should be sure before you start sayin' shit like that."

"Whose baby was it?"

"Mine."

I thought back to what Mercedes had said to me about how Sophia liked them. "Kinda old. Really rich." Just not in that order.

35

I WASN'T SURE IF the ringing was in my dream or real life. It stopped, but then it started again. I sat up. Stryker lifted his head quizzically from the foot of the bed. I reached over to the nightstand and picked up my cell phone. It was my father.

"Have you had breakfast already?" he asked.

"It's just seven o'clock," I said. "I haven't even gotten out of bed."

"I just landed from London," he said. "I want to see you."

"Are you okay?"

"Couldn't be better. Come to my house for breakfast. Nine o'clock. I'll have Pearline fix you french toast with glazed peaches."

He was gone before I could even answer.

———

MY FATHER AND I sat in his spacious sunroom on the second floor of his five-story town house. Many years ago he had purchased the town houses on both sides of him, then tore them down to give himself what he called "breathing room." Now there were two large grassy lots on either side of his house, and the open space gave this room direct sunlight through a wall of windows facing east. It was his favorite place to sit after breakfast.

Pearline, as usual, had outdone herself, cooking the perfect meal. I had put away two servings before my father finished his first. We now sat in soft leather chairs facing the climbing sun.

"There's something I need to tell you," he said. He had on a silk robe and slippers he had purchased on the last trip to Cairo he and my mother had taken.

I knew he had invited me over for more than just breakfast. I also knew he would wait until we got through the meal before he brought it up. He never liked having stressful conversations over a meal. He always claimed it was terrible for digestion.

"Is what you're about to say going to surprise me?" I asked.

"Most likely," he answered.

"In a good or bad way?"

"I can't be the judge of that."

"I'm ready."

"I had some extra time while I was in Paris," he said. "We played two matches at Roland-Garros, then had a chance to tool around the city for a couple of days before going to London."

"Okay."

"And during those couple of days, I had lunch with Julia."

"Excuse me?"

"Julia and I had lunch together the day before I left for London."

I was definitely surprised.

"How did this happen?" I asked.

"I told her I was going to be in Paris for a few days."

"But how did you know where to find her?"

He took a moment, then said, "We've been in touch. She's reached out to me several times, and vice versa."

Not only was I surprised, but now I was angry.

"What the hell is going on?" I asked. "You and Julia have been in touch for who knows how long, talking about who knows what, and this is the first I'm hearing of it? Jesus fuckin' Christ, Dad!"

"This is why I never brought it up."

"Why?"

"Because of the way you're reacting right now."

"How do you want me to react? Sing a Mary Poppins song and dance around the room? Of course I'm acting this way. Anyone in their right mind would feel the way I feel right now. My own father is talking to my ex two years after we've broken up, and I haven't spoken to her once."

"I know you find it hard to believe, but I'm very fond of Julia independently of your relationship with her."

"I don't have a relationship with her, remember? She ran away with that fuckin' stockbroker who went to Yale and has four god-damn names. Who the hell has that many names?"

My father sat there, calmly staring at me like he did when he was trying to be disarming. I'd been on the opposite end of this exact stare a thousand times, and it still drove me crazy that he would treat me like one of his patients.

"It's not gonna work this time," I said, "so you can cut the shit. You've been talking to the only person in the world who has ever broken—no, crushed—my heart, and you're sitting there staring at me like I'm some fuckin' lunatic and you have the answers to make things all right. Not going for it."

"Is the language necessary, Ashe?" he said calmly. "This is still my house."

"And I don't need to be in it," I said, standing. "I have my own."

"She still loves you," he said.

"So she said." I laughed. "She has a strange way of showing it."

"That stockbroker was just a diversion. It was not about him. It was about her needing an excuse to escape."

"I'm not gonna let you pull me into one of your sessions," I said. "Not today. You carrying on with Julia was dishonest and a betrayal. Period. End of story. No justification whatsoever."

"We weren't carrying on," he said. "We were communicating."

"Whatever you want to call it, I don't appreciate it."

"She's lonely," he said.

"She wouldn't've been had she not left me."

"She was even lonelier in your relationship. She felt overshadowed. Insecure. Not up to your standards. Her words, not mine."

I almost told him about the letter she had sent, but I didn't want to allow a conversation about what she had written to deflect my anger away from him. I wanted him to feel every scorching ounce of my fury. "I'm done," I said, turning to leave. "Thanks for breakfast."

When I reached the door, he said, "She's a sweet girl, Ashe. She never intended to hurt you. She wants to try again."

Those words chased me down the stairs and outside. It wasn't until I was inside the stillness of my car that I realized I was hyperventilating.

———

THE NEXT THREE DAYS I escaped to the solitude of southwest Michigan, where Penny Packer had a ten-acre compound spread on the pristine beach of Lake Michigan. She and her family were overseas at their other summer estate in the English countryside, but she had given me a standing invitation to use their Michigan residence whenever I wanted. The Packers had been to the compound only once that summer, but of course it was fully staffed and operational even in their absence. I had my own three-bedroom cottage on the northern part of the property, with a full, unobstructed view of the lake from every room, including the two bathrooms. When the sky was clear and the lighting just right, I could make out some of the Chicago skyline during sunset.

I had been to this part of Michigan before, the summer getaway for Chicago's elite families. At the time I had been working on a case for the Gerrigan real estate family, whose daughter had mysteriously gone missing. Only a one-hour-and-fifteen-minute drive from downtown Chicago, this side of Lake Michigan was not only sparsely populated but absent all the urban intrusions of honking horns, police sirens, and screaming ambulances. Entire families rode their bikes along deserted streets, and deer hopped and galloped freely across the wooded roads before disappearing into large tracts of forested land. The area's slogan was "Pure Michigan," and it fit it perfectly, as this was a place of serenity where you could breathe easily and escape the squeeze of city life. So, that was exactly what I did for three days. I didn't answer my phone but once to text Carolina to let her know that I was out of town catching some me time and would be back in a couple of days.

Everything I needed was available, including a fully stocked refrigerator and an attentive staff that cooked whatever I wanted around the clock and delivered it to my door before quietly retreating back to the main house. I left the cottage only to walk the private beach, where I watched the few sailboats glide by. The water was too cold to swim in, but I enjoyed feeling it run over my bare feet.

I had plenty of time to think about how I was going to handle Antoine Nelson, who'd served two years in prison and had now upgraded his life to that of a low-level dealer. Pink Lady had become all the rage with the young urban set because it was not only stronger than its more famous cousin OxyContin, but, for a faster and fuller high, addicts would crush and dissolve it and convert it to an inject-able form. The FDA had banned it a few years ago due to its link to an HIV outbreak in southeastern Indiana as well as cases of hepatitis C in other parts of the country. I would call Brittany Farrington soon and make arrangements to apprehend Nelson as quietly as possible.

I also took the time to think about Julia and her letter and what my father had said. Then I thought about Carolina and this surgeon she had begun dating. Then I thought about Mercedes. I missed her youthful energy. I finally admitted to myself that I still loved Julia and wanted to be with her again. But how could I ever trust someone who might just run away when things weren't working? I was tortured by thoughts of her being out there with someone else, debating art in a museum, singing old Prince songs on the radio, and watching tear-jerkers on Netflix or Amazon Prime. While so many people understood a part of me, she had gotten all of me. She under-stood the complicated layers of my relationship with my father and, most importantly, knew how to listen when that was what I needed. Could I ever find that again? And if I did, would I ever allow myself to be so vulnerable?

Carolina might be the one, and maybe my love for Julia just blinded me to the greatness of her potential. I wanted Carolina, but I was afraid I wasn't ready, incapable of giving her what she deserved. I'd been keeping her in the safe zone, but that also meant risking losing her. She wasn't going to wait for me forever.

While these thoughts and emotions raged in my head and heart, the meditative sound of the waves crashing onto shore gave me a sense of calm and the space in my mind to sort things out. I hadn't thought once about Walter Griffin and Sophia and Cephus

Redmond. But that all came to an end as I loaded up my car to head back to Chicago and my phone buzzed in my pocket.

"This is Gabby from Dryhop," the caller said. "You gave me your phone number. I hope I'm not catching you at a bad time."

I could tell by the ambient sounds that he was outside.

"I'm just jumping into the car," I said. "What's going on?"

"Other than the fact that Connor and Magnus call here every day asking whether or not you've been back?"

"Yes, other than that." I laughed. It felt good to laugh again.

"You told me to call you if I remembered anything. Well, I saw the man who was here with Bryce that day."

"He came back to the restaurant?"

"No, I saw him on TV."

"TV?"

"Well, I never really watch TV; almost no one does because everything's on the phone. Anyway, I turned it on last night to watch my friend who was being interviewed on the news about a floral shop he opened over in Roscoe Village. We dated years ago, but then he decided he wanted to be straight again and—anyway, that's another story for another time. So, I'm sitting there waiting for my friend's story to come on when I saw the man you were asking about. I didn't know he was such a big shot."

"What do you mean?"

"He's the head of the public school system. He looked very handsome standing there next to the mayor."

"Andrew Milton, the CEO of CPS?"

"That's him. They were making some announcement about closing more of the bad schools and sending the kids to the schools that had better test scores. It's all a racket, if you ask me. I think they're up to no good. But he was standing there next to the mayor. His hair had grown a little longer, but I recognized him right away."

"And you're sure it was Andrew Milton you saw with Bryce that day?"

"Not a doubt in my mind. I might forget a name. But I never forget a pretty face."

36

I WOKE UP IN the middle of the night and sat up in bed. I couldn't get Bryce Horner out of my mind. Stryker lifted his head from the foot of the bed, rolled over, and went back to sleep. I threw the covers off and walked down the hall to my office. I picked up the police report about Horner's death and sat in my recliner. Something about the timing of the drowning kept gnawing at me. I read the report three times, then booted my computer. Horner's next of kin was his sister, Kemberly Guyton. She lived in Los Angeles. I logged in to Facebook and got a hit immediately. Kemberly Guyton operated an interior decorating business called Kemberly by Design on Melrose Place. I sent her an instant message, and within seconds she responded.

Who is this?

My name is Ashe Cayne. I'm a private investigator looking into the death of a man in Chicago named Walter Griffin.

I don't know how I can help you.

Your brother knew him and died only two weeks after Griffin allegedly killed himself.

Allegedly?

I have a different theory. Can you talk?

I'm in Honduras right now sourcing fabrics. I will be home in a couple of days. Can it wait till then?

Sure. Please call when you can.

I gave her my phone number and email address, then turned off the lights and looked out the window toward the lake. The Ferris wheel's lights had been turned off, too, except for a vertical strip of red lights between the upright spokes. It looked so alone standing there in the darkness. I wondered how lonely Bryce Horner had felt going into that water just yards away. Had he known it would be the last swim of his life?

———

BURKE AND I SAT in the back of Stan's Donuts on Roosevelt Road while his driver stayed in the car parked at the bus stop. Burke was halfway through a cinnamon roll big enough to feed a family of four. I was taking my time with a double-chocolate old fashioned. The L trains rumbled above us every few minutes.

"You really think Griffin's and Horner's murders are related?" Burke asked, dipping a handful of the roll in his coffee.

"Seems odd, I know, but they share too much to be just a coincidence."

"How are you tying them together?"

"First, the timing. Griffin dies of an apparent suicide; then, just two weeks later, Horner washes up on North Avenue Beach."

"Victim relatedness?"

"Relatedness? You've been brushing up on your SAT prep."

"Lonely remnants of a Catholic high school education."

"Horner is best friends with Sophia Caballé, who is the mistress of Walter Griffin *and* Cephus Redmond. Horner knows that

Caballé is pregnant with Redmond's baby. Or maybe he thought it was Griffin's. It depends on whether Caballé tells him the truth."

"Do you think Griffin thought it was his baby?"

"I do. I think the half a million dollars in cash he borrowed from Cephus was for Caballé. And don't forget her million-dollar apartment Griffin bought with the help of Cephus."

"Jesus Christ, that's some expensive fucking."

"The last time I saw her she had a fifty-thousand-dollar crocodile handbag sitting next to her."

"Who the hell spends that kind of money for a handbag?"

"The crocodile was Himalayan."

"I wouldn't care if the damn thing had swallowed a Brinks truck. A waste of fuckin' money. Anyway, what are you figuring for motivation?"

"That's my problem. There's a lot of it to spread around."

"For example."

"Caballé. She has Griffin believing she's carrying his child, and he gives her half a million dollars. Then she puts the baby up for adoption. Griffin later discovers the ultimate betrayal when he learns the baby is actually Redmond's."

"Kind of thin, but possible."

"Bailey. Griffin knows where all the bodies are buried. He's been in the room when all the shit's gone down. Bailey is worried Griffin will cooperate with the FBI on the Cabrini land investigation. Bailey also is pissed because Griffin crosses him with the whole Andrew Milton appointment. Milton gets the CEO job, but Griffin takes a stand against it, maybe for reasons we still don't know. Griffin might know where the smoking gun is that leads to Bailey."

"Well, there's no denying the man knew a lot of secrets," Burke said. "His death had to make some people sleep better for sure."

"There's also the Russians."

"I thought you ruled them out?"

"Not altogether. He screwed them over money—a lot of money—by selling them that land that was worthless after the Olympics didn't come through. We both know how long their memory is when it comes to this shit."

"They're very dangerous and very connected," Burke said. "Be very careful."

We sat, trying to digest everything.

"What do you think happened to all the money he earned from selling that land?" Burke asked.

"Not sure, but obviously he ran through it if he needed a loan from Cephus."

"Have you heard from my friend's daughter yet?"

"Nothing. I really hope I can talk to her about the Cabrini angle."

"Don't worry. Alicia will call you. If she's anything like the old man, you can bet your bottom dollar on her."

———

I SPENT THE BETTER part of two hours sitting in my office with the lights out, looking at the lake and not making much progress in my thinking. So, I did what I liked to do when I needed to clear my head: I headed to the Jackson Park driving range. I had finished my first bucket of balls and was working my way through a second when my phone rang. It was Dr. Ellison.

"I hope I'm not catching you at a bad time," he said.

"Just trying to fix my slice," I said.

"Took me the good part of twenty years to fix mine."

"What's the last tip you have?"

"Make sure you take the club back on the inside, and make sure your body moves first on the downswing and not your hands."

"I like that."

"Well, I don't want to take up much of your time," he said. "But there's been something on my mind, and I can't shake it. I want to make sure I understand the findings with his hands."

"What do you mean?"

"I want to revisit their positioning."

"I don't have the report in front of me right now, but when I get back to the office, I can take a look at it. What's bothering you?"

"Well, here in the ME report, they wrote that the skin on his left hand was shriveled due to extended exposure to the cold water. But the right hand did not have the same appearance, nor did it have any abrasions. It had an old scar that had healed in the space between his thumb and index finger and a gold Rolex on his wrist. Then it mentions the gunshot residue found on the right hand."

"That makes sense, because the right hand was not in the water," I said.

"What was his dominant hand?"

"Left hand for sure. Very dominant. Writing, eating, golfing— all left handed."

"Doesn't make sense. He's a lefty, yet the residue is found on his right hand according to this postmortem. And he was shot in the left side of the head. Do you remember if the on-scene report showed the same thing about the residue?"

"Not off the top of my head. I need to go and take a look at it. Anything else I should be looking for?"

"That's it for now. Also, I'm trying to get a contact number for Fred Skinner. No one has seen or talked to him in a while, but I have a contact who's working on it."

"I'll call you when I get back to my office."

I finished the last bucket of balls and was satisfied that only one out of ten balls actually moved to the right. I could live with this percentage and save at least a couple of strokes a round. Mercedes texted me to see if I was available for dinner. Mechanic called to say he'd meet me in the office. My father sent a text asking if I was all right. I was still giving him the silent treatment, because I knew how much it frustrated him having to guess my thoughts and feelings.

When I got back to the office, the first thing I did was look at the supplementary report. Within minutes, I found the section that Dr. Ellison had asked me to check. Griffin's left hand had been submerged in water, but his right hand had not. They did a GSR test at the crime scene and found gunshot residue between his thumb and index finger and the index and middle finger of his right hand. I looked at it again to make sure I was reading it correctly. The autopsy report matched the crime scene report, but it still didn't make sense, considering Griffin was left handed. The entrance wound and the muzzle imprint from the gun had indeed been against the left side of his head. I dialed Ellison.

"You're right," I said. "This isn't making any sense. I have the investigative report in front of me, and it matches the autopsy. Residue found on the right hand, not the left."

"Are you certain?"

"Hundred percent. It's very clear here in the report."

"Not good," he said. "No way a dominant left-hander can shoot himself on the left side of his head with his right hand, unless he held his arm up, twisted it around over his head, and did it that way.

Let's say for the sake of argument that he did do it that way. It still wouldn't match the report. The trajectory of the bullet would be downward, not upward. The exit wound is higher than the entrance. The bullet went up, not down."

"You said Skinner was one of the best," I said.

"Not just one of the best, but of all time," Ellison said.

"So, how could he make a mistake like this?"

"Impossible. He didn't make a mistake at all."

"Then what do you think happened?"

"Either someone changed his report, he didn't do the exam, or the crime scene information is wrong. But only he can answer these questions. Someone tracked down his contact number up in Wisconsin." He repeated the number for me. "Give him a call. I'm sure he still has all of his files."

I called Skinner's number, but there wasn't an answer. I waited and called him back thirty minutes later, and there still wasn't an answer, and his voice mail hadn't been set up. I got the feeling that Skinner didn't want to be bothered. I decided I would call him in a couple of hours. I picked up Bryce Horner's report that Burke had given me to see if something new stuck out. Bryce Horner's sister hadn't called me yet. Maybe she wasn't back from Honduras or she'd simply forgotten. I found the phone number to Kemberly by Design in Los Angeles and dialed it. A woman answered and told me that Kemberly was not in the office. I left my cell number and told her it was an urgent matter.

I was about to text Mercedes when my phone buzzed. I didn't recognize the number, but when I picked up, I recognized the voice.

"Is this Ashe Cayne?" she asked.

"This is a surprise, Sophia," I said. "Never expected a call from you."

"For once, it's me doing the surprising," she said. "Are you busy tonight?"

"Depends on who's asking."

"It's just the two of us on the phone."

"What did you have in mind?"

"Why don't we start with drinks."

"Start?"

"I never put limits on an evening prematurely."

If I hadn't known any better, I would've thought she was flirting with me.

"Where and when?" I asked.

"The Aviary at ten o'clock," she said.

"I have to tell you that I turn into a pumpkin at midnight."

"Then I'll make sure I bring a purse to match that color," she said.

Just as I got off the phone, Mechanic came through the door, carrying a pizza box. He placed it on my desk and opened the lid. Half the pizza was pepperoni; the other half was bacon. I turned the pepperoni in his direction and pulled out plates and napkins from my desk drawer. Mechanic grabbed a couple of sodas from the fridge.

"You sounded urgent on the phone," he said, grabbing a slice and folding it.

"You free the next couple of days?"

"Depends on what I'm free for."

"How about tracking Sophia Caballé again," I said.

"I can manage that. What's going on this time?"

"She asked me to meet her for drinks tonight. I think she's up to something. I want to see if she's doing this alone or with some help."

"Where are you meeting her?"

"Aviary on West Fulton Market."

"That's the place with all those drinks that look like science experiments and cost thirty dollars a pop."

"She called the meeting, so maybe she's treating."

"You're being delusional. The last time that girl had to pay for anything was a piece of bubble gum out of a quarter gum machine."

37

I HAD JUST WALKED INTO Arnie's Gym and gotten my bag sorted in the locker room when my cell phone rang. It was a Los Angeles number. Kemberly Guyton was on the other end.

"This has been very difficult," she said. "Bryce's death was so sudden. The officers explained to me what they could, but it never made any sense to me."

"There's a lot that's not making sense," I said. "But I'm trying my best to put the pieces together."

"How can I help you?"

"Were you close to your brother?"

"Very. Bryce and I talked almost every day—if not speaking, then by text. He was the best little brother you could ask for."

"Did he ever mention Walter Griffin?"

"The name sounds familiar, but I can't be sure."

"What about Andrew Milton?"

"Andy?"

"Who was Andy?"

"Someone he had been seeing for about a year. Bryce fell hard for him. But it was a very complicated and stressful situation."

"In what way?"

"He was married, no longer in love with his wife, and was trying to come to terms with his sexuality. But it was difficult for him. He felt trapped."

"Did Bryce mention what Andy did?"

"He said something about him being involved in education."

It had to be Milton.

"Involved is an understatement," I said. "Andy is not just a teacher or high school administrator. He's the CEO of the entire school system. Numero uno."

"Bryce never mentioned that, but that's Bryce. Titles and things like that never impressed him. He cared about who people were, not what they had."

"What did he say about their relationship?"

"Andy kept promising he was going to tell his wife, but the timing never seemed right. Bryce was being as patient as he could, but it was totally stressing him out. He went through days when he would literally be depressed and wouldn't eat. I told him he needed to go talk to someone. He finally set a deadline for Thanksgiving. If Andy didn't say something, he was going to leave him."

"What happened?"

"Nothing. Bryce died before Thanksgiving."

"Did you believe your brother drowned?"

"No offense to the police officers, but not for a second. Bryce wasn't just a good swimmer. He was on the varsity team in high school. The only reason he didn't swim in college is because his school didn't have a team. But even when he moved to Chicago, he swam several times a week, mostly in the lake. I just couldn't believe he drowned in the water he knew so well."

"Do you have any of his belongings?"

"Such as?"

"His phone, for starters. I saw on the report that they found a cell phone with his clothes."

"Yes, along with the watch my parents had given him as a college graduation present. They would've been devastated if they were still alive. Our father died about ten years ago, and Mom died a year before Bryce."

"Have you turned on his phone?"

"Not for some time. I did for a while after he died. Somehow it made me feel more connected to him, as if he hadn't died."

"Where is it now?"

"In a box upstairs with his watch and a few other things I saved from his apartment."

"Do you know the code to unlock it?"

"I do. We always shared the same PIN."

"I need you to open the phone and check his call log. I want to see who he talked to the last couple of weeks before he died."

"Give me a second."

I could hear her rest the phone on a hard surface. While she searched for Bryce's cell phone, I pulled out Griffin's call log. A few minutes later she was back.

"It's dead as a doornail," she said. "I can plug it in and give you a call when it has some charge. Fifteen minutes or so should be enough time."

I hung up the phone and dialed Carolina.

"Do you have a few minutes to talk?" I asked.

"Sure," she said. "I'm just finishing up something here, then going home. What's on your mind?"

"Bryce Horner."

"Has something happened?"

"I'm in touch with his sister, who lives out in LA. I have her charging up his phone so I can see who he talked to the last couple of weeks before he died."

"Are you still thinking his drowning wasn't an accident?"

"Absolutely. Too much of a coincidence and too convenient. When I get some of the phone numbers, I need you to do your magic and let me know who the numbers belong to."

"You know, I really should start charging you for this. I could build a nice little nest egg for my retirement."

"We could be partners. Cayne and Espinoza."

"Has a nice ring to it."

"I would even put your name on the door."

"Only if mine came first."

———

TWENTY MINUTES LATER, KEMBERLY called back.

"I have the phone partially charged and his call log open."

"Scroll through and tell me how far back the log goes," I said.

"I'm scrolling through now. There are hundreds of them."

"Okay. I want to focus on the last two weeks."

"There still are a lot. Probably a little over seventy-five."

"Okay. Let's focus on the last week, then. Write down, in order, all of those calls from oldest to newest, and email them to me."

"I have to join a conference call in about fifteen minutes. It shouldn't last more than an hour. Once I'm done, I'll send it to you."

———

A LINE OF FOREIGN cars, one more expensive than the next, filled the valet lane outside Aviary. Women in six-inch heels and body-con dresses carefully marched their way underneath the long gray awning jutting out from an otherwise nondescript brick building that looked more suited for business offices than the city's most expensive bar. I pulled up behind a convertible Rolls-Royce, flashed my shield, and told the valet to leave me up front.

The hostess stood every inch of six feet and had been positioned just inside the door. Her hair had been cut into an asymmetric bob that matched the angle of her one-shoulder dress.

A shorter girl with bright-blue eye shadow and a black skirt that left little to the imagination looked up as I approached.

"Welcome to Aviary," the shorter hostess said. "Reservation?"

The tall girl looked at me before I could answer and said, "Follow me."

We walked deeper into the dark room, where well-dressed patrons clustered around low tabletops and lounged back in leather banquettes. The furnishings were meant to be a statement. Shimmery and modern, they let you know that this was a cultivated experience and at this moment you were in the only place that mattered in all Chicago. I spotted Sophia sitting at a table near the center of the room. Had I not known it was her, I would've thought she was a piece of art. She wore a black-and-white-striped sleeveless dress, and her hair had been pulled back off her face. She stood when I approached. I reached my hand out, but she stepped in closer and kissed me on the cheek. She smelled of something foreign and expensive. A large dark-orange bag full of gold zippers and buckles occupied its own seat.

We sat down.

"You look very nice," she said. "You should dress like this more often."

"I didn't want to show up at a fancy place like this and embarrass you," I said. "Reputation in your business is everything."

"No business tonight," she said. "I don't want to talk about your case or your theories or anything like that. I just want to have a relaxing night. Can you agree to that?"

"I'll try my best."

Her bag vibrated. She opened it, picked up her phone, looked at it, then put it back.

"Snakes instead of crocodile," I said. "Very reptilian of you."

"Are you always so fascinated with women's bags?"

"I'm more fascinated that someone would spend the entire GDP of a third world country to carry makeup and a wallet."

"Women love bags, Ashe, as irrational as it might seem. It's a very easy way for men to score points. You should try it sometime with your girlfriend."

"I don't have a girlfriend."

"I don't believe you. You're too smart and too cute to be unclaimed."

I shrugged. "Maybe I need to brush up on my handbag shopping."

The waitress came over to take our drink order.

"Can I order for you?" Sophia said. "I know what you'd like."

No woman had ever asked to order my drink. There was something about how she said it that was familiar and sexy and authoritative all at the same time. I nodded.

She ordered the three-course cocktail progression, starting with the Jungle Bird as well as the lobster and salted cod. She waited for the waitress to leave, then said, "So, who really are you, Ashe Cayne?"

"An unapologetic golf addict," I said.

"You're much more than that," she said. "You're a jumble of contradictions. You stood up to CPD and walked away with several million dollars because you wouldn't let them walk all over your integrity. You were engaged to be married until your fiancée ran away to Paris. You're a pretty good boxer, and you could've been good enough to have a real shot at professional tennis. You quote Shakespeare and poetry and hang out with a Lithuanian thug who can shoot a bee half a mile away."

"He might have a problem with you calling him a thug," I said.

"What should I call him?"

"A former thug who has residual thug tendencies when the situation calls for it."

She smiled.

"How do you know so much about my fiancée?" I asked. Even after all this time, hearing someone else talk about Julia felt like a solid blow to my rib cage.

"You're not the only one who does his homework."

"Did you know my ex?"

"Never met her but heard of her. One of my friends knew her college roommate. She's very beautiful."

"That's a unanimous consensus." I smiled.

"So, what really drives you, Ashe?"

"Why the sudden interest in me?"

"Reciprocity. You seem interested in my life, so I thought it only fair to better understand you."

"I don't like it when people hurt other people," I said. "And I really don't like it when they think they can get away with it."

"That's incredibly old fashioned of you. Are you still upset about your fiancée hurting you?"

"Of course I am. If I wasn't, I wouldn't be human."

"You need to move on. Lots of other fish to be caught from the sea. When one wiggles off the line, you have a chance to catch something bigger and even better."

"Is relationship counseling part of your PR offerings?"

"In the world of PR we deal with different types of client needs."

"Was Walter Griffin a client?"

She put her slender finger up to her red lips. "We agreed not to talk business tonight," she said. "You can't work all the time."

"When I have a client that's hurting and looking for answers, I find it hard to do anything else."

She slid closer to me and put her hand casually on my leg. "Relax and try to have fun," she said.

For the next hour, the drinks kept coming. One called Passion in the Ice came in a Bunsen burner–like device reminiscent of the ones used in high school chemistry class. The waitress and server heated up the drink, causing a plume of smoke to fill the top of the enclosed glass. She deftly explained that this infused the alcohol with fruit. Once the smoke had settled, the drink was ready. I tried cutting the alcohol with the food Sophia had ordered, but the alcohol was strong and winning the battle, and my head was feeling it.

"So, what did you find out about dear Bryce?" she asked.

"Nothing yet," I lied.

"Have you found anyone that can answer questions about him?"

"Unfortunately, it's slow going."

"Well, what kind of private investigator are you?" She smiled, flashing every kilowatt she could muster and confirming why men gifted her apartments and animal skins.

"A very patient one," I said. Right on cue, my phone buzzed. I looked down at it. Kemberly had sent me the email.

"So, are you close to solving your case?" she asked.

"I thought you said no shoptalk."

"That's my last question. I promise." She made the sign of the cross over her chest.

"In cases like this, you're only as close as you are far away."

"What does that mean?"

"You never really know how close you are until you actually close the case."

"Couldn't you have just said it like that the first time?"

"The riddle makes me sound more intellectual."

"I find smart men attractive," she said, resting her hand higher on my thigh. It made my muscles twitch just a little. I was certain she felt it.

"And you find rich, smart men irresistible."

"No, I find them very attractive," she said. She slid closer to me, to the point that her chest pressed softly against my shoulder. She put her mouth to my ear and whispered, "The ones I find irresistible are rich, smart, *and* handsome."

38

I WAITED UNTIL I GOT home to open the email and print it out. Kemberly had carefully listed all the incoming and outgoing numbers from Bryce's cell phone in the week before he died, as well as their date and time stamp. Two numbers appeared much more than the others. I circled them. Then I focused on the last day he was alive. There were only three calls. One was early in the morning. It was an incoming call and was one of the numbers I had already circled. The second-to-last call came in about fifty minutes later from a blocked number. The third and last call was one he had placed just seconds after the blocked call.

I sat Griffin's call log next to Horner's. I immediately recognized that one of the numbers I had circled on Horner's sheet was also on Griffin's. I had a suspicion. I took my cell phone and opened my text messages from Sophia. My suspicions were correct. It was her number. I wrote Carolina a text asking her to trace the other circled number as well as the last call Horner had made. I was about to send the text when I looked back at the logs. Griffin had also received a call from a blocked number the same day he went missing. I deleted my text and wrote a new one: Call me the second you get up.

I dialed Kemberly Guyton's number. She picked up after the first ring.

"There's something I forgot to ask you," I said. "Did Bryce ever mention Sophia Caballé?"

"All the time," she said. "They were best friends."

"Do you remember why they were so close?"

"Absolutely. They had a really special bond. They both were adopted."

I wasn't sure I'd heard her correctly. "Say that again?"

"My mother couldn't have any more children after she had me, and my father really wanted a son. So, when I was about five, they adopted Bryce. I forget exactly how it happened, but Sophia also was adopted when she was a baby. A couple of years ago, Bryce found his biological mother. They met several times and even formed a nice relationship. He's the one who convinced Sophia that she should look for her biological parents."

"Did she?"

"Yes. They both used the same company."

"Do you remember the name?"

"A place called Brighter Horizons. She had a friend who knew the owner, and they told Bryce about it. Bryce said it was expensive, but the owner was really good."

"Did Sophia ever find her biological parents?"

"From what I remember, she only found her father."

"Are you sure?"

"Positive. He was a very well-known businessman in Chicago."

"You remember his name?"

"Absolutely. His first name is the same as my uncle's. Walter. Walter Griffin."

And just like that, my entire investigation turned upside down.

———

MY PHONE BUZZED AT six thirty in the morning.

"Not exactly the second, but at least the minute I got up," Carolina said. "You sound tired."

"I am. I've been up all night."

"Everything okay?"

"I'm not sure."

"What do you mean?"

"I had an interesting call with Bryce Horner's sister last night. She said that Bryce was adopted, and so was Sophia."

"Does that change things?"

"The fact they were adopted doesn't, but them going to Brighter Horizons does."

"Isn't that the place up north where you followed her?"

"Exactly. But she wasn't pregnant and hadn't put a baby up for adoption."

"So, what was she doing there?"

"Trying to find her biological parents. She was adopted."

"Did she find them?"

"At least her father."

"So, now she's even more of a mystery."

"Worse than that. She's a complete conundrum."

"Why?"

"Because her father is Walter Griffin."

After a few seconds of silence, Carolina finally said, "Say that again?"

"Sophia was not Walter Griffin's mistress. Sophia was his long-lost daughter."

"Now what?"

"I'm not sure. I've been trying to figure out what that means, and at the same time I've been going through Horner's call log and Griffin's call log. Something's not right."

"Such as?"

"The day they each turned up dead, they received a call from a blocked number."

"People block their numbers all the time," she said.

"That's true, but according to Horner's last week of calls, he only received a blocked call once. When you look at Griffin's log for the last three weeks before he died, that one blocked call was the only one he had received also."

"I can get those blocked numbers, but it'll take a little time," she said.

"How long?"

"I'll put the request in when I get to the office this morning. Give me at least a few days."

———

I INTERCEPTED SOPHIA AS she walked out the door of Larry's Bootcamp Studio. She wore a pair of large dark sunglasses and a tight yellow ensemble that soon would be causing truck drivers to stop as if they had come to a red light. Her gym bag was leather and expensive looking.

"How was the workout?" I asked, stepping in behind her.

She stopped and turned. "Torture, but I survived."

"The torture of a bad conscience is the hell of a living soul," I said.

"Isn't it much too early to be quoting Shakespeare?" she said, taking off her glasses.

"John Calvin," I said. "Sixteenth-century French theologian."

She smiled, put her sunglasses on, and started walking. I walked beside her.

"I had you all wrong," I said.

"How's that?"

"Walter, the affair, the pregnancy. It made sense at the time. Everything seemed to fit."

"I tried to tell you, but you wouldn't listen to me."

We turned the corner, and she stopped near her parked Range Rover.

"But you didn't tell me he was your father," I said.

Her face tensed immediately, and her lips opened slightly.

"There's no need to deny it," I said. "I know all about you and Bryce and Brighter Horizons. And you don't have to worry about me saying anything. Your relationship to Walter Griffin is your business, and I'll respect that."

She looked away for a moment, then said, "How did you find out?"

"I talked to Bryce's sister, Kemberly."

Sophia looked at me. "It's true," she said. Her voice was quieter, more vulnerable. "Walter was my father. He and my mother met on an airplane. She was a flight attendant; he was on a business trip. They had a weekend thing. My mother got pregnant. She didn't want to have me. She was young, and Walter was married to his second wife. She was sitting in the doctor's office by herself, about to end the pregnancy—me. But she couldn't go through with it. She told Walter about me a month before I was born. They agreed to put me up for adoption. He had money and connections, so he took care of it. She went on being a flight attendant. Walter went on being a husband. I went to a family in Frankfort. I didn't know I was adopted until I was a teenager. I loved my family, but I always wanted to find my biological parents. It wasn't until I met Bryce and we became friends and found out we were both adopted that I got serious about finding my real mother and father."

"Which took you to Kristly."

"Amy's older sister, Stephanie, and I had been friends. Stephanie moved to New York for a job about six months after Amy moved here. Amy's the one who told me about Kristly."

"Have you found your mother?"

"Not yet. I traced her to Dubai. I went there for several months, looking for her. I couldn't find her. Amy and I went back to Robert to ask him if there was something more he could do to help me locate her. He said he would call in some favors and see what he could find."

"And the half a million dollars and fancy apartment?"

"Walter knew he couldn't make up for all the lost time, but he wanted to try to make things better. He wanted to take care of me and make my life better like he had his other children. He felt guilty. I was angry at him at first, but then I got over it. Shit happens. Nobody's perfect. I probably would've done the same thing had I been in that situation. My mother was only twenty-three when she had me."

"And Cephus Redmond?"

"He and Walter were friends from way back. He helped Walter buy the apartment, because Walter couldn't put anything under his name. Cephus agreed to help. Walter didn't want to hurt his wife and other children, and I agreed. There was no upside to telling people about the situation. His wife didn't do anything wrong. She doesn't deserve to have the memory of her husband twisted by a mistake he made so many years ago. Walter loved her, and he loved his children. I was just happy to have a relationship with my father. We had a really good time together."

"Do you think he killed himself?" I asked.

"Not a chance in hell. He loved life too much."

"What do you think happened?"

"I have no idea. But I would like to know who killed him, and I want them to pay for it. I think you're the one who can find out what really happened."

39

TWO CAMERAS MONITORED THE alley behind Brittany Farrington's town house, catching the flow of traffic traveling south and north. I had found the wires to both and had clipped them easily. I punched the code into the keypad, and Brittany's garage door opened. I backed the van into the empty bay. Brittany and Tammy would be out at dinner in Lincoln Park; then they would be having drinks with some friends at ROOF, the rooftop lounge at theWit Hotel. It would give me plenty of time to get the job done. I was in an old-school kind of mood, so I turned on V103 with Joe Soto on air, sat back, and waited.

———

THE TEXT FROM BRITTANY appeared on my burner phone a minute before eight o'clock. Pharrell Williams was just getting into it, feeling happy.

He's outside the garage.

Ok. Thanks. Have a good dinner. Don't worry, your secret is safe with me. I won't say a word to anyone about your little Pink Lady friends.

Thank you for being so cool about this.

I put my ski mask on so just my eyes could be seen, jumped out of the van, and walked to the control panel farther back in the garage. I had disconnected the overhead light so that it wouldn't come on when the door opened. Antoine Nelson wouldn't be able to see me in the shadows. I pushed the button, and the garage door groaned and slid open. He stood there for a moment, surprised to see the van; then he continued in. I needed him to come within fifteen feet before I made my move, so I waited until he was halfway along the van before I tapped the button to close the door. He stopped and looked back at the garage door, then turned and called, "Brittany?" I waited for the door to completely close before stepping from behind the van.

"What the fuck?" he said.

I already had the Taser gun raised and now pulled the trigger. Nelson screeched and moaned and dropped immediately to the ground. I quickly handcuffed him, then grabbed him by the shoulders and pulled him to the back of the van and threw him into the cargo bay before jumping in behind him. I'd had the van retrofitted from a workman's vehicle to one that had a steel cage with two-inch-thick walls and front and rear doors that unlocked only from the outside. Cameras were anchored in each corner so that I had a full view of every inch of the cage.

Nelson mumbled something unintelligible as I strapped him into the bench at his waist and then tied both legs. I jumped out of the van, locked the back door, then opened the garage door. After making sure the alley was empty, I got behind the wheel, then slowly pulled out of the garage. I took a right into the alley and found Nelson's motorcycle parked against the side of the town house. I waited for a couple wheeling a stroller to pass along Indiana before I got out, opened the back doors, pulled out the ramp, then rolled the bike into the van, jumping in behind it, then closing the doors.

"Who the fuck is you?" he yelled. "Where you takin' me?"

"You and I are gonna have a little fun. Take a trip down memory lane."

"Where's Brittany? Why the fuck you wearin' a Halloween mask?"

"Brittany's at dinner in Lincoln Park. She sends her regards."

"Let me go or I'm gonna fuck you up."

"I look forward to that," I said. "When we get to where we're going, it'll just be you and me. I know you like knives, but they're against the rules in our fight."

"What? Fuck you! Let me go."

"Be very careful what you ask for."

I opened the interior door of the cage that led to the front cabin, locked it behind me, and drove. I looked at the clock on the dashboard. It had taken only seven minutes since Nelson walked into the garage—the same time it had taken Demetrius Jackson to bleed out on that platform. It had been several tough years for the Jackson family, but the true wheels of justice had finally begun spinning.

———

"OKAY. NOW IT'S TIME to fuck me up."

I stood three feet in front of Antoine Nelson in a concrete-reinforced steel chamber with walls five inches thick and five feet in the ground. World War III could be going on outside, and you wouldn't be able to feel even the slightest tremor down here. I had purchased this nondescript house many years ago in a southeast Chicago neighborhood called South Works. It sat at the end of a small, anonymous street next to an enormous mass of vacant land that used to be a US Steel manufacturing plant before being shuttered almost thirty years ago when the steel market bottomed out. Four hundred and forty acres of prime lakefront property sat unused and neglected, as the city leadership could never agree what to do with it and commercial developers found the cost of remediating and repurposing the land too expensive. It was perfect for me, because not only was the land vacant, but the surrounding community had long been forgotten and ignored. What few people remained kept to themselves and didn't ask any questions. This was not a neighborhood where people lived, rather one where they simply survived.

I stepped in close, and Nelson put his hands up. I tapped him quickly on the right side of his chin. Not enough to knock him out, but it sent him stumbling back.

"Let's go, tough guy," I said. "Now's your chance."

He looked at me, raised his fists, and lowered his stance. He circled me for a few seconds, then threw a wild left hook my grandmother could've blocked. I ducked underneath it, rolled to my left, and stuck him with a left jab just underneath his rib cage. I could hear the air rush out of him as he bent over, gasping. I was tempted to finish him with a right uppercut but thought better of it. He was done. I grabbed him by the neck and dragged him to the east wall, where I had bolted in several manacles. I locked in both thighs first, then his lower legs, then spread his arms into a T and locked them in. He looked like da Vinci's *Vitruvian Man*.

"What the fuck?" he groaned. "You doin' this over some Pink Lady?"

"I don't give a shit about your little drug business," I said.

"Then what?"

"Demetrius Jackson ring a bell?"

"You his family?"

"No."

"What he got to do with this? You got some connection to him?"

"No."

"Then why the fuck you say his name?"

"Because you're a coward. You stabbed a kid because you tried to rob him and he kicked your ass."

"He should've gave me his shit, and he still be alive today."

"Or you could've taken a beating like a real man, and he'd still be alive today."

"I wasn't tryin' to kill his punk ass."

"Of course not. You just stuck a six-inch fixed blade all the way into his back just to make him hurt a little."

"He wanna play tough, he should've watched his back."

"Why did you do it, Antoine? You didn't even know the kid. Not like you had some previous beef. He was minding his own business, talking to his girlfriend. What made you think it was okay to do that?"

He looked at me, then looked away. He shook his head slowly. "He had it coming. He wanted to fight, then he should've finished it."

"Did you even consider that putting that knife in him could kill him? Done. Forever. No coming back. Or were you such a weak-ass little bitch that it didn't even matter?"

"Don't try some psychological bullshit with me," Nelson said. "I went and did my time. I paid my price."

"What a fucking thought," I said. "You're a joke. You think three lousy years of jail time is the equivalent of a kid losing his life?"

"I ain't make the rules; the court did."

I turned and walked toward the door. "You pathetic piece of shit," I said. "Not one ounce of remorse in your body."

I stepped through the door and locked it behind me. I opened an app on my phone and tapped a couple of buttons. The crime scene image of Jackson lying in a pool of his own blood had now been projected against the wall opposite the one Nelson was strapped to. I wanted him to see it every moment his eyes were open.

40

I HAD TRIED CALLING the ex-ME Frank Skinner for several days and never reached him. No answering machine. No voice mail. No return phone call. Nothing. I reached out to Ellison, who reached out to another retired pathologist and found an old address for Skinner in the town of Belcrest, just shy of two hours northwest of Chicago. I jumped in my car early one morning and headed out to the great open expanse of Wisconsin.

My GPS navigation guided me about fifteen minutes north of the border before instructing me to make a series of turns into a small town full of lush farmland and winding roads. I arrived at a large black mailbox that matched the address Ellison had given me. A long dirt driveway led me uphill to a gigantic two-story white farmhouse with shiny black shutters and several apple trees scattered about the sweeping front lawn. An old Range Rover with Illinois tags sat parked at the side of the house. I pulled in behind it and walked up the wide front steps. I rang the doorbell and waited. No response. I rang it again. Still no response. The chimes sang softly in the light wind. I walked around the porch and looked through the windows. There was no sign of anyone inside. I left the porch and walked along the side of the house toward the back. A building that looked like a smaller version of the main house sat off it about twenty yards to the right. I headed toward it.

"That's far enough," a voice said from behind me. There was no mistaking the seriousness of the warning. I stopped immediately.

"Turn around slowly and keep your hands out of your pockets where I can see them."

I did as instructed and found myself staring up the barrel of a long rifle aimed center mass. At the other end was a very large man with a face full of gray hair that had turned slightly yellow at the ends. He had broad rounded shoulders and a bucket fisherman's hat tilted on the side of his massive dome. His doughy eyelids drooped in a way that probably made him look tired and bothered even when he smiled. It didn't seem like he made a habit of smiling.

"Who the hell are you?" he said. "And why are you on my property?"

"My name is Ashe Cayne," I said. "I'm a private investigator from Chicago. I wanted to ask you a couple of questions."

"Ashe, like Arthur Ashe the tennis player?" he said, still holding the gun steady.

"Spelled the same way. My father's favorite player."

"Mine too. I played almost every day until I blew out my right knee two hundred pounds ago."

He lowered the gun.

"Let's go inside," he said. "I've got water on the stove."

I followed him up the steps of the back veranda and through a large storm door and a dark narrow hallway that could barely fit his wide frame. Several yards later we entered an enormous bright kitchen with aged oak furnishings. The entire space was spotless. A double Wolf stove anchored the back wall. Skinner set the rifle on the counter and instructed me to take a seat near the bay window overlooking an elaborate vegetable garden. A red barn sat off in the distance between two silver milk silos.

Skinner brought a tea tray over to the sitting area and placed it on a short round table between us, then slowly lowered his heft into a chair.

"How the hell did you find me?" he said.

"Dr. Ellison told me you were up here."

"Barry is a good man. One of the best pathologists I know."

"Mutual admiration club. He says the same thing about you."

"I miss Barry and the others," he said, less to me and more as if he was having a conversation with himself. "We had lots of good times."

"Why did you just disappear?"

Skinner grunted an attempt at a smile.

"That season of my life is over. A pathologist comes to accept the finality of things. It's what we trade in every day of our professional lives. We accept that the natural life cycle of all things must end. I don't carry any regrets."

I decided not to waste any time. "What about the Walter Griffin case?"

Skinner took a sip of coffee and looked out the window. He didn't register any shock at my question, almost as if he was expecting it. His heavy eyes moved slowly as he scanned the property. There was such a calmness about him.

"My grandfather bought this farm during the Great Depression," he said. "The man who owned it was named Dickers. Lost all his family money betting on the stock market when the crash of twenty-nine wiped him out. My grandfather was an internist. The Dickers family had been his first patients after he opened up shop. My grandfather was young and from the East Coast. Dickers took a gamble on my grandfather, an outsider, when no one else would. So, when the Dickers family had their hardship and no one else in the town would help, my grandfather bought the farm, even though he had never even seen a cow in person his entire life. Loyalty."

We sat there, looking out the window. I didn't want to rush him. Asking questions wasn't always the best way to get information. Sometimes you needed to let people have time with their thoughts.

"Why exactly are you here?" he finally asked.

"I've been hired by the family to find out what really happened that night."

He nodded, as if expecting that answer. "What do they know?"

"That their husband and father never would've committed suicide."

"Are they pursuing this for legal reasons?"

"They're pursuing it because they want to know the truth."

Skinner turned and faced me. "The case was a mess from the very beginning," he said, placing his cup down and clasping his massive hands. "I was at my vacation house in Galena with my oldest son. We had bought some new rods and had planned on fishing for a few days. My pager went off at six thirty in the morning. I called in to the office. They had a VIP on the truck and needed me back ASAP. I told them that my deputy chief was more than capable of handling it. But the word had come from up high. It wasn't a request. It was an order. I was to do the case."

"How high?"

"The Cook County board president. She wanted me directly involved."

"So, you came back and did the exam?"

"Not exactly. I instructed my deputy chief to start it while I was en route. Very capable. Trained at Wash U in Saint Louis. She had done thousands of exams. I trusted her. When I finally got back a few hours later, she was well into the exam. I got dressed and finished it with her. It was a pretty straightforward case. We had a very clear picture of the findings and cause of death."

"How about the heart petechiae?"

"What about them?"

"Were they consistent with a suicide by gunshot?"

"Did Barry read the report?"

"Yes. I asked him to give me his opinion."

"What did he say?"

"That not everything was adding up. There were heart petechiae but nothing in the eyes."

Skinner nodded and smiled without showing his teeth. "Barry would catch that," he said. "I'm not surprised."

"What does it mean?"

"It means that the likelihood of there being petechiae on the heart and not in the eyes is extremely rare. It means that a skilled and thoughtful pathologist would see the discrepancy and question it. It was sitting there the whole time waiting for someone to see it. Two years later, Barry Ellison is the one who found it."

"You say that as if you wanted someone to find it."

"I did."

"I don't understand."

"I was curious as to why the president of the board found it necessary to insist I do the case. In the ten years she'd held that role, she had never done that before."

"So, what did you do?"

"I called the mayor's office."

"Did you speak to Bailey?"

"No, I was told by one of his assistants that someone would come and talk to me."

"Did they?"

"She was waiting for me when I arrived. A rather tall woman. I was surprised at how young she was. She told me that Bailey was devastated by Griffin's death and that enough damage had been done to a lot of people already. It was in everyone's best interest that all of this go away quietly."

Amy Donnegan.

"So, they asked you to lie?"

"In a manner of speaking. A left-handed man is shot through the left side of his head at close range and at an angle consistent with suicide. But the gunshot residue is found on his right hand, and the petechiae on his heart indicate he was deprived of oxygen before he was shot. At the least, it should have been investigated."

"So, why did you cover it up?"

"I didn't have much of a choice."

"No disrespect, but that's an easy way out."

Skinner turned back to the window and fixed his gaze on something in the distance. Then he said, "There were over a hundred and fifty people who worked in that office, from janitors to secretaries to staff pathologists. They had families, bills to pay, living situations, stress. They came to work every day not making a lot of money, but what they did make was important to their survival. When I first took the job, the office was in tatters. It had lost its national accreditation because it was understaffed, bodies were all over the place in the cooler, stacked on floors, missing for days. They were still using an outdated paper log system that was inefficient and difficult to manage. It was a disgrace and an embarrassment. It took me the good part of five years to turn the place around. New hires, better training, new equipment. We built something that we could be proud of. In the sixth year, we got our accreditation back. That was a big deal and major morale booster for everyone. Things finally were where they should be. We started receiving federal grants; I was able to bump up everyone's pay—not a lot but enough to where it made some kind of difference. Then the Griffin case came through the doors."

He paused for a moment. I gave him his time.

"I had a choice to make," he continued. "The message that young woman delivered was perfectly clear. Either I help the case go away quietly, or I tell almost a hundred and fifty people that most of them will lose their jobs, get demoted, or come under tremendous scrutiny. Those were the two choices I faced. And it really wasn't too difficult a decision to make, all things considered."

"Loyalty to your staff."

"The same reason this farm has been in my family for three generations. Yes, I made the report fit so it would go away rather than let them gut the office and destroy so many lives as collateral damage."

Skinner lifted himself out of the chair with effort and walked over to a small oak cabinet against the wall. He opened a drawer and pulled out a thin gray folder and rested it on the table when he sat back down.

"I was hoping someone would eventually come," he said. "In all my forty years of practicing medicine, I've never deliberately lied or written something that was unethical in my work. Until that case. Not a day has gone by that I haven't thought about him and his family. The grief that comes with losing someone, especially in that way, can be immeasurable. They deserve the truth."

41

DRIVING THROUGH THE VAST WISCONSIN farmlands was a perfect backdrop for me not to be distracted and focus on my thoughts. I felt like I had so many pieces of the puzzle but still couldn't make them all fit. I couldn't get my mind off Bailey. Every time I turned the corner, he was there, but I couldn't get to him. He had a connection to Griffin, Donnegan, and Milton. He was smart enough, however, to reduce his exposure and push others out front to do his work. Then I thought about Griffin. It was clear he had been murdered, but who got him to Wolf Point, and how? Even after all this time of talking to those who knew him, I felt like there was something I was missing. Maybe I was looking for answers in the wrong place.

Shortly after crossing the Illinois border, I saw signs for Chicago even though I was still forty-five minutes away from the city. I turned up the radio and caught the signal to 104.3 FM, the throwbacks station. The early-nineties song "Ice Baby" came on. I picked up my phone and dialed the number to Lanny "Ice" Culpepper, the fearless leader of the notorious Gangster Apostles. If anyone had the pulse of the street, it was Ice. He could find answers in places that most people saw only in their nightmares.

———

I PULLED UP TO the front of Mr. Knight's Laundromat, next to the dilapidated Cermak Grocery in the tough K-Town neighborhood, a gritty area on the Southwest Side, where one would never expect to find the headquarters of the city's largest, most lucrative criminal enterprise. For the last quarter of a century, Ice Culpepper had presided over the toughest, most murderous gang since Al Capone's. Two years ago, Ice and his men held the distinction of being responsible for a third of all murders in the city, edging out their rival gang, the Latin Warlords, who trailed closely behind at 20 percent. It was an eye-popping statistic, even for a tough city like Chicago—two gangs responsible for half of all murders in the city and in control of 75 percent of the drug money that flowed in the streets.

I hadn't seen Ice for a little more than a year since Tinsley Gerrigan, a wealthy blonde North Shore woman dating Ice's nephew, had gone missing, and that nephew, Chopper McNair, had been found dead weeks later. Ice had moved his operation to this new location, but everything looked the same, including the Laundromat he used to clean his money and the black-suited men standing outside the nondescript side door that led to his second-floor office.

I pulled my Glock from my shoulder holster and slid it underneath my seat, then left the car and walked up to the men. They weren't exactly excited to see me.

"Where's your sidekick?" the bigger one said. He was the color of melting blacktop with large pimples in various stages of eruption on his bald head.

"Buying you some Proactiv," I said.

The bald guy turned to the shorter guy with dreadlocks, who hiked his shoulders.

"What the fuck is that?" the bald guy said.

"Acne medication for all those nasty pimples about to explode on your head."

He started to move his shoulders toward me, and I was ready to unload an uppercut to the right side of his jaw, but Dreadlocks stepped in front of him.

"We don't need no shit," Dreadlocks said. He stepped toward me, and I raised my hands. He patted me down, then stepped back and said, "Just go on in. Ice is expecting you."

I smiled at the bald guy, then walked up to the door and the ten cameras that were now focused on me. The door buzzed, and I opened it and started up the narrow staircase, atop which stood Dexter Barnes, a short guy, thin as a withered tree branch in the middle of winter and not much over five feet. The AK-47 strapped to his back weighed more than he did and was almost the same height. Ice's head of security led me through a waiting room fit for callers to the crown. An enormous lead chandelier hung from the center of the ceiling, the dark-cherrywood walls etched meticulously with some Greco-Roman pattern. Ice's secretary, Pam Elsworth, a well-appointed woman with close-cropped hair that had been dyed blonde, sat behind a neat desk and looked up as I passed. I flashed Pam one of my biggest smiles, and she struggled not to do the same, but I could see the approval in her eyes.

The security guard opened a door several feet behind the secretary, and another guy in a black suit patted me down.

"Felt pretty good," I said to the guy. "Ice ever decides to throw you out, Massage Envious is always hiring."

The guy's scowl never left his face. He turned so that I could enter, then closed the door behind me.

Ice's office hadn't changed an inch. Same oil paintings in gold baroque frames, same built-in bookcases elegantly lined with books that looked to be centuries old. Two guys sat in leather banker chairs in opposite corners of the room. Ice sat behind a desk statelier than the one Kennedy had made famous in the Oval Office. A lavender suit coat hung on the back of his high-backed chair, matching his lavender shirt, tie, and vest. He looked no different than when I had last seen him, thin hair swept back off his face and plastered down with pomade. His diamond-and-gold presidential Rolex hung from his narrow wrists. He had a plate of ribs, mac 'n' cheese, and collard greens in front of him. He took a bite of the ribs as I entered and sat in some chair that looked like it belonged in the Galleria Borghese in Rome.

"Didn't know you were into poetry," I said.

Ice swallowed, took a sip of soda, then said, "Who said I was?"

"The Laundromat used to be called Miss Beale's. Now it's Mr. Knight."

"And?"

"Thought maybe you were making an homage to Etheridge Knight."

"Who the fuck is that?"

Ice took another healthy bite of the ribs, careful not to splash anything on the lavender.

"Etheridge Knight, really smart Black poet. Wrote a book in the late sixties called *Poems from Prison*. Served eight years for armed robbery."

"He wasn't that smart." Ice smiled. "He got caught and did eight years. I ain't done a single day."

"Point taken." I smiled.

Ice took another sip of soda, wiped his hands, leaned back in his chair, and said, "So, what is it you want from me?"

I looked over his shoulder and noticed two pictures prominently situated on a short chest of drawers just off his shoulder. His deceased nephew Chopper beamed from one photo and from the other, two beautiful girls with Chopper's eyes and lips and their mother's light complexion and slender nose. They were a perfect combination of their parents.

"I know you've got your hands in some of the gambling around the city. You know Cephus Redmond?"

"Course I do. Cephus makin' a killin' over there with them car washes. Got damn near as much money as I got."

"Walter Griffin borrowed half a million dollars from him."

Ice smiled. "Who told you that?"

"Cephus."

"Ain't that a muthafuckah! Everybody knew Griff. He made a decent amount of money, but not as much as people thought he made. Them suits downtown would kick him down and let him in on some of those deals, but it wasn't like he was making millions a year. He made enough to live well, but he borrowed from different people to pay back the last person, and on top of that, he gave a lot of money away. One thing I can say about him is, he really tried to help people. Cephus tell you how much money Griff saved him and how he kept his fat ass outa prison?"

"Never mentioned it."

"Convenient. Cephus always been slick. Cephus been cheatin' the tax man for as long as he had them car washes. Not only does he take a big skim from the till, but he cleaned a lot of dirty money through there. Everybody know if you wanna clean your money,

Cephus your man. Clean it better than a Brillo pad. They was onto Cephus big-time. Word was the DA had an airtight case against him. They was about to pick him up. Everybody waitin'. Never happened."

"Why?"

"Why you think? 'Cause Griff pulled some strings downtown. Money exchanged hands. Case went away. Griff had that kinda pull."

"The kind of pull worth half a million dollars."

"Worth a helluva lot more than that," Ice said. "Ain't no price too high to avoid gettin' locked up and losin' everything. Griff saved Cephus's fat ass. That half a million dollars won't no loan. That was a damn fee for service. Had it been me, I would've charged him a whole lot more. And would've kept chargin' him the rest of his god-damn life!"

42

THE CIRCUMSTANCES OF WALTER Griffin's death were coming into focus, but I still needed a lot of answers. The East Bank Club occupied an enormous building in the upscale River North neighborhood just west of downtown. A luxury fitness center for the well heeled and well connected, it was as much a social hub as it was an athletic facility. Equal to its physical prominence was its cost of admission. What the rest of the city's fitness centers charged for an entire year, East Bank charged for a single month.

A little before seven o'clock in the morning, I waited outside one of the spin rooms for the class to end. Andrew Milton was the second person through the door, wearing dark biking shorts and a white T-shirt, his wet hair plastered down. He carried a water bottle in one hand and a towel in the other. There was no denying that he was tightly muscled and extremely handsome.

"I'd like to ask you a few questions," I said, approaching him.

"Not now," he said, not stopping. "Call my press team and schedule something. I don't do unscheduled interviews."

I had to almost jog to keep up with him.

"It's not an interview," I said. "It's related to an investigation."

That was enough to stop him. He toweled off his hair.

"Investigation?" he said. "I don't know anything about investigations."

"Bryce Horner."

"I'll meet you in the garage in twenty minutes," he said. "We'll talk in my car."

Twenty minutes later we were sitting in Milton's new Porsche Cayenne SUV. The car's ornate interior perfectly matched his tailored pinstriped suit.

"Why are you coming to me about Bryce Horner?"

"Because he was your boyfriend."

"I'm married. He was not my boyfriend. He was a friend."

"Who happened to also be your boyfriend."

"Is there a point you're trying to make?"

"Bryce Horner, an experienced swimmer, mysteriously washed up on North Avenue Beach on a Sunday morning. Did that bother you?"

"Of course it did. Wouldn't you be bothered if a friend of yours washed up on a beach?"

"Even more so if it was a lover."

Milton looked out the window and shook his head as a line of shiny foreign cars and tinted-window Range Rovers exited the garage.

"I'm the CEO of CPS," he said. "I've been happily married to the same woman for almost ten years. What I do on my personal time should not be a concern to anyone else."

"You're not understanding me," I said. "Who you were fucking is no concern of mine. My concern is how a healthy twenty-seven-year-old man who by all accounts was an extremely capable swimmer ends up drowning two weeks to the day after Walter Griffin's body was found partially submerged in the Chicago River."

"Walter Griffin?" Milton frowned. "What does he have to do with this?"

"That's what I was hoping you'd tell me."

"I have no idea what you're talking about."

"I think you have plenty of ideas. Let's start with the fact that you know that Griffin's girlfriend was a girl named Sophia Caballé, who also happened to be best friends with Bryce."

"Okay. That's none of my business what Walter was doing on his personal time."

"You also knew that Griffin was in a tremendous amount of debt."

"There had been rumors," Milton said. "He made some bad investments that hadn't worked out for him."

"You also knew that Griffin was the only one in the board of education who didn't vote in favor of your appointment."

"That was no secret."

"You knew that those few charges on his corporate card were minor mistakes."

"I don't make the rules. Whether it's three hundred dollars or three hundred thousand dollars, wrong is wrong."

"But not wrong enough to warrant a full-scale investigation that could've been handled with a simple phone call."

"That decision didn't come across my desk."

"No, but it was made in your office."

Milton shot a blank stare in my direction.

"You convinced Pete Dent, who happened to be a buddy of yours from law school, to bring the investigation even though it didn't fall under his jurisdiction. You did it because you hated Griffin, and you wanted to do anything you could to make his life more difficult."

"Walter and I weren't exactly friends," Milton said. "But I think *hate* is a strong word."

"Okay, fine. You were adversaries. Neither one of you liked the other. He didn't think you deserved the job, and you were jealous of his relationship with Bailey. He was the insider you were hoping to become."

"Is there a point to all of this?"

"I want to know who killed them."

"Them?"

"Griffin and Horner?"

"You think I had Bryce killed?" He screwed up his face.

"When was the last time you talked to him?"

"Two or three days before he died."

"Are you sure it wasn't the day he died?"

"I'm certain. We had a small disagreement and decided to take a couple of days. Let the dust settle." His shoulders dropped.

I decided to switch up, like a boxer switching his punching stance in the middle of a round. This was unorthodox, but it could catch the opponent by surprise and leave him vulnerable to a knockout punch unless he quickly changed his defense.

"What about Sunrise Holdings?" I asked.

"What do you mean?" Milton responded.

"Are you pretending like you don't know who that is?"

"I don't."

"How about Belvedere Technologies?"

"I know them."

"You awarded them a seventy-million-dollar contract, give or take a few million."

"So? We award a lot of big contracts, and that's not the biggest. We have an eight-billion-dollar budget."

"Did you and Walter ever talk about Belvedere?"

"All of our contracts of a certain size are reviewed by the board," Milton said impatiently. "It was approved."

"Do you know who owns Belvedere?"

"I don't privately meet with each of our vendors. I'm the CEO of CPS. I have an entire procurement department in charge of our vendors."

"You ever hear of Sunrise Holdings?"

"Never."

"They own Belvedere."

"So?"

"Just figured you might want to know who you gave seventy million dollars."

He blew out an exasperated breath. "Is all this going anywhere?" He started reaching for the door handle to signify our meeting was over.

I decided to take a stab in the dark. "I think you know who killed Griffin, and that Bryce did also. I think whoever killed Griffin had to protect themselves by eliminating Bryce. So, you ask if I think you had Bryce killed? My answer is that as much as you didn't want to, there was no other way out."

"Goddamn it!" he said, his face finally cracking. "You're wrong. I loved Bryce." His eyes narrowed and his voice quivered. "I wanted to spend the rest of my life with him. I was trapped and didn't know how to get out of a difficult situation. Do I really care that Walter died? Not at all. He had been given plenty of opportunities, and he squandered a lot of them. He wasn't a saint. He pushed people's buttons and wanted everything *his* way. But I was devastated that Bryce died. I loved him. I would never agree to kill him or have him killed."

Tears streamed down his face. I believed what he had said. At least most of it.

———

THREE DAYS HAD GONE by when I finally opened the door to the basement chamber. Antoine Nelson lifted the upper half of his slumping body when I walked in. His eyes were bloodshot, and his beard was starting to look like a bird's nest that had fallen out of a tree. The odor of dried urine hit me like a brick wall.

"You look like hell," I said.

"Where the fuck you been?" Nelson croaked. "This ain't no fuckin' game."

"Now you wanna be serious?"

"Damn right," he said. "Let me the fuck outa here. You made your point."

"For the life of me, I can't understand why you thought it was okay to call Cesar Jackson two days after you stupidly killed his son and tell him, and I quote, 'Your punk-ass son got what he deserved.'"

"What the fuck you want me to say?"

"Something you probably haven't done since you got out of diapers. How about the truth?"

"I don't know why I did that," he said. "I just did."

"You kill a man's son for no good reason, and you think it's okay to just taunt him like that? That's the problem with you young bloods these days. No regard for human life. You think this is a game. Death isn't an illness. It's final. No recovering from it or taking it back."

"I heard he was talkin' about comin' to get me."

"Okay. Seems logical. You kill my son, and my first thought is to come and get you too. Paternal instinct."

"I wanted to back him off."

"By taunting him about his dead son."

Antoine shrugged. "I'm fuckin' starvin'," he said. "And my mouth dry as shit. I need something."

"Give me a sec. I'll get a menu so you can order takeout."

"You got fuckin' jokes."

"Are you sorry?"

"For what?"

"Let's start with killing Demetrius, then work our way to posting all those IG photos afterward like you were some tough guy."

"I ain't sorry for shit," he said. "That's life in the street."

I looked at him and his indifference and thought about how Bailey and his cronies used and manipulated the school system to line their pockets while abandoning their basic obligation to educate those kids and give them hope and means to escape the clutches of poverty and the never-ending cycle of violence. In many ways these gangbangers were nothing more than a product of the hopelessness of the neighborhoods they grew up in and the schools that could've been a ticket out but instead turned into war zones where no one got along and survival was much more critical than learning. CPS had become a political football, tossed and kicked and fumbled by the Fifth Floor and the never-satisfied union. Meanwhile, wealthy men marauded the CPS coffers, then fled back to their gated homes with sweeping lawns and children riding their bikes on leafy cul-de-sacs without a care in the world.

I'd make it a point to try to give them what they deserved too.

I reached behind the door and brought in a bag from White Castle full of cheese sliders and frics. They were still hot. The aroma quickly permeated the chamber. I had a tall cup of soda to go with it. I could see the flicker of hope lighten Nelson's eyes. I walked over and placed it a foot in front of him. He'd have to be the world's greatest contortionist or break his spine in order to bend down and get it. He started to yell something as I turned around, but the door slamming behind me cut him off.

43

CAROLINA AND I SAT shoulder to shoulder at the tiny counter-top in Kyōten, along with five strangers observing the sushi chef's fussy preparations. The restaurant had only two seatings per night, set you back $220 per person, and offered a twenty-course meal that was *omakase*—the Japanese word for "respectfully leaving another to decide what was best." We had just finished the third serving, a delicious piece of fried tilefish with caviar and crème fraîche, the Japanese equivalent of an elegant fish stick. We cleaned our palate with a small sip of sake. My phone chirped. I ignored it at first, but then it chirped again.

"Go ahead," Carolina said. "You can read one message."

I opened my phone and read the text messages.

This is Alicia Gentry. I'm back in town. I can meet you tomorrow morning.

Where and what time?

10 AM at the Riverwalk. Top of the steps at North Columbus and Lower Wacker.

I'll be there wearing a black baseball cap.

Don't worry. I know what you look like.

"Everything okay?" Carolina asked.

"Yup. Meeting with that FBI agent tomorrow. The daughter of Burke's friend."

"You think she'll help?"

"They're usually pretty tight lipped. But I'll pack an extra dose of charm before I leave the apartment and see if that loosens her up."

Carolina smiled and took another sip of sake. "So, what's the big news you've been keeping from me all night?" she asked.

"Yours first," I said.

"But I asked you first."

"But I'm picking up the tab."

"Because you never let me do it."

"I'm just old fashioned that way."

"So, spill it."

"Remember that probiotic company I told you about that Barzan had me invest in?"

"The one you thought he was completely crazy for recommending?"

"No need to rub it in," I said. "The sale went through at record speed. Yesterday I got a very sizable deposit in my bank account."

"Which explains tonight's extravagance."

"Not really, but this might."

I reached under the table and lifted a small bag.

"What is this?" she whispered, her hand over her mouth.

"A small token of appreciation for all you do for me. You never ask for anything in return."

"Except for a decent meal."

"Well, you deserve more than that."

Carolina pulled the slender box out of the bag and untied the bow. She lifted the lid off the box and froze.

"Just a little thank-you," I said.

"I'm afraid to touch it," she said, her hands trembling.

I reached over and pulled the diamond tennis bracelet out of the box. The light caught it just right, and the sparkle looked like mini bursts of fireworks. She held out her wrist, and I clasped the bracelet around it.

"I'm speechless," she said, tears forming in the corners of her eyes. "No one has ever given me something so nice. And so expensive."

"You're worth every carat of it," I said.

She sat there, slowly rotating her wrist. "What am I supposed to do with this?"

"Wear it."

"But I can't even afford the insurance on this thing."

"You don't have to," I said. "I took care of that too."

She reached into me for a kiss. I turned my cheek toward her, but she grabbed my face with both hands and kissed me square on the lips. It was the first time I had felt her mouth on mine, and while it wasn't a long kiss, I savored the soft wet warmth of her lips.

"If I knew that was going to be your thank-you, I would've bought you the entire damn store," I said softly.

"You really surprised me with this."

"I love it when the plan comes together." We were both silent for a few moments. "So, what's your news?"

"I'm not sure why, but getting behind the blocked numbers is a little more difficult than it used to be," she said. "It now requires approval from someone higher up the food chain. Anyway, my person got through. That blocked call to Bryce Horner came from 509 North Oak Park Avenue."

She paused. I lifted my eyebrows.

"The home of Andrew Milton," she said.

"That's unfortunate," I said.

"Why?"

"Because Milton told me he hadn't spoken to Horner for at least a couple of days before he died. But he talked to him right before Horner died and blocked his number."

"Maybe he didn't want him to have his home phone number on account of his wife."

"Possible."

"The other number that was blocked to Griffin was a little trickier," Carolina said.

I looked at the bracelet as she moved her hand.

"What's wrong?" she asked.

"I thought it looked nice in the store, but it looks even more exquisite around your wrist."

She smiled and rested her hand on top of mine.

"Now the second number. It's registered to TSG Developers, LLC, a limited liability company formed in Delaware in 2002. It has a local address in the Ukrainian Village. The owner of the company is a man named Grigor Medvedev."

I smiled.

"You know him?"

"Not at all."

"So, why are you laughing?"

"My father would get a kick out of the name."

"Why?"

"Because it's the combination of the names of two famous tennis players. Grigor Dimitrov from Bulgaria and Daniil Medvedev from Russia. He'd recognize it right away."

"So, how are you and your father doing?"

"I'm not sure."

"What does that mean?"

I told her about what happened with him going to Paris and seeing Julia and not telling me before he left that he had intended on seeing her. I left out the mention of the letter. I didn't know why, only that I was falling in love with Carolina and I still loved Julia and I didn't know how I was going to sort that out. She took the news about Julia well.

"I haven't talked to my father since he came clean about his betrayal."

"Ashe, he's your father, and I'm sure he wasn't trying to hurt you," she said.

"He wasn't doing me any favors either."

"So, what are you going to do?"

"Try to find out why Grigor Medvedev was calling Walter Griffin on the day he died, and why he was calling him from a blocked number."

"And about your father?"

"What I always end up doing. Take the higher road and call him."

She winked and flashed a smile as shiny as the tennis bracelet. I knew this didn't change things between us. She was still dating that surgeon, and I was still going to hang out with Mercedes. But seeing Carolina looking so happy gave me hope for what the future could be.

"Mind if I share my personal, unbiased opinion?" she asked.

"Never." I smiled.

"Julia was a damn fool to let you go."

44

THE NEXT MORNING I ADJUSTED my black ball cap while I stood adjacent to the stairs that descended to the Riverwalk below. I was uncharacteristically a few minutes early, and I felt exposed, watching people crossing Wacker and heading to the Sheraton or across the street to NBC Tower. I faced north toward the bridge, expecting Alicia Gentry to arrive from that direction, but I heard my name called behind me. I turned and noticed a small blonde woman in leggings.

"So, what can you tell me about Walter Griffin?" I said as we began walking.

"Depends on what you want to know."

"Was he under investigation?"

"Not officially," Alicia said. "We had an interest in what he knew."

"Did it have anything to do with the Cabrini land deal?"

"It did."

"Was he involved in the deal?"

"He wasn't."

"Was Mayor Bailey?"

"I really can't comment on an active investigation."

"How about I tell you what I heard, and if you want to verify its accuracy, you let me know."

"I'm listening."

"Bailey pushed through closing Cabrini-Green and tearing down the buildings to make way for developers to be awarded leasing rights to the land. Some of those developers were Bailey's friends. Those friends also happen to have been very generous donors to his reelection campaigns over the years. Walter Griffin was not part of these arrangements, but he was well aware of them. He was also being investigated by OIG for fraudulent usage of his city credit card. They were pressing him hard. You all made him an offer. He tells you what he knows about Cabrini, and you get the OIG investigation dropped."

Alicia looked out into the river as several boats made their way through the calm water.

"Almost," she said.

"What part was wrong?"

"The OIG investigation."

"What was wrong about it?"

"Griffin did more than make a few charges on his credit card. He directly and purposefully influenced a contract made between CPS and a company that he consulted for."

"As if that never happened before," I said. "Are you kidding? That's how business is done in Chicago."

"It is," she said. "But it's still illegal. And if someone discovers it and wants to expose it, then it can be a big problem."

"Do you know who exposed it?"

"I do."

"But you won't tell me?"

"I can't comment on potential targets in an active investigation."

I thought for a moment. I liked Gentry. She was tough, but she was doing her best to help. If she was anything like her father, I could see why Burke liked him. She was doing her best to give me answers without directly answering my questions.

"I'm gonna think out loud for a minute," I said.

"You do that often?" she asked.

"Usually not in front of other people." I laughed. "Could give the wrong impression."

We stopped across the river from the Apple store, its iconic glass cube in stark contrast to the neogothic skyscrapers that rose from its shoulders, the Tribune Tower to the right and the Wrigley Building on its left.

"Walter Griffin helps a company he consulted for in the past or is still consulting for secure a city contract with CPS. Someone else catches wind of this conflict of interest and decides to expose what Walter's done to the OIG. That someone else is Andrew Milton, but you already know that. Milton isn't clean either. He has his own ethical lapses when it comes to awarding contracts to certain vendors. Of course, you already know that. So, your play to flip Griffin and get the information you needed on the Cabrini land deals wasn't to nail Milton. You want someone else."

She smiled. "You fish much?" she asked.

"Never took to it," I said. "Golf has always been my thing."

"My dad is a big fisherman now," she said. "It's a sport for him. He doesn't spend hours on that boat trying to hook a little bonefish or snapper. He wants a difficult catch like an Atlantic tarpon. It's big, high jumping, and incredibly strong. Fights like hell not to get pulled out of the water. The same can be said about what we do in the field office. We don't waste our time with the snappers of the world. We want tarpons. The bigger and stronger, the better the

305

haul. But the key is patience and the right conditions. Even the best fisherman can go out for days or even weeks and nothing bites. But that doesn't mean he stops fishing."

I knew exactly what she was trying to say. The Feds were going after Bailey. But they needed all the pieces to come together before they could pull him out of the water.

———

AFTER A LONG DAY of chasing loose ends that amounted to nothing, I finally made it back to my apartment. I put Stryker on a leash and took him for a night walk along the lakefront. It was closing in on ten o'clock, but there was no way I could go straight to bed. We walked all the way to North Avenue Beach, where I stepped off the walking path and sat down on the concrete ledge, looking out into the black water. I thought about Bryce Horner out there all alone, his body being pushed and dragged by the currents until they finally deposited him on the beach's sand.

Could Milton have killed him? Very possible. It wasn't uncommon for someone to kill their lover to protect a secret. I actually felt bad for Milton. It must've been difficult leading a double life—a married, successful man in public but privately a gay or bisexual man in love with someone he was either too afraid or too ashamed to reveal. Why had he lied about speaking to Horner on the day that he had died, and why had he blocked his number? Was he afraid that Horner would call him at home, or did he know Horner was going to be killed and didn't want his phone number in the call log as a last point of contact?

I sat there for a few more minutes thinking about Grigor Medvedev and how he might play into all this. I took out my cell phone and dialed Mechanic.

"Where are you?" he asked.

"On North Avenue Beach, looking out into the lake."

"Alone or with company?"

"With Stryker."

"Isn't it kind of late for the two of you to be out exploring?"

"I can't sleep. Too much on my mind. I need some help on a guy named Grigor Medvedev."

"I don't know him, but I could make some calls. What's your interest?"

"He was one of the last persons to call Walter Griffin on the day he died. He called him from a restricted number."

"What's his connection to Griffin?"

"I have no idea. That's what I need to find out."

"What are you about to do now?"

"Head back to the apartment with Stryker."

"I'll have an answer before you walk through the door."

Stryker and I walked back along the footpath, passing a young border collie and its owner also out for a late-night stroll. We made it to East Illinois Street where it fed into Navy Pier. Families had long gone to bed for the night, and young people in cars with throaty mufflers and loud music raced along the otherwise empty streets. We stopped at the light underneath the overpass and waited. I could hear the sporadic sound of rubber tires pressing into the asphalt on the road above us, then fading away as the cars rolled farther north along Lake Shore Drive. The light turned just as a turquoise Supra sports car pulled up to a stop. Its windows had been tinted jet black, and the chromed grille and hubcaps sparkled like crushed diamonds under the streetlights. Stryker and I walked in front of the car. Even the front window was too dark to see inside. Once we had gotten halfway across the street, I looked at the back of the car with its aftermarket spoiler kit and dual exhaust pipes. I figured it for some young car enthusiast who didn't have the money yet to purchase the real deal.

We had made it across the street, but for some reason I felt like I had seen that car before. I stopped and turned around to look at it again. That was when the window rolled down slowly, and the nose of a handgun sat there suspended in the darkness. Everything that happened next couldn't have taken more than a few seconds, but it felt like it took an hour. I saw the muzzle flash; then I heard the loud pop. I jumped back and pulled on Stryker's leash.

My only chance at safety was a large concrete pillar just a few feet away. The first bullet missed, but I was still an open target. Two cars were approaching the light from the opposite direction on East Illinois. They were too far away to shield me. My next move was pure adrenaline and reflex. The best way to avoid an ambush without any immediate protection was to jerk in the opposite direction you planned on going, then quickly move the other way. It was sort of like a fake on a basketball court or a running back in football trying to misdirect and avoid a defender. So, I took a quick step and made a body jerk opposite the concrete pillar and sold it as hard as I could, then changed directions and dived back toward the barrier. I heard the second pop while I was in midair but didn't feel anything as I landed on the ground safely behind the pillar. Then I heard the third pop and the immediate crash of glass as the window of a car parked behind me exploded.

Stryker let out a yelp, and I was able to grab him up and ball him in my arms. The Supra screeched forward, burning rubber as it lurched through the intersection in the opposite direction.

I wasn't able to catch the license plate, but I didn't need to. I knew where I had seen that car before. And I knew exactly why whoever was in it was coming after me.

45

MECHANIC HAD CALLED AS PROMISED before I got through my door. Grigor Medvedev was a Russian entrepreneur with his hands in many businesses throughout the city, all of them related to construction and real estate development. He had deep ties both politically and to the underbelly of the city. He was rich, savvy, and heartless. He had lots of friends and an equal number of enemies. I asked Mechanic to set up a meeting with Medvedev at a neutral location.

I turned on my computer and loaded the surveillance footage from the day Griffin had been killed. I was confident about which part of the tape I needed but upset at myself for not going back to the tape earlier and more often. Sometimes the answer was sitting right there in front of you, but until you adjusted the lens, you would never see it.

I fast-forwarded the video and watched carefully as it sped up to the point where Griffin's Cadillac came into frame. He pulled away from the nursing home and started making his way north. He drove past the Old Navy store, and that was when I saw it. I stopped the video and zoomed in. The turquoise car on the screen was the same Toyota Supra that had just tried to put several bullets in me.

The tinted windows, the aftermarket chrome and modifications, the single plate on the back, though Illinois was a two-plate state. It was making sense. This was the shooter. He knew where Griffin had been the entire time and had followed him just like he'd followed me.

I pushed the "Play" button, and the video resumed. The Supra followed Griffin as he turned onto Upper Wacker. I stopped the video again and dug through my notes. I looked for my conversation with Viola Griffin. Twice she had told me that her husband was going from the nursing home to Capital Grille to pick up dinner. But Griffin took a left on Upper Wacker, then wrapped around for a bit and turned on the access road heading east. That made sense if he was heading to Capital Grille. But he never made it there. Something turned him around.

I let the tape roll again just to be sure. Once he had turned onto Upper Wacker, the Supra was no longer behind him, or the video clip the cops had assembled was not long enough to catch it trailing. As he pulled out of frame, the video lasted another two seconds—just long enough to catch the shiny chrome grille of the Supra. It had reappeared. The tape stopped. There was no more footage of Griffin. His body would be found less than a hundred yards west, opposite the direction of Capital Grille, across the river, partially submerged in the water. I couldn't stop wondering what made him change directions.

I picked up my cell and called Burke.

"It's midnight," he growled into the phone.

"You can still tell time," I said.

"What the hell is going on?" he asked.

"A guy took three shots at me tonight over by Navy Pier." I succinctly gave him the rest of the details.

"Did you call it in?"

"No need. I didn't get the plate number at the time and didn't want to spend the next three hours going through paperwork with some rookie patrols. But I have the plate now."

"How's that?"

"Because it's the same car that followed Griffin the night he was killed. I found it on the surveillance footage."

"Jesus fuckin' Christ."

"My thoughts exactly." I gave him the plate number.

"I'll call you right back," he said.

"I think we need more footage."

"What do you mean?"

"The footage you gave me was assembled and edited from different cameras. I didn't think about it before, but I might be able to get more from the raw source footage. Maybe there's something there that was missed by the editor."

"I can't get that done right now," he said. "But let me make a couple of calls."

———

SEVERAL HOURS LATER I tapped the app on my phone. Antoine Nelson filled my screen. I had just left the chamber and released his shackles. I'd told him he had a rematch in the works. Now he was on the ground doing crunches. I counted thirty before he sat up and took a sip of water. A minute later he flipped over and did push-ups, slowly lowering his chest to an inch above the ground, then snapping back up. He stopped at thirty but looked like he could've done more. For all his street bravado, Nelson wasn't a total fool.

He knew he needed to be as ready as possible for the fight. But no amount of crunches or push-ups could equal the might of vengeance.

46

A STREET FIGHT IS much different than exchanging blows in the ring. There is no referee, and there is no being saved by the bell. The fight usually ends when one man is severely injured and the other decides he has delivered enough punishment. The biggest mistake the inexperienced make is allowing their adrenaline to send them into a wild early charge. If they're not able to injure or incapacitate their opponent, then the tide can quickly turn, and they become the vulnerable. Their breathing becomes short and labored, their legs get rubbery, and their punches weaken and slow, making them ineffective.

Cesar Jackson was not big by any stretch, but for a man in his midfifties, he was in good shape. A former US Marine, he kept his hair cut short, and several patches of gray had spoiled his otherwise youthful appearance. When I first contacted him, he told me he had to pray first, then talk to his son, which he did every night on his knees before climbing into bed. They both must have given him the green light, because here he was, wiry, tightly muscled, and ready to confront his son's killer.

We stood outside the chamber watching Antoine go through a series of stretches.

"Does he know it's me yet?" he asked.

"No."

Jackson nodded and continued to stare at the monitor.

"The first year, all I could think about was killing him," he said. "I felt like I was doing my son a disservice by allowing his killer to walk freely."

"What stopped you?"

"I wish I could say it was my faith. But it wasn't. It was my other two kids, Rayshawn and Juanita. It was bad enough they were growing up without their older brother. I didn't want them to grow up without their father too."

"Him dying a quick death is too easy a punishment. Long, intractable pain can be a lot more satisfying."

"I agree. I want him to hurt and know he's hurting and there's nothing he can do about it."

"Are you ready?"

Jackson turned to me. "I was born ready."

I tied his gloves, then opened the chamber door and let him in. I stayed back and sat in front of the monitor to watch.

Antoine stood up and stared at Jackson, a smile creasing his cocky face. He stood a good three inches better than Jackson and had him by at least thirty pounds. His gloves had been tied up, and he was ready to go.

"What you 'bout to do, old man?" he said.

"Whoop yo ass," Jackson said.

Antoine waved him off. "Man, you need to go 'head with that shit. What's done is done. You need to go on."

Jackson rolled his shoulders. "My son was a good boy," he said. "Minding his own business. He didn't want any trouble. You were the one looking for a fight. He gave it to you. It was over. But you couldn't take that. You took the coward's way out and pulled a knife."

"He should've been watching his back," Antoine said. He moved closer to Jackson. "Ain't no fight over in the street till it's over."

"He wanted to go see those mountains," Jackson said. "All he talked about was seeing those damn mountains."

"Well, maybe he seein' 'em from heaven," Antoine said. "Or wherever the hell he is."

Antoine made the first charge, but Jackson was ready. He slid under Antoine's right hook and met him with an uppercut just below the rib cage, then followed it with a quick jab to the back of the head. Antoine spun around and threw a quick punch that landed flush into Jackson's shoulder and backed him up a couple of feet. Antoine didn't wait long. He had been in enough street fights to know that it was always better to get the first hit in, draw first blood.

He led with a series of quick, wild punches, most of them missing, one grazing the right side of Jackson's head. I could tell by the way Jackson had protected himself and blocked most of them that he was not a stranger to boxing. He was patient. He threw a couple of jabs that connected with Antoine's upper torso, but he didn't rush. He paced and looked and waited. He let Antoine expend his energy, allowing him to get through that first adrenaline rush. Antoine taunted him, called him names, let his hands down, and implored Jackson to make a move. But he didn't. He just paced and waited.

That was when Antoine made the mistake. He cocked his arm back and threw a hard punch, trying to put his entire weight behind it. Jackson was too fast, ducked and rolled. Antoine had thrown the punch so hard that he was wrong footed, his legs completely out of position to respond to a counterattack. Jackson knew this and moved in. The first punch he landed was a solid left to Antoine's face. It hit him square in the eye. I could hear the crunch of the orbital bones just above the eye socket. Antoine's head snapped back. That was real pain. Jackson wasted no time. Novices would hesitate and admire their handiwork. Not Jackson. He advanced again, dropped a little, then sprang forward and landed a right blow to Antoine's jaw. The sound of splintering bones was unmistakable. Antoine would be eating through a straw for the next six weeks.

Antoine was hurt badly. He tried covering his face with his gloves, but Jackson's punches were too quick and too strong. Blood poured down his face as he stumbled and screamed for Jackson to stop. Not a chance in hell. Jackson backed him up against the wall and unleashed a flurry of jabs to his face. Left, then right, deftly alternating sides, doing serious damage. I could tell he was familiar with working a heavy bag. Jackson wasn't interested in Antoine's body. He wanted his face. That had been his strategy from the out-set. A body shot could slow someone, but a shot to the head could be the kill shot. The pounding continued until Antoine crumpled to the ground. Jackson continued the barrage, jumping on Antoine and delivering the punishment. I admired how he went about his work—quietly, efficiently.

When Antoine's body went completely slack, I got up and entered the chamber. "Don't kill him," I said, grabbing Jackson and lifting him up. "That would let him off easy."

Antoine's face was covered in blood. His lips looked like sausages about to burst. "I can't see anything," he screamed. "I can't see."

I reached down and pulled his eyes open. His pupils were dilated and nonreactive. His optic nerves were crushed, and both retinas in the back of his eyes were likely torn.

"I can't fuckin' see!" he screamed. "I can't see nuthin'!"

"And you won't for the rest of your life," Jackson said calmly. "My boy will never be able to see those mountains, and you won't either."

I felt tremendous relief hearing those words and even greater satisfaction knowing the last image Antoine had seen was the avenging face of Cesar Jackson, father of the innocent kid he had callously murdered. Most people would never understand or approve this version of justice, but this wasn't about most people. This was about the victims and their families, who no longer had a voice and whom the system had let down so egregiously. The same system had let down Walter Griffin and his family, and soon I would deliver to them the justice they'd long deserved.

47

I SAT AT MY desk in my apartment, looking at the empty boats anchored in the harbor in a perfect grid. They bobbed and tilted to a rhythm of their own in the midmorning sun. In just a few months, the lake would be completely empty, and the winds would violently churn the water. I looked down at Julia's letter on the desk. I wanted to hear her voice again, smell the shampoo in her hair. I kept hearing my father say that she still loved me and wanted to try again.

I picked up my phone and opened my Instagram account. I searched for her name and found her page. She had made it private. The Eiffel Tower was her profile picture. I wouldn't be able to scroll through her posted photos unless I followed her and she accepted my request. I stared at the blue "Follow" button on the screen. The second I pushed it, she would be notified of my request. I closed my eyes, leaned my head back, and breathed slowly. After several minutes, I opened my eyes and called my father.

"I'm sorry," he said.

I was taken aback. I could count on one hand how many times he had said that to me.

"What I did was well intentioned, but it was wrong," he said.

"Apology accepted," I said.

"I've been thinking about you."

"You could've called."

"I wanted to give you your space."

"How are you doing?"

"Except for this sore right knee and a plummeting first-serve percentage, I'm holding up all right."

"What's new in your life?"

"I'm just getting home from getting my car washed. I leave for Indian Wells tomorrow with a couple of guys. We got courtside tickets for Stadium 1. If we're lucky, we'll get Serena's match or Nadal's."

"I'm sure you'll have fun. But why would you get your car washed, then leave it at the airport? By the time you get back, it's gonna be dirty, just sitting there in the garage."

"I like coming home to a clean car," he said. "The valet always keeps my car parked in the interior, so the wind and dust won't reach it."

I had to smile. Classic Dr. Wendell Cayne. He thought of everything.

"I'm moving on," I said. "I've lost too much time thinking about what Julia did and what could've been."

"It still could be. I was telling you the truth when I said that she still loves you and wants to give it another shot."

"I'll always love her too," I said. "But I don't know if she's right for me. There are some things in life, no matter how hard you try, you just can't get over."

"This is your decision to make. What anyone else thinks really doesn't matter. At the end of the day, it's your life, your happiness. You should always be in charge of that."

I don't know what it was, maybe just where I was emotionally, but those simple words caused my body to relax and my heart to feel free.

"Let's have dinner soon," I said.

"I'll have Pearline fix one of your favorites."

"I love you, Dad."

"I love you too, son."

I disconnected the line and looked at the blue "Follow" button still sitting on my screen. Julia was somewhere out there 4,130 miles away. One push and she would be in my apartment again. I looked down at Stryker loyally sleeping at my feet. He lifted his head and looked back at me, his tail coming to life. I closed the Instagram app, got up from my desk, and grabbed the leash. I chose to take a step forward. And maybe that meant I was finally ready to move on.

———

THE MEETING HAD BEEN arranged for high noon. Sergei Yeltsin had offered his bakery as our meeting place. Mechanic had accompanied me. Sergei welcomed us into the back room. Grigor Medvedev sat at the small circular table in the middle of the room. He was quite ordinary looking, thin, average height with black circular glasses and chestnut-colored hair that had been pulled back and tucked behind his ears. I could see him teaching art history or a romance language on a small liberal arts campus. Three of his men hung back, posted in the corners of the room. I knew they were armed to the teeth, but I wasn't worried. Mechanic could draw and shoot all three before any of them could unholster their gun. Besides, Burke and about twenty officers were posted in unmarked cars surrounding the bakery. He had run down the Supra's license plate. The car belonged to a guy who had been on Medvedev's payroll for years.

I looked around the room. Yeltsin had added a new movie poster to the wall. This one was a shot of Jennifer Lawrence and Bradley Cooper in *Silver Linings Playbook*. I looked at Yeltsin, who nodded and smiled without showing teeth. Introductions were made; then Yeltsin left the room and closed the door behind him.

Medvedev took a sip of tea. The arms of his jacket pulled back a little. He wore gold-and-emerald cuff links in the shape of a lion's head. They were expensive but not gaudy. Quiet wealth.

"You have a famous last name," I said.

"How's that?" he replied.

"The tennis player."

Medvedev smiled a set of perfectly bleached teeth. "It's not an uncommon name," he said. "Maybe here in the States, but not back home. But no, Daniil is not my relative."

"You know tennis?"

"Very well, but I'm sure you didn't ask me here to explore my knowledge of tennis or its famous players."

"You're right. I wanted to find out directly from you why you tried to kill me last night."

Medvedev craned his neck back and widened his eyes. "I don't know what you're talking about. I was home last night with about ten other people, having a birthday dinner for my brother-in-law. You are mistaken."

I pushed the folder across the table in his direction. He looked it over for a second, then picked it up. He pulled out the three photographs of Vladislav Nijinsky and examined each one carefully, his expression never changing. He placed them back in the folder and smiled softly.

"Two nights ago, someone fired three shots at me just across from Navy Pier," I said. "That man in the photographs owns the car where the bullets came from. That man also has been on your payroll for ten years. And he followed Walter Griffin hours before he was killed."

"If I wanted to have you killed," he said, looking at two of his men. "I could do it right now."

"Impossible."

"Why is that?"

I nodded to Mechanic, who stood there leaning against the wall like he was half-asleep. "Because you only have three guys to my one."

Medvedev smiled his understanding. "Let's talk," he said.

"Let's start with your connection to Walter Griffin," I said.

"What connection?"

"Let's not waste time playing this game. You called Griffin the day he was killed."

Medvedev shrugged. "So what if I did?"

"Why were you calling him?"

"He's a businessman. I'm a businessman. Businessmen talk."

"About what?"

"That's not relevant to this conversation."

"Were the two of you working on a deal?"

Medvedev stared back at me. He was not denying it.

"It had to be something pretty important for you to call him on a Sunday," I said.

Medvedev smiled, then reached out and lifted his glass of water, took a sip, and rested it back on the table. Just as he did that, sunlight beaming through the ceiling windows caught his cuff links, and I noticed an inscription running along the lions' heads—GEM.

The second I saw it, I knew where I had seen it before. GEM was one of the Sunrise Holdings entities that I'd found in the Offshore Leaks database. "You have to follow the money," the anonymous informant had said when he'd told me to look into Sunrise Holdings. And the money was big. Seventy million dollars big. That money led back to Medvedev.

I now had a handle on the likely motivation behind the murders of both Walter Griffin and Bryce Horner. But I still didn't know exactly who had pulled the trigger and how they'd created the opportunity to do so.

———

WHEN I GOT HOME that evening, a small envelope had been slipped under my door. I gave Stryker several hugs, threw my keys on the kitchen counter, and grabbed a Sam Adams. As illuminating as the meeting with Medvedev had been in solidifying the connection between Medvedev, Sunrise, Milton, and the $70 million contract, I still had no proof who exactly had killed Griffin or how it had been carried out.

But something had been tugging at me from the back of my mind the entire time. I thought back to my conversation with my father that morning. He had gotten his car washed the day before leaving for California to watch a tennis tournament. It didn't make much sense to me, just like it hadn't made much sense when Carolina first told me Griffin had phoned a car wash on the day he died. At the time, I'd seen it as proof that Griffin's death wasn't suicide. A man planning on killing himself doesn't go get his car washed that morning.

But now I wondered if it signaled something more. I found Griffin's call log. I started with the first number that morning and called each one. It wasn't until I reached the ninth number that I had my answer. No one picked up the phone, but the answering machine kicked in. The voice on the recording clearly identified the business: Diamond Sharp Car Wash.

Griffin and Cephus Redmond had spoken the very morning Griffin had died, and Cephus had conveniently forgotten to tell me that.

Why had Griffin driven east that afternoon, in the direction of Capital Grille, but ended up west at Wolf Point? I was starting to see the sequence of events take shape, and I hoped the raw source footage Burke had delivered would provide the final clue.

I opened the envelope, pulled out the black flash drive, then went to my computer and plugged it in. A lot of the footage was too grainy or dark and unusable, but there were stretches that were clear and the resolution surprisingly good. I could tell the difference between the video that had been collected from commercial security cameras and the footage from the police observation devices. The private cameras had much better resolution. I sat there for two hours straight, combing through it all, fast-forwarding, rewinding, pausing the action when I thought I saw something. Nothing struck me as unusual.

Then I thought it might be more helpful to have something to compare this footage to, so I loaded up the edited video Burke had previously given me. I set up both videos next to each other on the screen, started from the beginning, then played them simultaneously. It quickly became evident what had been missed or not included from the source footage in the final edit. My eyes got blurry from looking at the screen, but I pressed on. I had almost reached my third hour when I saw it.

I played with the video adjustments a little until it was clearly visible and identifiable, and then I knew I had the linchpin of my case: a small red Lexus convertible that followed Griffin's car all the way from Calgary until it disappeared onto the access road running beside Lower Wacker.

48

IT HAD BEEN ALMOST three months since the Griffins had walked into Hammer's Gym and asked me to find their father's murderer. I'd known it wasn't going to be easy. I'd known there would be powerful people with powerful allies making powerful moves to keep Walter Griffin and his treasure trove of secrets buried forever. There were infinite reasons why a human took another's life, but when you collected and distilled the motivations behind murder, they really fell into a few buckets—jealousy, hatred, money, and sex. Antoine Nelson had murdered for money and jealousy. The murders of Walter Griffin and Bryce Horner had hit the quadfecta.

I pulled up to the elegant home in Oak Park, just a twenty-minute ride from the city when the traffic on the Eisenhower cooperated. The lawn had been meticulously cut and edged, the flowers making their last show of brilliance before the cooler air blew in and swept them into hibernation. The red Lexus sat in the driveway by itself. I parked behind it, then scaled the wide limestone steps leading to the front veranda.

The door opened before I could hit the buzzer. Francesca Milton stood there in a pair of black dress pants, a gold silk blouse, and long curly red hair that made her blue eyes pop against her creamy skin. She was even more beautiful and composed in person than she had been in the few photographs I'd been able to find online.

"My husband's not here," she said.

"I'm not here to see your husband," I said. "He's probably just pulling out of the East Bank Club on his way to the office."

"Then how can I help you?"

"I'm Ashe Cayne. Private investigator. But you already know who I am. Mind if I come in and talk for a moment?"

A hesitant smile slightly turned up the corners of her mouth. She stepped back and opened the door so I could enter. I followed her through several spacious rooms until we reached a formal living room with beamed ceilings and several refurbished stained glass windows. We sat in two large wingback chairs. She took the chair with an oversize black handbag sitting next to it. An ornate pink marble coffee table sat between us.

"How can I help you?" she asked, once we had settled.

"I think you know why I'm here," I said.

She raised her perfectly waxed eyebrows.

"I saw your car on the surveillance footage," I said. "You had been following him from the nursing home."

"And who would that be?" she said.

I smiled. I would play along. "Walter Griffin."

"And why would I want to follow Walter Griffin?"

"To protect your husband's secrets."

"I don't need to protect my husband," she said. "He is more than capable of taking care of himself."

"Until Griffin was about to expose his affair with Bryce Horner."

"You've come to my house to talk to me about my husband's sex life? You're not breaking new ground. I have known Andrew for almost twenty years, married for ten of them. I know who my husband is and what he does."

"This wasn't just about a little roll in the hay," I said. "This was about money and power and revenge."

Francesca Milton offered an accommodating smile. "You've built up quite a plot," she said. "Very Shakespearean of you."

"I do like my Shakespeare," I said. "It took me a while to piece it all together. You were pretty clever. Up to a point. The only piece I couldn't figure out was who helped you on the inside with the ME reports. One death a suicide, the other an accidental drowning. All the blocks were lined up to make the suicide a reasonable conclusion. Well-known insider, facing humiliation with exposure for an OIG investigation. Griffin wasn't destitute, but he definitely had some financial problems. Anyone on the outside wouldn't find it too hard to believe that a man with his problems and secrets would finally give up and just end it all. Then there's Bryce Horner, your husband's lover, who dies doing what he loved doing most out in the open water. Very believable on the face of it, with the riptide and all. Very smart."

"But not smart enough for you," she said.

"You made some small mistakes, left tiny footprints where you hadn't intended. Dryhop Brewers was a mistake. Going there and talking to the host, inquiring about your husband. He remembered everything. You blocked your home phone number and called Horner the day he was killed. Small things that by themselves wouldn't mean anything, but when you look at the overall picture, they're like tiny blots of glue that hold everything else together."

"Walter wasn't the saint everyone painted him as," she said. "He had his hand in the jar just like everyone else. He was fine when he got a share of the take, but he was too greedy. He wanted to be in on everything. Nobody gets a piece of everything. When he wasn't part of the action, he tried to muscle his way in."

"Is that what he was doing with Andrew? He was about to ruin your husband's golden ticket. Belvedere Technologies, subsidiary of Sunrise Holdings. Seventy million is a lot of money for a CPS contract. How much was Medvedev kicking back to your husband?"

She stared at me, then smiled.

"Walter had been given a lot of opportunities like everyone else. All that city land he bought at a steal. Andrew's deal was none of his business. He was put there as CEO, and Walter should've left it at that. Instead, he threw a fit, and when he couldn't get his person the gig, he tried to block Andrew. When that didn't work, he went hunting, looking for anything to make Andrew and the Belvedere contract look bad. Even the threat of the OIG investigation didn't convince Walter to back off."

"An investigation over a few hundred dollars?"

She smiled. "That's what they made people believe. But that was just to get the investigation open. Only a few people knew that Walter had approved several contracts that went to firms he had active consulting relationships with or had worked with in the past. Walter should've recused himself, but he didn't. Those contracts were worth millions of dollars to the same firms that had him on the payroll. If the truth came out, he was definitely going to jail. He knew that."

That tracked with what Alicia Gentry had told me. This was the missing piece I hadn't totally figured out, but it now made sense. Bailey had hand selected Milton to be CEO of the school system even though there were better candidates. The CEO controlled an $8 billion budget. With Bailey's person in charge of the budget, that meant there was plenty of opportunity to funnel money and contracts into the companies and individuals Bailey had chosen. Bailey sat on top and directed operatives like Milton. That kept him several arm's lengths away but still in charge. Then those who got the contracts passed along the kickbacks to Bailey. That was going to be difficult to prove, but I was convinced that was how the scheme worked.

"Since we're being so transparent, how much money was Bailey kicking back to you guys?" I said.

"Andrew and I have worked very hard to get where we are. I never wanted to come to Chicago, but I gave up a very comfortable life to move here to this cold city and support my husband. Walter was against Andrew's appointment from the very beginning. He made a big show of it. He wanted people to believe he was opposed to Andrew because he didn't find him qualified. Bullshit. Walter knew how to play the game. He was against Andrew's appointment for one simple reason. He wanted *his* person in that office, who would then control the system's multibillion-dollar budget. Greed. Walter wouldn't let it go. Eventually, he became a bigger liability than he was worth."

"But a liability big enough to murder?"

"Do you mind if I smoke?" she asked.

"It's your house. Not exactly great for the paintings."

She reached down and grabbed her bag. She pulled it open, reached in, and came out with a small pistol.

I needed to buy some time. "Nice touch," I said. "State pride."

"Meaning?"

"Springfield Hellcat. Highest-capacity microcompact nine millimeter in the world. Eleven plus one, right?"

"I only need the one."

"Confident."

"I didn't kill Walter or Bryce," she said. "But I am going to kill you."

"I know you didn't pull the trigger on Griffin. You and Cephus Redmond worked together on this. You had a plan. Griffin called Cephus that morning, maybe to ask for more money, and Cephus told him to meet him at Wolf Point. His children told me their father was a germophobe and never would've stepped foot near a dump like Wolf Point. He went there because Cephus asked him to meet there. Medvedev's guys were following him. I think plan A was for Medvedev's guys to kill Griffin on his way to the meeting point. But Griffin changed his mind and headed east first, toward Capital Grille, where he was going to pick up dinner. Eventually, he turned around and drove to Wolf Point, and now plan B kicks in. You're following Griffin the entire time, keeping track of what's going on. And if your call log was checked, I bet it'll show you were in constant communication with Cephus and probably the Russians. The Russians don't take Griffin out, so now it's up to Cephus. Griffin never would've expected Cephus to physically harm him, so he has no suspicions about the meeting. He gets caught off guard. Cephus strangles or suffocates him to unconsciousness, but he wants to make it look like a suicide, so he shoots Griffin. Griffin owned two guns, but neither of them was used to kill him. That gun belonged to Cephus, serial number scratched, never used in a previous shooting, so it was virtually untraceable. He did his best but made a couple of mistakes. Put the gunpowder on the wrong hand and didn't realize that strangulation could be discovered during the internal autopsy exam, even if there weren't any external marks. You might not have shot Griffin or seen him murdered, but you damn sure helped coordinate it all. That's still murder in the blue eyes of Lady Justice."

"You're a very stubborn man, Ashe," she said.

"I've been called a lot worse."

"Several warnings were sent to you to back off. But you wouldn't listen."

"Ya know, I just have a really difficult time giving in to intimidation. Family trait, I guess."

"One that's gonna cost you your life."

"Maybe, but not today."

She extended her arm, but the gun was still too far away for me to swat it out of her hand. I needed a couple more minutes.

"Did your husband know you did it?" I asked.

She smiled. "Keep Andrew out of this."

"Of course, protect the golden goose. Why did you have to kill Horner?"

"I didn't kill anyone. I've told you that." Her fingers tightened on the specially textured grip. Her knuckles whitened.

"You didn't kill him, but you had him killed."

"He got himself killed. He broke the rules, didn't understand the importance of discretion. He was upset that Andrew wouldn't leave me. Andrew was never going to leave me. That's not how this arrangement works. Bryce wouldn't accept that. He threatened to expose Andrew, thinking that would get Andrew to change his mind. Andrew was in love with him, but he wasn't a fool either. We worked too hard to get where we are."

"So, why was Bryce talking with Griffin?"

"Bryce and Walter met through a mutual friend, and that's how Walter discovered Andrew's affair. Walter wanted to use the affair against Andrew to get the OIG investigation dropped. Bryce thought that by helping him expose Andrew, it would force Andrew to choose him over our marriage. Andrew and I are partners for life. He tells me everything. When Bryce figured out his little plan with Walter wasn't going to work, he came clean with Andrew."

"Lower the gun," I said. "You're not going to use it."

"I most certainly am," she said.

I heard a footstep just outside the door. I didn't turn because any sudden movement might startle her into pulling the trigger. But I knew who was there.

"How did you and Cephus connect?" I asked.

She smiled. "Because we had a common problem. Walter. Walter had called in a few favors and helped Cephus with his tax situation. Cephus paid him well, but Walter wanted more, including a million-dollar apartment downtown. Cephus knew that Walter was going to keep asking for more, because his leverage wasn't going away. People talk. Sometimes too much. Andrew had heard that Walter called in favors to help Cephus with his tax situation. Bryce knew that Walter had purchased that expensive apartment for his girlfriend."

It was possible that Sophia had never told Bryce that she was Walter's daughter.

"So, you put all this together and reached out to Cephus?" I asked.

"Only after it became apparent our interests were aligned."

I nodded, then said, "If you don't lower that gun, you're going to be in a lot of pain and without use of your right hand for several months, maybe more."

"Is that so?" She laughed.

And that was when the explosion tore open the still air. It happened in seconds: the gun flew across the room, and her hand collapsed on itself. A small squirt of blood splattered the pink marble. Her scream was almost as loud as the gunshot.

I looked at Mechanic standing there, not a hint of expression on his face.

"It's only the index finger," he said calmly. "I was in a charitable mood today. I spared the rest of your hand so you could still dial your husband's number from prison."

49

"HOW DID YOU GET this reservation?" Carolina asked. "Wendy from my office said they were booked solid for two months."

We were sitting on the upper patio of RPM Seafood, overlooking the river as a couple of Shoreline Sightseeing boats trudged by and a phalanx of people walked below us on the water's edge. The temperature couldn't have been more perfect. We were separated by a candle, half a pound of chilled Alaskan king crab, and a ramekin of melted black truffle butter.

"No restaurant is ever totally booked," I said. "That's just what they throw at you over the phone. They always keep one or two tables open per seating just in case."

"And you happened to be the just in case."

"No, Bill Rancic is the just in case."

"Isn't he the owner?"

"He is."

"Isn't his wife Giuliana, that pretty fashionista?"

"She is."

"How do you know him?"

"Penny introduced us at her golf club. He hits the ball a mile."

"So, he's better than you?"

"He hits it long, but I hit it straight."

"What good is straight if it doesn't go far?"

"A lot better than long if it's out of bounds behind a fence in someone's backyard. And for the record, I never said my ball didn't go far."

We nibbled on the crab and swirled our Trimbach Riesling, which released a pleasant minty apple and jasmine fragrance.

"So, are you happy with how the Griffin case turned out?" Carolina asked.

"Plus ou moins."

"Translation?"

"More or less."

"The more?"

"The family has confirmation of what they knew all along. He didn't commit suicide. That doesn't give them closure, but there's some gratification knowing he didn't just wake up that day and decide to take his own life. And once Lady Justice has her say, Francesca and Cephus will probably spend the rest of their lives looking at the sun through a barbwire fence."

"The less?"

"I think Bailey was in on it, but unless someone talks, there's no way to get him. He'll get away with it for now. And without Griffin, the FBI might never have enough to nail Bailey on the Cabrini land deals."

"You want him."

"Bailey? Badly. He's the devil, and he's not even in disguise. He's the reason I'm not on the force anymore. He's turned the department into his political weapon. It's all about power and money for him. He runs the city like a feudal lord. At some point he's gonna make a bad mistake, and his entire house of cards is gonna come crashing down. I'd bet anything he was the one who sent those two guys after me that night I went to pick up my pizza."

The waiter cleared the discarded shells and presented us with warm, wet napkins. I admired Carolina's bracelet. The candlelight caught the diamonds at a perfect angle.

"What about Medvedev?" Carolina said. "He just gets away with all that money and the kickback to Milton?"

"He'd better stuff himself on as much Beluga caviar as he can."

"Why?"

"Because he doesn't have a lot of time left to eat it."

Carolina raised her eyebrows.

"He took a run at me."

"But he missed. Thank God."

"Doesn't matter. Mechanic isn't happy. And he for sure won't miss."

"So violent."

"Only when necessary."

The waiter refilled our wineglasses and let us know that our entrées would be out shortly.

"When did you figure Francesca Milton was behind it all?" Carolina asked.

"Not till the end," I said. "That blocked call to Horner from Milton's house didn't make sense to me, but then I saw the red Lexus on the Griffin surveillance footage. The cops had cut it down to the frames where Walter's car was visible. Whenever he rolled out of frame, they just stopped the tape and cut to the next shot. But when you waited a few seconds after Walter passed out of frame, you could see the red Lexus. That's when I knew she was in on it. I just didn't know her role in it all. That's why I needed to confront her."

"How did the cops miss something as important as that?"

"Depends. If it was an honest mistake or simply sloppy work, sometimes you don't see what you're not looking for. They were focused on Griffin and where he was going. They needed to confirm the timeline. But if it was intentional, then that means someone coordinated it all. Given how Bailey manipulated the autopsy report, I wouldn't be surprised. It's unlikely we'll ever know."

Two waiters approached us with our plates. They first set down Carolina's chicken paillard and root vegetables. Then came my Spanish branzino without the head. The grill marks had been lightly burned into the skin.

Once we had commenced eating, Carolina announced, "I'm single again."

I raised only one eyebrow.

"He wasn't right for me," she said. "He liked to go to sleep with his socks on."

"That says it all."

A large boat with tinted windows sailed by. Several couples sat at a long table on the upper deck. The men wore tuxedos. The women had been all done up in elaborate gowns and jewelry from the vault.

"I'm single too," I said.

She tried raising only one eyebrow but couldn't.

"I like her," I said. "She's a lot of fun. But we're at different places in our lives."

"And where exactly are you?"

"Thinking of a solution that would jointly end our singleness."

"I have one. Less thinking and more doing."

I reached into my back pocket, pulled out a Frommer's guide to Marrakech, then slid it across the table.

"So, you're ready for your trip?" she asked.

"Almost."

"What do you have left to do?"

"Convince you to go with me."

She rested her hand on mine and leaned into me. "Thought you'd never ask."

ACKNOWLEDGMENTS

Thanks again to Detective Socrates Mabry and others at the Chicago Police Department for their invaluable insights into procedural information that helped me get most of it right on the page. Any mistakes I've made are mine alone. Thanks to Dr. Sharon Lieteau for all her medical help and consideration while taking my ideas and giving them real context. Megha Parekh has been a wonderful editor who has read and made suggestions with a discerning eye and an understanding of the story I've tried to tell. I thank you tremendously for helping my story sing better on the pages. To all the other editors, like Laura Barrett and Caitlin Alexander, as well as the art designers and those who help with marketing and publicity—your efforts are equally important and very much appreciated. My family always deserves a big thanks for allowing me to sneak away for hours on end to get lost in my imagination and the stories it creates. Thanks for your unparalleled support and understanding, and know that you're always number one for me. I hope you find the ride on these pages worth it all.

ABOUT THE AUTHOR

Dr. Ian K. Smith is the #1 *New York Times* bestselling author of *Shred: The Revolutionary Diet*, as well as *Super Shred: The Big Results Diet*, *Blast the Sugar Out!*, *The Clean 20*, and twelve other books, with millions of copies in print. Dr. Smith's critically acclaimed novel *The Blackbird Papers* was the 2005 BCALA fiction recipient of the Honor Book Award. His other highly praised novels include *The Ancient Nine* and *The Unspoken*.

Dr. Smith, a graduate of Harvard, Columbia, and the University of Chicago, is the medical contributor and cohost of *The Rachael Ray Show*. He has written for *Time*, *Newsweek*, *Men's Fitness*, and the *New York Daily News*. Dr. Smith has served on the boards of the President's Council on Fitness, Sports, and Nutrition; the American Council on Exercise; the New York Mission Society; the Prevent Cancer Foundation; the New York Council for the Humanities; and the Maya Angelou Center for

Health Equity. He currently serves on the board of public broadcasting station WTTW in Chicago.

Keep up to date with Dr. Smith by visiting his website at www.doctoriansmith.com and following him on Twitter (@DrIanSmith) and Instagram (@DoctorIanSmith).